DROCHAID

Four university friends visit Jerusalem and return home sharing a secret which will change their lives and those under their influence. After his father's death, and before taking up his own place at university in Edinburgh, the son of one of the four finds himself at the centre of a dangerous quest. Evil swirls around him as he encounters a mystical ferryman with superhuman strength, a strikingly beautiful girl who befriends him, his father's contemporaries who he meets for the first time, and a professional hit-man employed by one of them to kill him. In a race against time, and in his naivety unable clearly to distinguish friend from foe, he receives his father's sole legacy, a box apparently only containing a candle. The quest takes him to Jerusalem and Southern France; to Whitby, the Hebrides, Walsingham and the Norfolk salt marshes. 'Something almost lost to the world remains'.

DROCHAID

SCOTT McKENZIE

Unicorn Press

First published in Great Britain in 2023 by Unicorn Press
60 Bracondale
Norwich
NR1 2BE

tradfordhugh@gmail.com
www.unicornpublishing.org

A CIP record of this book can be obtained from the British Library

ISBN 978 1 739164 00 3

Design by newtonworks.uk
Printed in the UK by T J Books, Padstow

Contents

Dedicated to my wife Helen,
something almost lost to the world remains.

DROCHAID

1

*Ronan MacDonald's promise. Sunset: time to begin his journey
up to Drochaid, the bridge. Then down to the Ferryman's house.
The Ferryman's challenge and their struggle.*

He had promised himself that this was how it would be. Many times he had promised and many times he had rehearsed. He had made a covenant in the depth of night and now he would keep it.

He knelt in front of a small selection of his possessions for a long time in the candlelight. Then, one by one, he carefully placed them in a canvas bag and fastened this by its leather straps. The leather was ancient, dry and left some brown dust on his fingers. The bag smelt faintly of the sea. He knelt for a long time in front of the bag and the candle and looked at the room. The large, frayed rug by the fireplace had always been there, the room had always existed in his mind. It had no beginning, how it came there was a mystery and he could not envisage its ending. The rug was countless red shades as if it had absorbed the firelight over the years. It had the odour of dust and warm earth. The odour of sanctity. It held the memory of a child seated amidst a halo of dust particles which scintillated in the filtered sunlight. He seemed to have been born there, in front of the fire. On a warm, red island surrounded by dark oak boards which were a scarred, broken and decayed record of the life they had carried. Dark green paint clung to the wooden boards of the simple dado. The grooved boarding was a cold green ocean in his memory.

The light from the window told him that the time to begin had come. He lifted the candlestick and as he did so he awoke from his reverie like the breaking of a spell. The serenity of the steadily flickering flame was instantly broken by dark swaying shadows which made the room lurch drunkenly in front of his eyes; leering and irreverent. He blew out the candle … "… dona nobis pacem". The candlestick was old and brass, so it seemed, although it had a warm, coppery hue. It was cylindrical and fluted like a Doric column, the candleholder was supported by a wreath of cast acanthus leaves. It had been a present from his father, for his confirmation. The heavy, round base bore the inscription, 'I am the light of the world'. The base hinged open so that the candle could be placed inside. When he had completed this action, he wrapped the candlestick in red velvet and, undoing one of the straps, placed it in the bag with the rest of his belongings. The room was darkening fast.

Gently clasping the bag to his chest he went softly downstairs, then quickly out of the house and through the garden gate and up onto the moor. He looked back once to see the small, white house rocking amidst the rippling pastures. Windows gleaming red in the fading light. He would keep to the high ground if he could for the whole length of the island until he reached the shore. The sun was setting as he began and a powerful, wet wind was gusting over the moor. It brought him scents of spring and of the sea. Something primordial stirred in him and he sensed evil, he could not say why and he shivered at the feeling. Then he understood that death had stolen over the moor in the wind like a squall of rain. The death of someone near. He had sensed it as it passed him by. He felt a contraction in his throat and tears rose into his eyes, to subside again like waves receding from rock pools. He had chosen the most difficult way and the worst time. Everything was perfect. The relics of his past and of his childhood lay in neatly tied cardboard boxes, except for the few he carried. From the most north-westerly point of the map he was being drawn towards the centre.

At that latitude the night was never quite black and the moonlight guided him along a windswept ridge for several miles. It was often wet underfoot and difficult, yet several hours passed before he grew tired. Still, he would not rest until he reached the place he had appointed and as he breasted the next ridge he caught an indistinct glimpse of the spot. It was called Drochaid, the bridge, because it was an ancient Celtic graveyard. There were no dwellings now, only a level part of the moor surrounded by a dry-stone wall and the beginning of a road which ran down from the hill through a glen, which became a sea loch, to the place of his departure. It was several months since he had been here and a year would pass before he came here again. A young man of eighteen years rarely thinks of things past nor gestures of remembrance, yet that was why he had come this way. With little difficulty he selected a headstone against one of the walls and laying down his burden, knelt in front of the grave. His knees sank into the wet earth and the air was filled with the scent of damp peat, heather and gorse. The place seemed purified by incense, the mist a benediction, the wind a litany. Here, decay seemed to be overcome by regeneration. He thought, "… in sure and certain knowledge …" and prayed and then lifted his eyes to the stone. It was a plain enough memorial, rectangular with a Celtic cross in bas relief at the top and, near the base, a small cross with triangular arms within a plain escutcheon. All as specified, even the epitaph which was inscribed:

HERE LIE THE EARTHLY REMAINS OF THE REV. JOHN MACDONALD.
MINISTER OF DUNLAITH CHURCH 1983–1996.
DEPARTED THIS LIFE 6 JUNE 1996 AGED 58 YEARS.
"NOT EVERY ONE THAT SAITH UNTO ME, LORD, LORD,
SHALL ENTER INTO THE KINGDOM OF HEAVEN BUT HE
THAT DOETH THE WILL OF MY FATHER"

The young man knelt there for many minutes, all the while his eyes were closed and his lips moved but no sound was audible. The mist was turning into a steady rain. Another minute, then he rose abruptly, shouldered his pack and without looking back set off down towards the sea. Down and down he dropped through the echoing glen until he sensed the tang of the sea in his nostrils, refreshing and astringent, and felt his heart beat in his chest. As soon as he had cleared the last stand of stunted pines the sounds of the sea broke over him. The cries of wading birds and gulls and the steady heartbeat of the surf. He had arrived near the tip of a small peninsula, or aird, where the mainland could be seen dimly across a narrow channel in which the dark green Atlantic rose and fell. Today, like a serpent's back and oft-times as a seething cauldron. The brief northern night was now losing its struggle with the dawn. The young man gazed over the water and his lips moved.

"Feumaidh mi falbh. An-diugh. Caite a bheil an t-aiseag."

He knew that on the other side of the inlet to his left an immense waterfall thundered down a sheer cliff into the ocean and that in spite of its power the autumn gales often blew the cascading water back hundreds of yards in-land; to fall on the moor like driving rain. When he was a child he had heard that not far from here two shepherds were lifted bodily by the wind and blown across the hillside like dry autumn leaves, sucked between ragged outcrops of rock and thrown into the rapacious sea. For many years thereafter he imagined the ringing roar of the wind that must have enveloped and deafened them, the terrifying helplessness as they were, at first dragged, then swept along by an unfathomable, invisible force. The scrabbling of bloody fingers on soil and rock. The stunning, numbing, blood-blinding impacts and the sickening plunge to icy oblivion.

A harsh, fearsome environment which bred a hard fearless people. Well, there was some truth in that. They were also characterised by the way they blurred the edges between the physical and the metaphysical in their landscape and in their music and song. Seas, stones and skies held spirits, Celtic and Christian. But it was equally true that the vigour of the people was now largely wasted by poverty, internecine strife, foreign wars, betrayal, and exile. The spirit so often consulted now came in a glass bottle and the social system which operated on family, honour and trust had largely been replaced by a pathetic dependency on an uncaring and impersonal state.

Further around the coast out of sight to his right an immense rock arch, eroded by the sea, thrust out into the ocean like a cathedral buttress.

In summer the shrill toccata of countless, nesting sea birds echoed between its walls like organ music. After a while his eyes found what they were seeking. Just where the moor ran down to the rocky shore, was a small, circular structure of random grey-brown whinstone. In its shape, hardly a traditional island dwelling. It was the Ferryman's home and place of work and, some said, his cell.

There had been a ferry here before documentary record, and there was an ancient oral tradition whereby ownership passed to the eldest son. As far as anyone knew a wife and a small family had always been able to subsist from the Ferryman's trade. But, with the depopulation of the island, crossings had dwindled to a trickle. The present incumbent lived alone, almost, it seemed, as an anchorite. In the absence of an heir it was said that God's providence would mark a traveller for the role when the time came. Well, that was just the speak of old women and in faith there was little in the tale to charm a traveller setting eyes on the place for the first time. A rotten wooden jetty against which knocked a rusting thirty-foot tender with a central wheelhouse and, by the jetty, a tiny corrugated iron shed stuffed with oil cans and an accretion of corroded metal were the sum capital equipment of the concern. There had been an occupational tradition in our young man's family also but that, he thought, was over now and over forever. He was eager to be gone. Even so he paused and took a deep breath. Here was stillness, with only the suck of the waves on the pebbled shore, and the scent of pines, of iodine from the sea and the aroma of smouldering peat blown in the wind. His gaze turned to the thin filament of smoke coming from the single, central chimney of the Ferryman's house. Of the occupant he really knew almost nothing except for the gossip that he was a semi-recluse who spoke little and was given to unexpected swings of mood. It was said that he was temperate in his habits and it was somehow accepted that he was pious. A word that now so embarrasses the world that its usage is more often met with derision than with respect.

He drew near to the house past a tumbled down and gateless stone wall which had once served to protect a few vegetables from the sheep.

He located a path through the grass to the bare wooden door which he struck three times. Some startled crows took to the air, cawing and he stood and waited. Some time passed and just as he was about to strike a second time a call like an ancient sword drawn slowly from a rusty scabbard came from within. It was a human voice and one as deep and as sad as the ocean.

"De tha thu'g iarraidh?"

"Tha mi'g iarraidh a dhol an tir mor."

The voice came close to the other side of the door.

"I am not going to the mainland this morning. Co tha sin?"

"It is Ronan MacDonald," and then in desperation, "the son of John MacDonald of Dunlaith and I must cross today."

A few seconds later the bolt was drawn and the door thrown open. The Ferryman issued forth, stooping as he did so to clear the low doorway. Straightening to his full and considerable height he placed his hands firmly on his hips, leant forward and surveyed our traveller, whom we must now call Ronan, with an inquisitive stare.

"Is it just so?" was all he said.

Even by Highland standards he was a large, powerfully-built man. On first sight his most remarkable feature was a cowl of long white hair which streamed back with the wind. His forehead was heavy, furrowed and weathered and his temples concave. Beneath his firm lips flowed a prophetical beard of grey-white, cut sharply across at the base of his broad neck. Those who had occasion to talk with him were soon aware that there was an intensity about his eyes that made it uncomfortable to meet the Ferryman's gaze. And still he stood and surveyed his visitor. For some inexplicable reason, Ronan felt that his position was becoming faintly ridiculous and that he needed to re-assert the seriousness of his request.

"It is an early hour, I know, but I have to be away now if I am to reach my destination."

He was speaking too quickly and the off-shore breeze seemed to snatch his words away and jumble their meaning. Yet the Ferryman's voice cut cleanly through the air.

"Well, well, John MacDonald's son there you are. You are no doubt a fine, big strong fellow but must you really be wanting to fly the nest already. Why not bide with us a while yet, I'm thinking that the world is not for you so soon."

The youth, as is the wont of all youth, was stung by what he perceived as the paternalistic tone of the Ferryman. It was, he thought, an affront to his dignity. By what right was this stranger so familiar. He spoke more insistently.

"I have already walked over from Dunlaith and need to be at Murravaig station in two hours, if you would just …"

"Atweel, atweel, John MacDonald's son and do you but think you can fit all providence into a railway timetable. Well listen, this is just the way of it and the way of the world, providence the caman and us the ball and lives cast into the wind with each of His strokes."

Slowly he stretched out his arm so that his white shirt sleeve rippled in the breeze. The arm was unnaturally still, as the head and talons of a hovering kestrel when all about is noise, change and motion; power resides in stillness.

"See yonder boat, now when I push her against the tides or drive her into the wind it is to little avail. We both struggle and strain and sweat and become unhappy and dispirited. Yet little progress have we made and no joy. Yet if I say no, I will not travail today but will wait until the current shows me the way, then, all is at once easy. The voyage is pleasing and the journey swift and sure. And if sometimes, John MacDonald's son, you do not always arrive precisely where you intended, you will find that providence may have allotted you a finer destination than you could have chosen. Aye, one long journey for your family is perhaps enough this season. This is a day, John MacDonald's son, to bide at home, and wait."

Ronan's rising impatience as he listened to the Ferryman had been checked momentarily by the mention of the 'other journey' in the young man's family. He turned inward upon the image it provoked. Women hugging their fluttering black dresses and shawls against the cold, wintry blast. Men, heads bent clasping black hats against black ties. Their grey hair blown pathetically by the wind under a grey furrowed sky. A bottomless grave, a stone Celtic cross, sea spray, the smell of fresh earth. Polished brass and oak spotted with rain drops. The uneven rows of bowed heads and behind them, in the distance, beneath the rowan which struggled for life against the graveyard wall, a figure of a man, watching. A big man with white hair who makes the sign of the cross, and then slips slowly away. A man not unlike the one who was now standing before him. And yet, any connection seemed so improbable it drifted, just as fleetingly, from his immediate thoughts. He turned again to the business in hand, he felt sure he knew what lay behind the Ferryman's reluctance.

"Look, if it's a matter of money, I could pay you an extra sum, say, for your inconvenience."

Ronan, to do him justice, regretted this remark as soon as he had made it. The Ferryman set his gentle, seal-grey eyes upon Ronan with a look that made him force down a blush. There was a marked contrast between the soft way the old man looked at his own hands and the undoubted power they still retained. Huge lumps of whinstone that they were. He rubbed his palms together and Ronan could hear the dry, rubbing noise of the calloused skin, and then the Ferryman's voice.

"You and I will wrestle for it will we not, the first to cry hold is the loser."

Youth, it has been said, is forever impetuous and ready to risk all for an ideal. Even so, the young man's first thought was that this Ferryman was indeed, as some said, a madman. Yet there was something reassuring about the old man's eyes and the way he now sat down upon a grassy mound, first placing a brass key on the top of an adjacent rock. In some way Ronan found the man almost comforting. He felt there was something important he would say to him, but could not define it. The Ferryman, sitting upright with arms folded, nodded his brow to the rock and then turned to face our young man.

"There is the key; begin or be gone."

Ronan had made his mark in scrum and scree and considered himself a canny, couthy lad, and powerful for his years. He had never fought any man in anger. Yet the strangeness of so doing now, on this bleak shore, in the misty, ambiguous half light between night and day, hardly occurred to him. It was a challenge. A chance that no youthful blood, be it presbyter or poet, could resist. And, was he not his father's son? He would try not to hurt the old man, a brief tussle, say, and one quick fall on the turf. That would take the wind out of him.

"So I will then," he shouted with an anger that surprised himself. Forced, artificial anger to put smedum to his kindling.

The old man arose slowly and smiled, it seemed, at the seriousness of the other's resolve. He was still smiling as, drawn together, they circled each other. Stooping, arms extended in a ritual dance, their feet lost from time to time in the rising mist. The young man felt that he was no longer treading on the earth but was drifting slowly in a circle around his opponent. They were like two planets locked in each other's orbits. Time and place became uncertain. Then the old man's arms swept around him. Like immense, broad oars leaving a wake of silver bubbles as they plunged through the air. He held Ronan in his embrace, like a child. And Ronan struggled like a demon to be free.

The young man's preconceptions had left him totally unprepared for the crushing strength he now encountered. The more furiously he struggled the tighter his opponent's grasp became. He gasped a "damn you", although more in growing fear than in malice. He was so close to the old man's heavy chest that the Ferryman's reply sounded like the rumble of an approaching avalanche.

"Aye, you curse me now, but the time will come when you bless me."

Ronan felt like a mountain of rock was inexorably sliding onto him. His very bones began to creak under the strain, but he would neither give in nor could he break free. An immense time seemed to be passing as the very rocks were ground to dust under the burden of their millennia. Whilst this young creature of bone, sinew and blood was gradually aware that he was profoundly tired, yet he must always struggle on under the commitment of his flesh and never cry hold. His awareness of external stimuli gradually faded. Now and again he sensed the encircling, impassive mountains forming a purple-brown amphitheatre against the sea, or a silver white flash of a wheeling seabird. He heard, again and again, the lonely cries of a curlew. Once in a while, when he caught the salt spray in the air, its astringency forced him back into the world and he was aware that, unlike himself, the old man neither strained or groaned nor palpitated nor gasped for air. Instead, the Ferryman's breathing and heartbeat came slow and regular, deep in his chest like a sanctus bell. He held Ronan calmly, strongly, yet not unmercifully.

At first the young man only thought of the passover which he must make. Gradually, through the seemingly interminable fatigue, pain and frustration, his aggression, arrogance, pride, vanity, desire, his very existence in the world, began to slip from him. He became resigned to the peace of death and felt no surprise that he longed for it. The only reality became his adversary. Almost a stranger yet almost a father. Their struggle became a common bond. Although beyond Ronan's comprehension, his opponent now tightened his grasp until the young man's sinews cracked. For the first time the Ferryman's voice was tinged with the beginnings of anxiety.

"Will you not relent now, and go home?"

Ronan's reply was slow in coming, indistinct yet just audible.

"I will not … I will not."

"You have your father's heart, Ronan MacDonald. Aye and maybe you have his obsession."

As he drew out these words the Ferryman braced his legs and raised Ronan into the air and onto his huge chest. Whether the embrace was in peace or in anger Ronan never knew for in that moment he sank into oblivion.

And in the deathlike sleep he dreamt. He dreamt of his father's thin ascetic face silhouetted against the armour of God, white collar and black jacket, and his greying black hair and grey eyes. A study in black and white. A voice was saying "I never knew you", slowly, repeatedly. And that voice was the Ferryman's voice and he appeared to Ronan in robes of gold and anointed in irresistible light. And out of that light stepped his father this time with a flaming sword in his right hand and in his left a black, domed casket. And the lid was open but when Ronan tried to look inside, its contents were now in shadow or now hidden beneath unbearable light which seared the eyes with exquisite pain. Time and again the open casket was offered to him until he fell exhausted to his knees and wept.

2

Two men seated in a Cambridge college room discuss a contemporary they first met by chance in Jerusalem. They share a letter from him.

"It is not common in life to be the recipient of a communication from the dead."

This was spoken by a man whose advanced years had yet failed to diminish his essential clarity and vigour. He spoke with that assurance and calm which comes from age and from learning. Attributes sometimes confused with knowledge and wisdom; which are rarely the province of man. Yet he luxuriated in the syllables and dwelt lovingly on their meaning as one who has suffered enough to appreciate the value of comfort, companionship, relaxation and intellectual stimuli. He spoke with the full yet soft and measured tone of one to whom free speech has become a privilege and to whom power and influence have become a right. His speech was devoid of accent or dialect but in spite of the macabre content there was a detectable smile in his voice.

"Even from a spirit who, whilst seeking the most sublime anonymity, left a wake of enigma and controversy in the world."

Turning his head a little to the side the speaker addressed these last words to an obvious contemporary of his seated in an adjacent armchair. The two men were seated in the study of some private rooms in St John's College, Cambridge. The speaker was a sometime Reader in Byzantine History, and the College President. The other chair was occupied by a cabinet minister whose portfolio also designated him Minister for Culture and the Arts. October sunlight filtered into the room via a single gothic tracery window and selected some items from the semi-darkness; the brass nail-heads on the green leather arm chairs, a strip of deep red carpet, the polished surface of an oak reading table, a finely-turned walnut music stand and a row of ponderous leather-bound volumes.

The shadow of the transom and mullion of the window formed a dark crucifix on the opposite wall. The minister looked at it whilst resting his chin on his clasped hands, somewhat in the aspect of prayer. He cleared his throat with a long but barely audible sigh.

"A Bishop of the Scottish Episcopal Church and, for that matter, a renowned theologian, does not simply abandon all for an obscure living in the Western Isles without public remark. Even his ability to secure that ministry, given his background, is a mystery." Then, after further contemplation, "I can't understand why any civilised person would want to cut themselves off from the current of city life."

"I can empathise with that, for the religious, spiritual person. I have some insight, there was a time that I thought I was chosen for the spiritual life."

James made a steeple of his fingers and rested his fleshy chin on the point. "How so, Andrew?"

As Andrew answered he had an intuition that he had already confided too much. "My first degree was in Divinity."

At this the Minister lifted his head from his hands and stared at the other with unfeigned surprise.

"You were a Divinity graduate?"

"Yes," with a half smile at the other's discomfiture, "briefly, a couple of years before you and I met in Jerusalem."

"Ah. Laude Jerusalem …"

"Quite."

"It seems, Andrew," the Minister continued in a more confidential tone, "that this is a season for confessions, both verbal and written."

Andrew leant slowly forward in his chair. "In this matter, James, this particular spirit retains a sepulchral silence." With this said, he slid his hand into a breast pocket and delicately drew forth a plain brown envelope. He held it out to the other man. There was absolute silence in the room for up to thirty seconds before he moved in his chair to accept the letter. He could not have accepted the Host with any greater reverence. As he began to remove the letter from its envelope he was aware of a dull rasp as his companion locked the study door and removed the key. Andrew sank back into his chair to meet the enquiring glance of the other who held the still unfolded letter in both hands.

"Just a precaution. Undergraduates bursting in, one never knows."

"Into the President's apartments?"

"We live in egalitarian times."

"We live in degenerate times. Times when, perhaps, even the bonds of lifelong friendship begin to decay."

Andrew smiled at the other with disarming warmth as he briefly clasped his hands "Not between us James. We have that strongest of all covenants; mutual dependence."

Their eyes met as Andrew settled back deep into the shadow of his chair. As his companion unfolded and began to read the letter, Andrew was able to observe him from the obscurity of his darkening corner. His friend's face was illuminated by the evening light except where the shadow cast by the letter fell across his features, just below the eyes. The effect was to concentrate the eyes which, in fact, were the only animated part of his figure and which seemed to express millennia of human longing. For knowledge, for truth, for spirituality, for temporal joy and power, for salvation from pain and death, for peace and for forgiveness. The text of the letter was simply but elegantly written in dark blue ink on cream paper. It was headed 'John MacDonald, The Manse, Skeasaig, Isle of Ramasey'. It was addressed to 'Sir Andrew Farquharson, St John's College, Cambridge' and it ran thus:

Well Andrew, I need hardly remind you that there is a time and a place for everything under Heaven. The harvest has been gathered in and 'Auld Suthy', my WS, will have sent you this, providing the fornicating old sinner has not pre-deceased me. I make no apology for the melodrama of this gesture which I know will offend your impeccable good taste. You will be reassured to learn that you will be spared any further histrionics from me.

You and I and James Galbraith have drunk deeply of antiquity since that faraway chance meeting in Jerusalem. So much so that our very bodies have become rags with the stench of grave mould. Oh Andy, did we develop and focus the spirituality of our youth? Sunny days lolling by the Cam on Granchester meadows in cricket whites. You reading Aquinas ... me, the pre-Raphaelite poets ... such claptrap. The sunlight glinting through the green willows and the dank scent of water. That dark-eyed nymph from Long Road College who told me she would die for you and then promptly married an accountant. Long bicycle rides to the fenland abbeys: Barnack limestone against flaming orange skyscapes. The excitement of May Balls of pink champagne and confidences. Of heated theological debate across warm ale by the inglenook of the Pike and Eel. The shared anguish of Finals, the word always reminds me of rain glistening on wet cobblestones and the smell of damp plaster. Then that year in Jerusalem, when James joined us and it all began. Was a lifetime of raking through arcane dust worth three such souls? With apologies to Nietzsche, we stared into the Abyss and the Abyss stared into us. How can I ever tell you what was concealed even, believe me, from myself. For I have found the truth that I was seeking.

Know then that we were in error in our perception of history. It exists only in the present. It is a reality when time is opened by us in the present. When the book is closed history ceases to exist even before the dust has settled. We carry all time within us. Know also that the history of events and knowledge of them and of thought is a living tree whose roots are Arcadia and whose branches, just a few, just one perhaps, are today and forever. Know above all my lineage, yes my lineage, which shed tears in Gethsemane and my inheritance which will never die and my legacy which is with you now.

You two fellow travellers forgive me I cannot help you lest I destroy you. It is time to abandon your darkness. Light will vanquish darkness, my friends, believe in that and that I truly love you. For I send you the inheritor of my line of my power, my son in whom I am well pleased.

The room grew almost dark with the gathering evening whilst James continued to contemplate the letter in his hand. He cherished it with the same scrutiny he had been wont to give to source documents in Hebrew, Sanskrit, Aramaic, Hellenic Greek, Occitan and Latin in an effort to find the true meaning of the writers. By the angle at which the letter was held it could be seen however that he was not in fact re-reading it but looking through the page into darkness. Looking for a light in his darkness.

With obvious effort, James returned to the present when a small table lamp was switched on casting a pool of faint light across the chamber.

"Always so pseudo-enigmatic."

The words came from Andrew but James could not discern his features which were obscured by the darkness behind the lamp.

"Yes, yes, enigmatic. Although not disingenuous I believe. He was the most inspired antiquarian scholar and theologian of his generation." Saying this, James looked pointedly towards the other's chair and added, "I believe he found something. That is, what he was searching for."

A few moments later the other replied out of the darkness; "And also a son."

"That seems, if you pardon the expression, inconceivable. You know as well as I that his wife, poor Rachel, who never shared that part of his life, died almost 20 years ago. That we, his closest friends, never knew he had any issue. I say again, inconceivable. How old is this child? Where has he been and where is he now?"

"Well, these questions may provide their own answers. Real life human beings usually do interpret themselves in the end."

"But to what end and to whom, Andrew, to whom?" As he said this, the Rt Hon. James Galbraith became increasingly animated to a pitch which would have made his colleagues wonder had it been exhibited on the floor of the House where he was famed for his imperturbable demeanour. Without pausing for a response he continued, shaking slightly with the effort of control; "With your leave, I will make enquiries. I am, as you know, not without influence. This concerns, I need hardly remind you, the work, the dreams, yes dreams, of a lifetime." James leant forward and returned the letter to his lifelong acquaintance. He had memorised every word. As their eyes met he slowly whispered; "We must find this child, and quickly."

Andrew took the letter and slid it into his breast pocket. "You know, James, you sound just like Herod Antipas."

The two spent the remainder of the evening in silence. Seated, immobile in the pool of light shed by a single lamp in the darkness. Keeping, as it were, a vigil.

3

Ronan recovering from his struggle with the Ferryman wakes to find himself in bed in an old croft house. He is visited by a beautiful young woman.

Ronan awoke to perfect darkness and to stillness. The stillness was not silence because he became aware of the sighs and whispers of the sea as it breathed like a troubled sleeper in the darkness. And the darkness was not blackness because, imperceptibly, he became aware of the coming dawn and of his surroundings. He gave a half-conscious thanks for the gift of life renewed. Renewed each day as a birth from the darkness of the womb and as much a miracle. These thoughts ran on until they were drowned by his flooding senses. For the first few moments of wakefulness he thought he was encased in a wooden casket. Upon further examination he became aware that he was in a box bed of the type common to the croft houses and turf-thatched black houses of the previous century. The room had a low-pitched ceiling which inferred that the eaves of the house were tolerably near the ground. The bed was built in under the eaves and the bed ends were the walls which separated the room from two other chambers. By today's standards the room was hardly more than a very wide corridor. The opposite wall to the bed was dominated by a deep, splayed window possessing two panes of glass which glowed with the light of dawn. The surface of the room was mostly a resinous dark wood cladding. The window was framed in a bare stone opening in a wall which was roughly plastered, whitewashed and completely unadorned. The wind slid around the sides of the iron window frame with a gentle, lilting voice which brought him a scent of the sea and of coolness.

Ronan's clearing thoughts now returned to his own mortal architecture and to the events which had preceded this inexplicable repose. The confusion of events was remembered as a darkened dream, although he knew these events to be true. He also knew himself to have been a fool. Slowly shaking his head and placing his hands over his eyes he murmured "what devil can have possessed me?"

Then, seized by a momentary misgiving he feverishly examined his body and in doing so discovered that at some time he had exchanged his clothes for a heavy, grey flannel night-gown. Bemused yet nonetheless reassured by his brief anatomical survey he gently sat up and swung his legs over the edge of the bed. His head felt light and his legs tingled but that gradually passed, he had not been killed at any rate. Youth and health are not as easily vanquished as the innocence they bear. The bedside served as the half wall of the corridor which was the only floor space. The floor was uneven stone flags worn smooth by the generations. A runner of faded brown carpet disappeared under the panelled oak doors at each end. He was in an old croft house for sure.

As Ronan got to his feet he immediately winced as a sharp pain shot through his thigh. He had evidently torn a muscle in the struggle, damned fool that he was. How long now before he could continue his journey? Momentarily furious with himself he limped violently to the window. There his face was at once bathed in warmth and light as the sun gently rose from a cleft in the hills. And his frustration and bitterness fell away from him. He gazed at the wind washing over the glistening moors, elbowing aside the gorse and softly running its fingers through the heather. The gorse was fading yellow-scented and the heather flowers were passing. Summer was playing its last act and winter was poised to make its entrance. Still, all inside his small room was peace, warmth, cleanliness and order and, above all things, simplicity. There was a profound silence, made infinitely more precious by the sighing of the wind. Something almost lost to the world remained here.

After some moments, one grey-purple cloud passed over the sun and he shivered.

"So, you have risen from the dead?"

Beauty, purity and honesty are facets of the same phenomenon. If one is lost, the other two cease to be. They co-exist in a fragile and elusive trinity. Why do we not add innocence; simply because innocence is not an attribute of mankind, through whom sin has stolen into the world. According to John Calvin the young lady who thus addressed Ronan may not have been innocent but beautiful she undoubtedly was. That rare example of beauty which demands a sharp intake of breath followed by total aphasia on behalf of the observer. Firstly, she was tall and held her head high and her shoulders proud and looked bravely and openly at those she spoke to.

Secondly, she was slim and well formed with a flawless complexion and lustrous dark eyes which spoke of someone not yet 25 years of age. Thirdly, though this has never been a popular view, who can deny that the face will unfailingly convey a noble ancestry and that the eyes betray intelligence with equal accuracy. This lady's porcelain features spoke of a will of blue steel and her eyes of a wild Celtic ancestry already old when Columba brought redemption from the shores of Dalriada. A thousand years of Celtic and Romish Catholicism, of Episcopacy and the Presbyterianism of the Covenant and even Saxon and Norman cultural and economic imperialism had washed over her without leaving a mark. She was still every bit as dangerous as the lethal, basket-hilted brands of the sons of Kenneth Alpin. Yet she was innocent of her power as a wild creature of its rending ferocity. She was as the sparrow hawk, whose impact on the collared dove, at a velocity approaching sixty miles an hour, often instantaneously decapitates and disembowels the prey. And she was as vulnerable as that hawk who in its rushing flight is sometimes fatally impaled on a blackthorn bush. Hanging crucified on the bloodied thorns. Fourthly, she was dressed and groomed with devastating dignity. A simple, brown calico dress with many small pleats about a drop waist swept from the high neckline to her fine ankles and feet, set off by slim calf-leather brogues. One did not look for heels on those shoes, she did not need them and any such fuss would have seemed a nonsense which could only impede her youth and vigour. Fifthly, sixthly and seventhly: her hair. John Knox was wont to quote St Paul on women's hair but in this case the lady's hair was not only her pride but a powerful image of her sex, sensuality and inner power. It flowed down over her shoulders like a mountain cascade with as much trapped sunlight, waves and buoyancy as the living water. It ended with a splash of curls just above her waist. Its colour would have defeated the palate of a pre-Raphaelite painter and sent the poor man distracted with grief. Not auburn, not chestnut but somewhere in that warm red spectrum yet ethereal; and incandescent as if it would sear one's fingers in the flames. As he looked at her, Ronan knew that such pain would be a trivial price to pay.

For the first time since he had woken, Ronan realised that he probably presented a rather sorry and unkempt appearance. His hand felt the downy stubble on his chin and then went back to his side where it reminded him of his rough-woven night gown. As if to further discomfort him, his strained thigh failed him as he turned to face his visitor, and he was forced to limp a pace to the wall for support. The girl smiled and watched, but said no more. By contrast, Ronan felt gross, clumsy, oafish and grubby. Although, if he but knew it, he was rather picturesque in his dishevelment. In an almost contemporaneous oil painting of MacRaes dancing on a firelit castle roof, the evening before the battle of Sherrifmuir, there is a young clansman half Norse, half Scot. He stands out by his fine features, broad frame and blonde hair. Thus was Ronan, whose ancestry drew as much from Somerled and the Norse colonisation of the Western Highlands as it did from the Clan Rannald Lords of the Isles. His thick, sandy hair and peppering of freckles gave him a boyish innocent appearance. His eyes, perhaps, a little too intense. Such is the Celt, incurably introspective and fatally romantic. To this end, let us divulge one of our young female observer's secret thoughts. In his long gown of rough grey wool he seemed to her to embody the young Bishop Aiden; newly consecrated and setting out from Iona on his mission to evangelise Saxon Northumberland. This, indeed, was how she was always to remember him. But make no error, this girl held her counsel as safe and dark as the mysterious green ocean.

When, after some moments, Ronan felt that he could trust his clumsy tongue not to betray him, he spoke. And what he said was only too obvious.

"I fear I may have acted foolishly yesterday and caused you no little inconvenience."

"Yes, but you are young yet."

Ronan resisted the urge to reply to the effect that she herself was hardly his damned grandmother. Thankfully, for him, his Scot's pride was still somewhat deflated by recent events.

"Could you tell me please how I have come over to the mainland and how I came to be here and where exactly am I and may I know who you are and who I have to thank … and …?"

His voice tailed off in his confusion and he stopped with an embarrassed smile. Which was the best thing he could have done, for they both laughed at once and this broke the tension.

"All in good time, all in good time. I believe a hot bath followed by some breakfast is the first requirement; and, one more question you might ask Ronan MacDonald, is just who had to put you into that woollen night-gown."

Then Ronan stopped smiling as a hot flush passed across his cheeks. He knew from her smile that she was enjoying his embarrassment, but he cared not one jot. Then the girl blushed charmingly at her own forwardness and they both laughed again. Laughter is the world's best physic next to love, and Ronan felt immediately better and even forgot his injuries. Which was all very curious for one who had been so badly wounded.

4

The young woman tells Ronan how she knows about him and explains about Lachlan Mor the Ferryman. She gives Ronan a small wooden box, a legacy from his father. The box appears to contain only the remains of an old church candle.

Ronan was seated in the weak autumn sunlight on a rough wooden bench beside a girl with no name. The bench, and Ronan, drew support from the white-washed stone of the cottage wall against which they leant. The cottage door was open and a chocolate brown sheep dog sprawled lazily across the threshold, gradually abandoning the unequal struggle to support the weight of his eyelids. Ronan had just bathed and eaten and shared the dog's delicious languor in the sunlight. The girl presented a disarming picture of highland domesticity seated near a basket of drying peats, her lap smothered by an enormous woollen shawl which she was darning. The browns, russets, purples and shadowy greens of the scene travelled through the brain like a bolt of Harris tweed along a waulking bench. As he let the colours and the thin waulking song of the wind unravel in his mind, Ronan glanced at the girl. Curled up on the far end of the bench, she had kicked off her shoes and folded stockingless legs underneath her as she worked. Her head was bowed in concentration. You would think, he thought, that we might be an old married couple sitting here like this and never mind that our acquaintance is but a few hours and that she has spoken barely a handful of words to me. But when he looked at her again, her pretty feet and shapely calves and her hair tumbling forward over her face and the smooth nape of her neck made

23

for young men to kiss, damn them, she never looked less like any married woman he had yet set eyes on. And to think, he thought, that I don't even know her name.

"To think", he said aloud, "that I don't even know your name and who to thank, although you seem to know something of me."

"Yes, that is correct."

Blast her, was she teasing him again; and spoken without even looking at him too. She's a veritable froth of words this girl. Ronan, however, exercised an uncharacteristic diplomacy and ventured a further amiable smile and address to the creature without a name or face.

"Will you not put a poor man out of his misery and answer just a few of his questions, I am like to die of curiosity if you don't and a saint like you would hardly like such a sin blackening her soul."

She smiled at that and turned her face half towards him so that she looked just like the illustration of a fairy he had seen in a child's picture book. That child was him, reading on his mother's lap. His poor, beautiful, tragic mother. Glimpsed occasionally through a dream, but always with him. When this girl looked at him, he became that child again.

"Why you are hardly more than a child," she teased, "though you call yourself a man proudly enough." And she added quickly to diffuse his rising rancour, "Although you are a couthy enough lad, Ronan Mac-Donald, and I will answer your questions. You will have to forgive my seeming rudeness. I am as little used to visitors as you are to fainting fits." Laying aside her work she smiled.

"To begin with let me help you introduce yourself. You have forgotten to do so, and it is only polite that you should. You are Ronan MacDonald, bachelor of the parish of Dunlaith. Your father was John MacDonald who was born in Dunlaith, unlike his son who was born in Edinburgh. Your father rose to pre-eminence in the Church of Scotland but, amidst some controversy, your father gave up what you might call public life and soon after returned to a ministry in the parish of his birth. That was shortly after your birth. You attended Skeabost school until the age of ten years whereupon you were boarded – an ugly word don't you think? – at Loretto. At the ripe age of 17 years you returned home, almost a stranger in the village, and the following year … the … following …"

Here both her smile and confidence deserted her. In truth she had not meant to go so far. She wrung her hands, and fidgeted as she searched for the right words. Help, however, was at hand as, almost in a dream, Ronan softly completed the narrative.

"And I came home to find father ill and near his last. He married late in life. Married a second time, for his first love, you might say, was the Church. And the pain of her death when I was but five years old came back to me when I saw him. It was like an old wound bursting afresh. I walked over to Ramasaig and down the glen by the river, still mumbling its devotions, past the ruined crofts, where generations of pain and suffering and joy are returning to the land, and sat by the bay where the water surges over the basalt rocks like a marble bath and the heron stands like a stone. And I was three days and three nights by the shore in a cell-like, shell-like cave known as teampul calum ceille."

Neither of them knew that she had taken his hand. But as she did so she was able to speak again. "That was after the funeral, folks thought you had gone to stay in Kintail, with your mother's sister. In the evening, after the sun had set over the Outer Isles, you would light a fire on the shingle and sit staring into the embers until dawn. When you returned, it was learned that you were to sell the old house and that you would go to university. Not to St Andrew's, to read divinity as … as …"

"As my father would have wished."

"As your father would have wished, but to Edinburgh, to read medicine. And …"

"And this is as far as I have managed to proceed in my famous journey."

As he said this he seemed to come back to the present and to himself. "I say 'famous journey' for what I believed was my own heart's secret seems known to half the world." Ronan, it must be said, struggled now even more to grasp the events of the past two days, and was not equal to the task. A lapse of some minutes ensued wherein the girl looked increasingly regretful and uncomfortable and Ronan simply stared at her, vainly trying to associate his thoughts. She gently, regretfully, withdrew her hand. When he spoke, it was not without bitterness.

"Well it was nice of you not to spare the pain of my recollection. Although you might just have added that my father and I drifted apart in the year preceding his death and that in fact … in fact … we parted unreconciled. You certainly have a remarkable, surgical precision about you."

She clasped her hands under her chin in a spasm of anguish and opened her mouth to apologise, but Ronan continued with rising warmth. He swung growling around to face her.

"I think you had better tell me who you are and how the devil, and devil it is like, that you come to know such things."

Without warning, she smiled at him again. Not that ambiguous, impish smile where you never knew if you were laughed at, but with a smile of simple friendship and concern. Yet again, Ronan's permafrost melted in spite of his every effort to blast them both with freezing bitterness. Is it possible that years of sadness and loss can be gently erased by the administration of one smile? It is like, he told himself, the administration of the consecrated wine for the remission of sins. Suffering and death which can only be remitted by the payment of sacramental love. A smile, a kiss, powerful physic for the soul. But in this world, a smile and a kiss can quite as easily deliver the body and soul to everlasting death. So now, we first think to take such coin in the palm of our hand and assay its value, just in case it is false, before we drop it into our pockets as pure gold. This we should do if we were wise as serpents but it seems to us so base to doubt such gifts, such innocent gifts, as a smile; and a kiss.

She kissed him. As a sister might, on his cheek, and then withdrew a few feet. When she spoke she smiled still.

"Do not look so fierce, Ronan MacDonald." Ronan had never felt less fierce. His face tingled soft and warm and scented where she had kissed him and he felt an uncomfortable fear in his chest. He waited and listened.

"I am Mary Dalbeith from Glenelg." Ronan was a little taken aback at this point to find that she had held out her hand for him to shake. He took it and shook it somewhat stiffly. The formality was a contradiction to the crass society of the present. Ronan respected it and she smiled at his seriousness.

"Having graduated in Life Sciences from Edinburgh, I have now commenced my Doctorate in Ecology and have rented this cottage to undertake some field work on sea otters, the pressures on habitat and food chain, pollution, predation, that sort of thing. This is all very boring I'm afraid, but now to the interesting part. My good friend who owns this cottage, Lachlan Mor, came to tea yesterday morning and with him brought you, flat out in the back of his Land Rover. Well, Lachlan knows more about healing than any doctor, so when he said; 'Lass, just you keep the child warm and in bed, but watch him close for a night and in the morning he will be none the worse of it', who was I to argue? Over his tea, for he wouldn't take a dram, just like him, he told me that you and he had a 'wee bit of a wrestle' and that you had almost got the better of him. No mean feat with Lachlan Mor. Ronan gasped audibly.

"Are you saying that the Ferryman brought me here and that you are an acquaintance of his ... and that he owns this property?"

"Ronan, my dear, glad as I am to learn that you have been paying such close attention, how will I ever get this story out if you keep inter-rupting? I will lose the narrative, tire of it, abandon it and probably go indoors and read a book." Ronan shrugged his shoulders and leant back against the wall.

"I agreed to look after you, feed you up – very domesticated of me don't you think – let you rest and then send you on your way. Now Lachlan, as you must know, is an old friend of your father's and ..." Ronan sprang upright on the bench.

"I know no such thing, nor do I hardly believe it. My father and the Ferryman ..."

"Well I have some reading to get on with, so if you will just excuse me ..."

Ronan held her wrist, but gently, "I will not interrupt you again, please go on." Their eyes met, and she sat down.

"As I said, Lachlan, a friend to my mother and my friend since child-hood," – here she looked straight at Ronan – "being also an acquaint-ance of your father, told me something of your life after he had delivered you – that makes you sound like a parcel, or a baby – and was sitting on this bench with a mug of tea cradled in his huge hands. With simply a 'come down to the shore if you have any difficulty', Lachlan, as usual, was off back to the Island. And that, Ronan MacDonald, is all there is to tell. Well, almost all for he asked me to give you this. It is from your father." So saying she drew from her sewing basket, a small wooden box with a domed top, like a miniature chest and held it out to Ronan.

Once again, Ronan had to address another paradigm shift in the order of his known world. His amazement was so apparent that the girl, Mary, could not help remarking on it.

"Have you seen this before?"

As he answered the sun slid behind the clouds and a dark wind stirred the blonde hair over his eyes.

"Only in a dream, a dream of great pain and suffering of the spirit."

"About your father?"

"Yes ... and about me."

"Lachlan would say that they are the same. But then, he is like a bridge with the past. His church is the Celtic church, pre Romish, and he has the language, liturgy and observances of Columba's faith. His family has always kept this pure. Agreed, that this is almost incredible but, it is true, the fashions and technology of the last millennium are but a passing dream to him. He contains all church history within him; he is both arcane and shining new. He holds the world together, past and present, with his great arms. And when he meditates on all he has been given from Christ, it gives him great strength, liberation and power."

Her voice had become as quiet and as regulated as her breathing. When Ronan spoke the softness of his own voice comforted him.

"You sound almost like a disciple."

"No, not a disciple; simply an inheritor."

She looked away to the horizon where the moor ran out of sight, under darkening clouds, between the mountains down to the shore. It had become overcast and cold. Ronan's hands were white and bloodless where they clasped the small casket yet he fought his fatigue and confusion to frame the question he must ask.

"Lachlan's connection with my father, please explain it to me."

She did not turn to him but sought out his hand again.

"I know almost nothing of that except the box you have in your hands. There may be little more between them than that; Lachlan your father's messenger and, perhaps, a common history."

"You seem to tell me a lot, but it is really little enough and little sense in it. What you may know, you do not say."

She looked at him closely then. Inspecting him. As a knight who tries a sword, parrying and thrusting in the air and, with an air of disappointment, returns it to the swordsmith, finding it dull and heavy, not keen and mettlesome to the arm.

"Ronan, you look weary. All this has tired you, and you far from strong yet. We will go in out of this cold wind and warm ourselves by the range. I will read and you will doze *in cathedra* in the Ferryman's old arm chair. First, you must open the casket. I'll admit that I am as pandorean as any girl and if you don't do so at once I will simply die of curiosity."

Ronan's limbs did indeed feel heavy so he let himself be guided by the girl. He placed the casket on his knees and examined it. The lid had two brass hinges and there was a small rusty hasp securing it, but no lock. The wood was so black with age and wear that it was impossible to say any more than that it appeared very old and that the wood was remarkably dense and hard, like bog oak. He felt that perhaps, he knew not why, the wood had been hewn from the great forests of Caledon, long since grazed into extinction by sheep and deer, and now replaced by mile after mile, rank after monotonous rank of sterile sitka spruce. Only vestigial clumps of the ancient forest survive on loch and river islets, sacred places where the Celtic saints were laid to rest amongst the last remnants of a squandered inheritance. Cherishing through the last millennium, something of infinite value now suffocating in meaningless squalor. A symbol of something precious almost lost to the world. Something of infinite importance; yet quite simple. Ronan looked again at the casket and became aware that his mind had been exploring patterns of thought quite new to him. The events of the past three days, he felt, must be having some effect. It almost seemed that every time he opened his eyes his perspective on the world had altered. He glanced at the girl but she remained resolute. There was nothing for it but to look inside then, so, struggling against a strong instinct to cast the chest far, far from him into the blustering wind, he undid the hasp and slowly lifted the lid.

Whatever he had expected to find could not have prepared him for the anti-climax. Inside the dark box, wedged at an angle across it was the remains of an old church candle. It was some seven inches long with a blackened wick at the molten end. The bees' wax was yellow and, in parts, ingrained with soot. Ronan held the candle between forefinger and thumb whilst he examined it and then returned it to the casket. He could feel Mary's sense of disappointment.

"Well, it must have had some kind of emotional value to my father, perhaps it was from his last communion, I don't know. But I will look after it as a keepsake, as he obviously did."

Mary liked him for that, smiled, and stood up smoothing the creases from her dress with the palms of her white hands.

Later that evening they sat by the range, a black lump of smoking cast iron which commanded attention as the provider of heat and cooking on chilly evenings. The firelight was amplified in her hair, to which it took second place as a source of warmth and comfort. Ronan sat in a thread-bare, fustian armchair and gazed into the firelight. Mary sat cross-legged on a pile of cushions absorbed in her reading. Again, Ronan was overcome by her elfin quality. As she sat with bare knees and fiery tresses spilling over her face she could have been a study from a romantic poem; La Belle Dame Sans Merci, perhaps. She sat a little to his right, almost leaning her left shoulder against the arm of his chair. At once Ronan was overcome by an impulse to kiss the nape of that slender neck and he began, quietly and carefully, to lean forward in his chair. Inch by inch he neared his goal. He was just within six inches of her when a fearsome and deafening noise at his left ear make him spring to his feet and swing around. In his stealth, Ronan had not considered the sheepdog who, he imagined, was fast asleep on the floor. Rarely in his life had Ronan wished to kill anything as much as he wished to murder that beast, as it stood, paws braced, alternately growling and barking.

Mary surveyed the scene with a half smile. "You are fortunate he did not nip you. They do that, you know, to subdue the sheep; and you look pretty sheepish at the moment."

"Why, I was only getting up to go to bed," he lied, and, to be fair, hated himself for saying it.

"Well, as long as that is all you were getting up to. Before you turn in Ronan, I should tell you that the day after tomorrow I am going back to Edinburgh. Of course, you must travel up to town with us, that is, if you are fully recovered. If you don't feel strong enough yet I am sure Lachlan will not mind if you stay on here for a few days. I will be travelling with a friend who has been staying in Oban. He is arriving tomorrow morning. You will like him, I think, he is a historian with a special interest in the Western Highlands."

Ronan thought himself a damned fool. It was obvious, to all but him, that such a pretty girl must have a lover, lovers perhaps, yet he could not help but ask,

"Have you known him long, your friend?"

"Oh, long enough. Good night, Ronan, pleasant dreams."

5

In London, James Galbraith looks out over the river from his eighth-floor flat on Chelsea Embankment. David Garrett, wakes in his less salubrious lodgings south of the river. He receives a summons from Galbraith and later that day the two men meet in a quiet wine bar.

Dawn in a large city has a peculiar horror to the sensitive or, perhaps, over-sensitive mind. James Galbraith stood by the window of his eighth floor flat in Pimlico Court. He had bought it before the new Docklands developments were available and, at the time, it was unusual for its panorama of the Thames from Chelsea Bridge to Tower Bridge. On balance, he preferred it to the more trendy newcomers. He sympathised with its architecture which reflected the moral restraint, austerity and stylised motifs of the 1930s. It was convenient for the House … and its inhabitants were discreet.

Sky and river were of indistinguishable grey on this oppressive September morning. Through the partly open window drifted the smell of exhaust fumes and the growing rumble of traffic. The fumes made his stomach contract and the slamming doors of delivery vans and the shouting of their drivers made him nervy and anxious. There was a crash of glass as a milkman or drayman landed a crate and someone was whistling a tune from an old West End musical in that queer warbling manner popular in the tap rooms of forty years ago. James moved to the window and closed it. Its double glazing plunged him into a near silent, fragrant, air-conditioned microcosm. He did not want to be reminded of social history, he did not wish to glance behind him on his 'lonesome road'.

Life had given him privileges and he knew how to use them. He had never indulged in what he termed the 'class guilt' of the 1960s. Whilst others were indulging in the new social freedoms and mind-expanding experiences of that era, he was, literally, doing his archaeological ground work in Jerusalem. Since that time his solace, his obsession, had been the distant past. If you looked far enough back in time life became timeless. The core science, philosophy, beliefs and politics of all ancient societies, he found, were compelled to historical repetition rather than variety. It was intensely comforting. There were gaps in our understanding of the past of course but even these missing pieces of the puzzle would fall into place, given time. As he thought this he bit his lip and was annoyed to taste that he had drawn blood. One quest could not wait. James did not have the required amount of time to begin again. He held his large, fleshy palms upward and gazed down at them as if he could see two piles of sand held there, but gently escaping through his fingers.

The day was so dull that James could see his reflection in the window glass. His features could have been noble but were somewhat spoiled by the soft, chubby cheeks and chin which gave him the appearance of a magnified schoolboy. His hair was straight, short and mousy; his complexion pale and, it has to be said, oily. He was blessed however, with wide shoulders and a good chest. Like many, so called, portly men he was surprisingly light on his feet and his dress, if uninspiring, was always immaculate and compensated for his indifferent grooming. Some women could no doubt have warmed to his more boyish and vulnerable qualities, but women were not a feature of his life.

The room behind him reflected his preoccupation with the Near East and his finely cultivated tastes. Finished in a pastel green wash with deep green carpets it was furnished with select artefacts recovered from a life-time's study of the ancient civilisations of Mesopotamia. The illumin-ated niches in the large drawing room contained sensitively chosen urns, statuary and other archaeological items. The soft furnishings suggested Islamic brocades and chintz. This morning James wore a dark red silk dressing gown and red leather slippers which gave even him a slightly oriental appearance. His gaze ran out to the jumbled suburbs south of the river. Beyond Battersea park and Dulwich common, the last leafy-green vestiges of the great North Wood the Normans had known, and on to the sweating, crumbling bedsitter lands; Peckham, Balham, Tulse Hill, Streatham and so on. Uncountable shadowy roofs and chimneys silhouetted here and there against clouds of sulphurous smoke oozing upwards through the heavy, grey sky. Roof-tops like ranks of black and rotten teeth symbolising pain, decay and complete hopelessness.

The aroma of freshly-percolated coffee was gradually drawing James's attention from the window. He broke his concentration and drew a phone from his dressing-gown pocket and began to key in a number he knew from memory. Whilst he was waiting for the connection he was drawn once again by thoughts of fresh coffee, warm croissant and a yielding Chesterfield. As he was turning away he gave the horizon a last glance and whispered "We must be sure that our housing policy always keeps us one step ahead of the mob. Such locations are simply breeding grounds for those who may vote us out of power one day, if we chance to lower our guard. And they quite spoil the view and depress one's spirits. They are nothing less than a vision of Hell."

* * * * *

"I appear, finally, to have been cast into Hell."

These words were whispered by a sleeping man as he reluctantly awoke to his own, anonymous torment. The mildewed and flaking plaster above his head reminded him that he was staying, for it cannot be called living, in a terraced house not far south of the river, which the planners and politicians like to refer to as an abode given over to multiple occupancy. Or even, bed-sitting rooms. From such innocuous phrases, however, it would not be easy to identify this dissected corpse of grimy London brick and jumbled slate, this abused child of Victoria's reign. Just to hear this man whisper was to experience the horror of the place.

"Through how many cantos of the inferno I have tumbled it is difficult to say and with how many vile demons I have battled, and lost, I cannot

recall. Yet these leprous, mould-stained walls, the characteristic stink of rotten cabbage freshened with sewage and the unceasing cacophony of infernal noises makes the situation quite clear ... and quite, quite ...”
He was interrupted by the ringing of a telephone. Not nearby but two floors below him. The telephone stopped and there was a pause followed by the sound of the floorboards outside his room door and a sharp rap on the door. Then came a man's voice in a thick Dublin accent,

"You in there, telephone, an' look sharp will you, I'm waiting for a call myself."

More suffering floorboards, then just background noises, the squeaking of a radio, the muffled clangs of outraged plumbing, the low background throb of a diesel engine and the sharp cries of children shouting profanities in the street. The closest this place ever came to silence. Satan rides amongst noise and clamour; spirituality resides only in quietness.

The man who had joined the lost cohorts of the damned rolled out of bed. His movements were remarkably fluid considering that he also had to extricate himself from the deep pit which had formed in the middle of the sagging bed and lumpy mattress. He didn't sit up first, but simply, automatically, was on his feet within seconds. Old habits die hard for those who have been institutionalised by blind obedience to authority. Two quick thoughts struck him. First, "Just look at me standing to attention like a tin soldier, and in this slum, what a joke." Second, "The damned don't get telephone calls, it must be a mistake." He considered going back to bed but, like the Duke of York, when he was up he was up. Anyway, the only bathroom was two floors down. He retrieved a thin towel from the windowsill, opened the door and within a minute was cautiously holding the receiver to his ear.

* * * * *

That afternoon a black cab drew up outside La Bohème, an appropriately named wine bar in Covent Garden, and decanted a middle-aged man wearing a pin-striped suit. To give him his due, James Galbraith would have been uncomfortable if any of his friends or colleagues had seen him enter such an emporium of cultural bad taste. The fact that they were unlikely to do so was precisely the reason why he had chosen it today. The Rt Hon. J. Galbraith's acquaintances were more used to accosting him in one of his St James's clubs or, more occasionally, in selected public rooms near the Palace of Westminster. However, the more casual acquaintance would hardly remark spotting the Arts Minister in somewhere as sufficiently trendy as La Bohème ... particularly if that gentleman were conversing with an apparent denizen of the arts underworld. It had been planned thus, with James's characteristic thoroughness; and ruthlessness.

At 3.30 on a Tuesday afternoon, the place was three-quarters empty. He bought a scotch and dry ginger and settled himself at a vacant table. Bars, like life, can be three-quarters empty or one-quarter full. This one was three-quarters empty. Converted from an old warehouse in the 1960s, and re-born several times subsequently, the efforts of the marketing men had not been spared. The basic idea seemed to be the auditorium of a fin-de-siècle grand opera house. The idea had not been realised. The crimson flock wallpaper was festooned with fake operabilia. Prints of theatres from every capital city hung around as did framed programmes. An aria sounded tinnily from an overworked stereo. In a glass case behind the bar a collection of mildewed opera glasses stared forlornly out at the customers. And the patrons themselves seemed equally self conscious to have been captured from their workaday lives and balanced uncomfortably on red velvet chairs under imitation oil lamps. James was involuntarily reminded of when he had been asked to open a restaurant adjacent to Guildford's new theatre. It was named, he recalled, the Jolly Farmer and customers were compelled to dine seated in plywood hay wagons which they entered by short flights of steps. Folk music and bar staff dressed in rustic smocks and leather gaiters added to the bizarre nature of the place. The glum, slightly guilty faces of the hay wain diners reminded him of the drinkers in La Bohème. To him it had all the joy and charm of a deserted bus station.

"This is a pleasant spot you have found, James."

James, hiding his momentary unease beneath his usual armour plate, found himself looking over his left shoulder at a youngish man wearing what he quite rightly guessed to be his only mid-grey lounge suit. James continued to be uneasy until his guest had moved around the table to face him. What James knew of this man made him distinctly uncomfortable to find him standing behind his left shoulder. He had appeared, quite unobserved and even seemed to have escaped the notice of the other drinkers. He certainly looked unobtrusive. Medium height, medium build, grey crumpled woollen suit. On closer inspection, however, there were tell tale signs of his provenance. His ginger hair cut to a length where his head looked almost shaven, a blue scar on his left cheek told of a deep wound and he wore a Paratroop Regiment tie. There were other signs of his more recent background which James instantly studied and analysed. The suit in which he had 'quitted' the Army had grown larger of late as the man's, still muscular, frame had grown thinner. His shoes were somewhat 'on their uppers', and the laces much knotted in repairs. The suit had not enjoyed the luxury of dry cleaning for quite some time. Finally, James noticed with gratification that the signet ring which had lately adorned the man's left hand was absent. That the Peckham pawnbrokers must now have acquired a gold ring with a square-fielded monogram which rotated to reveal the Masonic cipher, James adjudged that their meeting had been perfectly timed. James rose to shake hands.

"Thank you for arranging to meet me at such short notice. Please sit down Garrett, I'll get the drinks. Still the same tipple for you I take it?"

Garrett sat down. He was grateful enough for James's offer to buy the round but as for thanking him for coming at short notice, they both knew that Garrett's life afforded infinite opportunity to attend meetings, providing the tube fare could be found, or the distance could be walked in time. Garrett was also keenly aware that it was James who had arranged this meeting and he was sensitive enough to bridle inwardly. Pride, however, was a luxury he was learning to live without. That he had nothing better to do was not, of course, the reason he had come today. Shortly after the Ministry had invited him to end his military career he had been foolish enough to visit James's Lodge. At the time he was staying in a hostel off the Bayswater Road and it was the nearest one he knew. It was soon borne in upon him that the bonds of freemasonry do not transcend the class system; certainly not in James Galbraith's Lodge. However, James appeared to take an interest in him. At first he thought is was because they had both been to Winchester, but now he was not so sure. On that first meeting James had given him some fatherly business advice and a few contacts. On the basis of these he had gone into partnership with one of James's contacts, in setting up a security firm. Very sound, James had said, in these unruly times. Sound it may have been but not so his partner who made himself invisible with all that remained of Garrett's pension settlement, leaving him to fight an army of creditors. When the creditors had gone, so had Garrett's future.

Although he had never reproached him, Garrett clung to a vague hope that James might just feel guilty enough to help find him some sort of position. Nominally a Captain in the Paratroops, he had in fact spent much of his army career on special operations in some of the world's worst trouble spots. He had spent sixteen years developing a career specialism which would never find its way onto a curriculum vitae. You see there was not much call for Garrett's line of work in civilian society; that of delivering sudden and violent death with immaculate precision.

He watched James return from the bar with two shorts. Whilst James smiled amiably, Garrett, as was usual, betrayed no emotion.

James sighed contentedly as he eased himself into a chair opposite him. As he raised his tumbler of Glenfiddich he contemplated Garrett over the glass. Highland malts were now so far beyond Garrett's means that they had a near symbolic meaning. He had first acquired a taste for them during his time of optimism and achievement which seemed to have occurred to someone else several lifetimes ago. Yet he knew it must have been him because he remembered the scent of the hills and the subtle palate of heath and lichen as soon as his glass touched his lips.

The smooth, peaty esters and the warmth of the spirit created emotions of Garrett's sense of loss which almost unmanned him … much as James had calculated that it would.

"I forgot to ask you if you have lunched yet Garrett?"

"Yes, thank you, I ate early," lied the other. But he could not help looking at the pastries and gateaux imprisoned behind the glass bar counter. He longed to liberate them and, to his annoyance, his stomach articulated the conspiracy.

"Well, I've ordered us some cream pastries and chocolate cake, I hope you will not embarrass me by making me eat alone."

Once the white-aproned waiter had laid the cakes on the table James became solicitous about the other's circumstances. He smiled as a dentist might just before probing an exposed nerve.

"How's that fiancée you told me about, any wedding bells yet?"

A slight contraction of Garrett's lips and a heaviness in the eyes was all that might have conveyed the pain engendered by this question. Its effect was not lost on James. Albeit that James might be his only presumed friend and confidante, Garrett still replied as guardedly as he could. He explained that his girl had tried to understand his fall from grace and to be supportive but when the money had run out too … well, it was very hard for a girl from a respectable background to cope with it all. Money never seems that important … until you don't have any.

"Is there another man involved do you think, or might there be a chance of you two getting back together?"

Another layer of pain was thus skilfully applied. James knew that simply increasing the other's desperation was not enough. It must be seen that society itself had conspired in Garrett's downfall. That class enemies, in the guise of privileged and beautiful youth had conspired to ruin him and that it was only by striking a blow against this foe that he would recover his true position and dignity. The seed of alienation and victimisation could now so easily be sown in Garrett's suggestible mind. It would be no difficult task to direct his resentment against certain individuals in particular and perhaps, even against women in general.

Thus James talked, sympathetically, about the reactionary officer class, of the monetarist bank managers who had foreclosed on his business loan, on the faceless bureaucracy that withdraws social security benefits. He castigated the friends who had deserted Garrett as callous, chinless wonders, self-seeking social climbers. The girls, he subtly suggested, were vapid, disloyal creatures who cared more for money than a man's true affection and regard. James shook his head, spread his palms and sighed; Garrett began to grind his teeth.

There was a pause in the conversation during which, and not for the first time, Garrett gazed upon the cream cakes arranged invitingly on the other side of the table. They lay on white plates with gilded rims. The dark, rich, soft, aromatic chocolate and the crisp, buttery pastry made an irresistible contrast with the fresh cream which peeped out from between their folds. As the conversation continued Garrett's eyes were drawn to the cakes with increasing frequency. This was also increasingly accompanied by a growing, deep-rooted sense of personal injury and injustice. Eventually, he was forced to watch the other man lift one of the delicacies to his mouth and bite into the chocolate, into the pastry and into the frothy Devon cream. James licked his lips audibly and then wiped them with a napkin. Then, as in a dream, as if his own wish fulfilment had willed it to happen, Garrett saw James's pin-striped arm and fleshy hand lift one of the plates and offer it to him by a raising of the eye brows. As Garrett put his hand forward James also leant towards him and took Garrett's hand in his.

"Fortunately, I believe I may be able to put some employment your way. Some very well paid employment."

Garrett shifted uncomfortably in his seat, gently disengaging his hand as he did so. He began to listen very carefully to what the other was saying. His quickened breathing betraying that heightened attention. As he spoke, James slid the plate of cakes to Garrett's side, and smiled. Garrett was grateful for the excuse to wipe his hand on a napkin before taking a chocolate éclair.

It was growing dark by the time Garrett left the wine bar. As he did so, he did something he had not been able to do for almost two years. He hailed a taxi cab. As the cab drew near the kerb he lunged absent-mindedly towards the door quite failing to observe a young office worker, inaudible amongst the traffic, bicycling his way homeward. But whilst the cyclist's shout was still hanging in the air, Garrett had swung around and grasped the handle-bars. The bicycle stopped as if frozen, thereby avoiding impact or injury, yet the rider was clearly transfixed by the intensity of the gaze which met his own.

"Cor mate, you look as if you've just seen the devil 'imself."

The cyclist's words broke Garrett's reverie and he relaxed. Yet he did not smile. "I believe I just have," he said.

6

Description of Drumelzie House. Freddie Goldberg and Charles Meldrum meet and walk down the drive to its imposing Bear gates.

Drumelzie House rises proudly from a triangle of gently rolling meadow land at the confluence of the Talla Burn and Neidpath Water. Streams of memory, fairie remains of the prehistoric glaciers which have bequeathed such a romantic and enticing landscape to this part of the Scottish Borders. Drumelzie stands sentinel at the very end of Glen Craik, both its child and its guardian. Climate and landscape here blend with the old red sandstone of the house. Here are the gently rolling hills that inspired the forgotten authors of countless Border ballads. They remain our finest examples of the now extinct Middle-Scots language which lingers on as dialect scotch in the howfs and markets of the region. The 'dowie dens' and wooded glens have always been an inspiration for writers and poets, notably Walter Scott and the Ettrick shepherd-poet, James Hogg. Yet the countryside seems peopled with ghosts of human strife. In his tour of the borders Wordsworth wrote of Tweedsdale that it was 'more pensive in sunshine than other country in moon-light'. It is certainly a landscape of isolated farms, murmering trout streams and lonely, glittering lochans whose carpets of water lilies are shielded from the sight of man by its melting knowes. The place names are more eloquent of landscape and history than any treatise on the area: Blackhope Scar, Priesthope Hill, Auchen-corse Moss, Tweedsmuir, Craik Cross Hill, Glentress, Yarrow

Water, Baleberry Knowe, Teviothead, The Grey Mair's Tail, The Devil's Beef Tub, Otterburn, Saughtree, Hobkirk and Smailholm. The melancholy atmosphere of the House and lands of Drumelzie derive not only from the knowledge that Drumelzie is probably the oldest inhabited house in Scotland but that it was also the family home of the Stuarts, Scotland's most famous hereditary royal line and its most ill-fated and romantic family. At the end of the tree-lined driveway which approaches the House stands an ancient pair of wrought-iron gates ...

"These are the gates, right? Let's just stow the history lesson for a moment, and tell me about the bloody gates. They are, in case you've forgotten, why we are standing in this God-forsaken park soaking up a bone-chilling mist. Your informant forgot to mention that in his romantic monologue. Who writes such garbage anyway?"

"That was from a leaflet promoting the House and its estate written, I believe, by the current earl himself."

"Well he ought to know better than regurgitate such rubbish. Pure cliché and probably historically inaccurate. Why didn't you use archives, that's what we pay you for?"

"I did, but I thought you would be interested in some local atmosphere first. And I thought it was rather well written – of its genre. But then you always had such immaculate and flawless prose Freddie."

"Cut the sarcasm and gimmie the griff, Charles, unless you'd rather be writing tourist pamphlets for a living."

Two men held this conversation as they crunched slowly down the gravel driveway towards Drumelzie House. They were both approaching their middle years but were separated by a generation in their mode of dress. The taller and slimmer of the two was Charles Meldrum. He was clean shaven, with a stork-like quality. His face was sallow and his cheeks concave. He wore a time-served tweed jacket which had been drawn into a singular shape by his habits. Namely that of walking with a perpetual stoop, acquired rather than congenital, resting his left hand in the side pocket and transporting various reference works and writing implements in the other pockets. Through time this had caused the front of the jacket to be drawn earthwards by the bulging side pockets and the tail to be lifted heavenwards by the spinal curvature. The fact that the garment had survived such indignities for so long was a profound testament to the resilience of the material. The Harris Tweed Marketing Board would do well to consider publishing Charles's cadaverous frame in the media in preference to the beautiful people and bright young things which speak rather of the transience of lesser man-made materials. A good-quality tattersall shirt, a knitted woollen tie, green worsted trousers and tan English brogues completed the picture. But this almost donnish appearance belied Charles's accidental profession; that of historical advisor to what he called the mass electronic media. Television and cinema, mainly. Charles had learnt to analyse the facts and present them in the sensational and synoptic morsels which give appetite to those of limited attention spans. Unlike everyone else he seemed to meet in his work Charles was not a media enthusiast. He was a cynic with a ready wry wit but he had grown accustomed to the comfortable income, and he knew to which side of his bread the butter had been applied.

The other man was an ageing love-child of the flickering screen and, it must be said, a ruthless businessman. Short and stocky his slightly greying hair was cut short to the head to disguise a receding hairline. In contrast his short, well-manicured beard was rather darker with only a dusting of grey. The immediate first impression was that the hair had fallen by force of gravity from his head down to his chin. His hips and stomach were heavy and barely restrained by the Gucci belt of his designer jeans. He wore heavy, thick-soled boots which, like the enormous four-wheel-drive Jeep he drove, had seen very little off-road work. He wore a heavy cotton shirt, open at the collar to reveal a glimpse of gold chain, and an open, quilted leather waistcoat. All seemed to say that here was a man who, like a Sumo wrestler, had lowered his centre of gravity so as to help him push others around, without being knocked off course himself. Freddie Goldberg owned and directed a small British film company which, as Freddie said, focused on popular television documentary as its vertical market. This, in the main, meant the production of bite-sized, 25 minute screen-fillers which placed the minimum intellectual demand on the audience. "Always play to the lowest denominator," he was fond of saying, "after all, that's how politicians get elected." Freddie liked transatlantic buzz words and telling people how it filled him with angst to be a lapsed Jew. The fact that Freddie was descended from generations of lapsed Jews and could not have related even one of the tenets of that faith to save his life, was conveniently overlooked. Nonetheless, the pose gave some colour to a character which would otherwise have been completely etiolated by the single-minded pursuit of money.

The two men stopped walking. They had reached a point in the driveway where it began to broaden out into the ornamental courtyard which framed the house front. At that point their way was barred by two immense, wrought iron gates. The gates were flanked by the massive stone piers which supported them. On the top of each pier, a heraldic stone bear, clutching an escutcheon, stood guard. The two men were dwarfed by the scale of the ironwork and masonry. As they gazed upwards the autumn mist began to clear from a lucid blue sky which they viewed through the black and gold framework of the gates. The sun had little warmth at this time of year and Freddie reluctantly zipped the front of his waistcoat as he turned towards Charles.

"Just run the story past me again, Charles, I want to get the feel of it."

"Well, as a political and moral gesture, the family have ensured that these gates have remained closed until, as the saying goes, a Stuart monarch once again reigns over Scotland. They were last opened in 1745. The Earls of Drumelzie supported the Stuart monarchy, that is the hereditary royal family of Scotland, and in the 1745 rising they naturally espoused the Jacobin cause ..."

"What kind of bin?"

"Jacobin, it's from Jacobus, Latin for James."

"But you told me last time that his name was Charles Stuart."

"Yes, it was, but his father was James II, Charles was known by his enemies as the Young Pretender."

"What was he pretending to be?"

"Well a sort of regent for his father."

"Was he mad?"

"Mad? No, no quite sane as far as the sources tell us. In Anglo French, 'a pretender' is the name for the claimant to the throne."

"Charles, my dear, excuse me for observing that this is all getting rather balls-achingly complicated and not quite the stuff snappy documentaries are made on. Now let me give you the story as I see it and you just nod or grunt.

"The Stuart family is forced to flee Britain to escape a corrupt and decadent English aristocracy. Prince Charlie vows to return one day to repair the honour of his dad. He spends years in France amassing a vast army. When the time is ripe he lands in Scotland and sets up court in Edinburgh. Whilst there he visits the family country retreat at Drumelzie House where he falls in love with the earl's beautiful daughter. They embrace as he leaves for his last battle, never to return. Fallen on the bloody field, defeated by millions of English horse and treachery. His dad dies of a broken heart, as does his sweetheart and the kind old earl slowly locks the house gates never to be opened until the curse of the Stuarts is lifted by the ghost of Bonnie Prince Charlie marching down the drive at the head of a phantom pipe band."

"That's how to summarise a story. Pretty neat, huh?"

The dry, lugubrious Charles Meldrum had long since ceased to be surprised by any pebble which this pedestrian world might cast into his pond. Yet, even he was momentarily numbed by this bludgeoning of the historic events. Eventually he recovered the capacity for speech.

"Freddie, even I must caution against journalistic licence on this one. We are talking about one of the seminal events in Scottish history, even more tragic than Flodden, the carnage of Culloden Moor, the end of the clan system and sequestration of the Scottish titles, the prescription of Scots culture and the butchery and persecution of Cumberland. A holocaust that enabled the Clearances, the supremacy of Calvinism and the virtual conscription of highlanders into the English regiments. True, Freddie, elements of Charles Stuart's adventure had a tragi-comic element but ..."

Charles's voice trailed off with a sigh of exasperation. He was at once aware that almost from his second syllable he had vastly exceeded Freddie's own astoundingly short attention span. His client had simply turned his back on Charles and started to walk away. Charles, after a brief tussle with his pride, hurried after him. Freddie smote the air with a clenched fist ...

"I want you to check out a Goldberg tartan for me, I'm going to present this short in a full highland outfit. If you can't find Goldberg, get someone to make something up ... and I need a clan crest and motto."

Charles had come up level with Freddie's left shoulder.

"How about a red deer in full flight."

"That's a great visual, what about the motto to go with it?"

"How about, 'Follow the Fast Buck'."

"Yeh, that's ..."

Mr Goldberg stopped and half turned to face Charles, his solid designer boots scrunching on the gravel.

"You have just illustrated why, Charles, that in the immense pissing game of life, you will almost certainly come last."

7

*A September evening and Andrew Farquharson is fishing. He is
interrupted by James Galbraith. Andrew encounters a boy on a bridge
dropping pebbles into the water below. Later that evening he drinks port
with James Galbraith before returning to his hotel where he reads
the report of a postmortem examination.*

It is 7.35 pm on a soft and still September evening. A golden glow on the
eastern hill tops is turning orange. No wind. No noise except the soporific
murmuring of water on stone. Water and stone. Sightless eyes could see
a fern-framed, dank spring at the base of a rock face. Or a secret waterfall hidden in a mossy, mountain cleft … betrayed by freezing steam.
Or a brass faucet drip dripping into a stone drinking trough capturing
a wide world of blue sky. A cast iron pump dribbling onto cool flags in
a deserted courtyard. The sound of a single drop of water deep in the
forest. Unseen. Unheard. Mist condenses on the bud of a birch tree and
drops onto a worn out stone. The stone becomes a river. It washes away
the sins of the world. A hand, withdrawn from a stone piscena, allows one
drop of sanctified water to echo around the empty chancel. Innocence.
Longing. Sin. Guilt. Redemption. Forgiveness. Death. Resurrection.
Water running over brindled stones. Water running; drifting slowly.

A hand is holding a ten-inch length of cylindrical cork-covered wood;
about 1½" diameter. From this extends an eight-foot length of bonded,
split cane, tapering from about ¾ of an inch at the grip to around ¼ of an
inch at its tip. It is hexagonal in section and jointed at half its length by
brass ferules. The cane is varnished. When the craftsman was creating it,

he would just place the tip of his forefinger in the warm shellac and then smear it slowly along the length of the cane. The cane had twelve coats of varnish and the blue silk bindings for the line rings had eighteen coats of varnish. In doing this, the craftsman shared something of himself with the artefact and, inevitably, with the user. Without the reel, the rod weighed just seven ounces. And with the reel, it balanced in the hand with an animation which gave life. Although its purpose was quite the opposite.

The user raised the rod swiftly, adding momentum by pulling out the line with his left hand, until it was extended over his head where he stopped its movement. He drew an arc of flashing line in the air which straightened momentarily as it ran out horizontally behind the rod. When he felt that almost imperceptible moment of potential energy the man brought the rod sharply forward. At the optimum moment, as the rod tip dipped, he opened his left hand and shot thirty feet of line cleanly over the water. A small sedge dropped like the gentlest thistle--down, down onto the rippling water. But at its heart was a steel barb.

A few casts later, the fisherman reeled in his line and walked to the gravelly bank. The water trickled from his waders as he sat down slowly on a lichen-encrusted rock. The ponderous nature of his movements betrayed a man who was no longer in the first flush of youth. He sat on the rock and remembered. A few hundred yards upstream was a deep pool overshadowed by Neidpath Castle. As a boy he would swim in that pool, jumping from the rocky outcrop at the base of the castle. He remembered the other boys jumping and splashing in the water, their smooth naked bodies shimmering in the sunshine like young trout. A less sophisticated, less suspicious world. All day long the river would steal past like time. Like an accelerated glacier the crystal depths of the River Tweed were rolled between moor and meadow as the water slid with gathering momentum towards the rocky Berwickshire coast. Liquid, languid time.

The noise of a fish leaping downstream brought him back to his purpose. He would venture a nymph, and let the current take it to the shade of some overhanging branches on the far bank. It was very late in the season for this, but often he had found that taking a chance is the only way to succeed. Just as he was putting the finishing touches to a clinch knot he became aware of movement in the long grass behind him. He turned slowly on his rocky seat to discover James Galbraith making an uneasy progress over the tussocky river bank. He was somewhat out of breath when he reached Andrew Farquharson. If Andrew was surprised to encounter his acquaintance in this remote spot, he did not betray the emotion. The contrast between the two was marked. James, puffy, unsteady out of breath and clearly out of his milieu in grey flannels and grey wool overcoat. Andrew, poised, wiry, lined and ascetic. Sandy hair, flecked with grey. Blending with his environment in tweed breeks, Aran sweater and waxed fishing waistcoat. The only colours which betrayed him in the landscape were the yellow, red and white feathers of the two dry flies hooked on the side of his deer stalker. It was clear to him that James was exceedingly pleased with himself.

"There you are Andrew, a fine piece of detection work, don't you think?"

"Well, I see that you have been talking to the hall porter at my hotel. Fishing guests always have to leave details of their whereabouts, if they are wading alone. It helps the gillie to locate the corpse if one is late for supper. And no doubt you obtained the fax number of my hotel from the College Bursar and then simply asked them to confirm my residence."

A cloud passed over James's expression. "You might have let me savour my moment of triumph a little longer."

"I'm sorry James, but I always get rather belligerent when my retreat is intruded upon. Even by those whom I love. The last individual to thus intrude was banished into outer darkness to weep and wail. He, like you, could not comprehend the spiritual reconstruction afforded by the last evening rise at the close of the season. The time of which, I might add, is ebbing through my fingers as we speak. No doubt this is an … emergency."

"Damn it all, Andrew, this is an indifferent welcome and no mistake. It's more than trout we have to catch, or it will be the worse for both of us."

Andrew turned once to glance longingly at the river, sighed, then laid down his rod and gestured to an adjacent tuft of dry grass. Gathering his coat around him, James sat down. He looked carefully around him before he leaned forward and spoke in a confidential whisper.

"I have run our prey to earth."

"As you said you would ... and for heaven's sake, James, do drop this cloak and dagger mien, we are hardly secret agents. It's all very unsettling."

"Now look Andrew, your blasé approach to this problem is fairly unsettling *me*. You, of all people, know just how much is at stake. In John's letter he wrote 'I cannot help you lest I destroy you. It is time to abandon your darkness'; and he talks of his son as 'the inheritor of his line and of his power' ... the meaning is clear enough."

"In life, James, the meaning is rarely clear. However, I suppose we do need to find out whether the boy is involved."

"That at least, if not more, and I need some assistance."

"Go on."

"If it transpires, on further investigation, that the boy can ... injure us. What then?"

"What indeed!"

"Do you see, Andrew, we simply cannot take the risk. Having gone thus far, we must ensure complete and permanent silence."

"My dear James, only the grave is so silent."

Neither man spoke. Time passed. A cloud of tiny insects was dancing in some shafts of dying sunlight by the water's edge, by tomorrow they too would be dead. The river began to roar in Andrew's ears. He heard himself speak.

"Whatever you decide, James, is between you and your conscience but you will leave me out of it."

"It's rather too late for such scruples. The good fortune which took us from penniless undergraduates into positions of power and wealth could just as easily wither on the vine ... unless we take appropriate precautions. We know that John was as close as death, but a son, I am reliably informed, is often the inheritor of paternal confidences. I will leave nothing to chance. Not when there is so much yet to achieve."

"At the last, are your position and possessions so very vital to your existence? After all, a hereditary Galbraith dynasty seems a somewhat unlikely proposition."

"Andrew, luxury seems to have softened you and affected your memory. Had you been exposed as I have recently, to a particularly disgusting example of poverty and disgrace, it would have proven a chastening experience for you. You cannot return from whence you came, you just wouldn't have the stomach for it my dear."

Andrew stood to his full height and gazed down upon this sometime chance acquaintance now so inextricably linked with his fate. From partners to parasites. Not for the first time he questioned the path he had taken. Assuming a burden too closely woven to ever be cast aside, even for a moment, even in the bedchamber. The shadow it seemed had fallen between him and his immortal soul. He could not trust, even to love; and, without redemption, he knew that the central law of the universe … was waste. James was smiling up at him. A bad sign, as when the hyena smiles. Night was stealing to wrap its velvet cloak around them with the dank scent of river water. He felt deeply tired.

James shivered, glanced at his watch and spoke again. "If we can be completely and unquestionably assured that the boy knows nothing, all well and good. But if not, well, you have acquired influence in the Fiscal's office and with the Chief Constable and certain of the Judiciary for that matter – although I do not intend that matters will require their intervention. Perhaps the most satisfying aspect of giving is when the opportunity arises to call in one's debts." He stood up. "Now that's settled, lets warm ourselves up with a couple of whiskys back at the hotel."

"Thanks, but no. I'll just stop here for a while yet. You go on."

James shrugged, smiled and gathering his coat clear of the wet grass picked his way heavily back to the lane where his grey Range Rover was gently disappearing into the beckoning dusk.

Andrew heard the engine noise dwindle until it was finally silenced by an intervening hill; and he was left alone. He collected his landing net and slung it over his shoulder, then picked up his rod. Looking to the west at the fading light he half turned to go, and then stopped. It was that breathless time of evening when the scales of day and night, of good and evil, are in equilibrium. Like a slow tide, stilled just before the ebb. Small bats began to swoop over the water gathering flying insects. They could not quite be seen and not quite heard, only perceived by a slight uneasiness in the inner ear. He could hear some cattle nearby tearing grass rhythmically in the silence like rending cloth. Andrew considered the nymph lying in the palm of his hand and glanced at the river, flowing into the past. He turned again towards the water. Once in mid stream, he fed some line into the air. It whispered softly in the humid atmosphere as the nymph was gently laid on the water. The current took it under and across to the far bank where it sank into some black and shapeless pools overhung with gorse. After less than a minute, there was a tentative, soft pull on the line, and Andrew's heart quickened. The trout, he knew, had taken the nymph and turned downstream. In half a second it would feel the weight of the line, taste the barb in its mouth and spit it out. The time to strike was now. Andrew tensed his wrists and prepared to sink the hook into the pink flesh of the trout's palate. He did not move. Seconds passed. Some minutes passed, then he began slowly to reel in his empty line. He was smiling sadly as he whispered, "an offering for the God of the river and the natural world"; then later, "a sin offering". He began to breathe deeply and felt a rare sense of peace.

The water gurgled and slapped against his waders as he returned to the shore. He dismantled his rod, returning it to its canvas case, and tucked the reel into his waistcoat pocket. He had waded some distance from his car to a point in the river where an old, cast iron pedestrian bridge crossed the water. It had been built in the last century to permit foot travellers to cross to Cleuch Station about half a mile away. Both station and railway had long since disappeared and the Station Master's house was now a water bailiff's cottage. The water was black and the tracery of the bridge grey and indistinct in the gathering twilight. Andrew made his way to the bridge and began to take the track leading to Cleuch, where he could then walk back along the road. He had just found the track when his attention was drawn by a series of slight splashes in the river. Becoming curious he searched with ears and eyes until he located the noise as coming from the direction of the old bridge and at almost the same moment he noticed a small shape on the bridge, about half way across. A slightly lighter grey in the dusk. He was tolerably near to the bridge so, shrugging to himself, he laid his things on the path and climbed the three wooden steps which led up onto the footbridge. From that vantage point he clearly saw a small boy, in the middle of the bridge, leaning against the iron parapet and dropping small pieces of shingle, one at a time, into the water below. The boy was sideways to him and he saw that he was dressed in grey trousers and a navy blue sweater a couple of sizes too big. He was slim, had tousled fair hair and was about eight years of age. Andrew searched about for a parent or older companion but could neither hear nor see one. The boy was clearly far too young to be here on his own at this hour. Andrew moved towards the middle of the bridge and, at the noise, the boy turned and walked a few paces towards him. As they faced each other Andrew experienced a tightening about the heart. Yet, the man smiled at the child to show him that he meant no harm and asked him if he was alone there. The boy seemed quite at ease and looked innocently up into Andrew's face as he replied, but when he spoke, his voice was flat and heavy with an un-childlike sorrow and loss.

"Yes, I'm alone."

"Well, old chap, I'm not sure you should be wandering about here at this hour. Where are your parents?"

"My parents are both dead."

Andrew was thrown quite off beam by this answer but he had a conventional and erroneous notion that children feel bereavement less deeply than adults and cope with it more readily. So, he decided to put a bold front on it.

"Oh dear, I am sorry but someone must look after you. Suppose I just see you safely home, you can't have come very far. Now, in which direction do you live?"

The child searched Andrew's face, as if looking for a sign. The nocturnal breeze from the river blew the boy's hair across his eyes and from time to time he would brush it away with the back of a small hand. There was no indication that he had heard Andrew's question but after a moment the child seemed to have made up his mind about something and came a step closer. He was clearly cold and trembled from time to time.

"No one looks after me, no one at all, and I have no home."

The darkness was gathering and Andrew began to be concerned about finding his way back, yet he could not find it in himself to be impatient with the boy.

"Come now little man, these are strange things to say. If you have run away I won't tell, you know, and I'll make sure you don't get into trouble. The best thing is just to sneak back before anyone finds out. You'd rather be snug in a warm bed I'll bet and I certainly wouldn't want my son alone here at this Godless hour. Now, what do you say?"

For the first time, the boy began to show agitation and began to put some animation in his voice.

"Do you have a son?"

"Well … no, no I don't but what I'm saying is shall we …"

"If you had a son, would you make him frightened and unhappy?"

"What a question. No, of course not." Andrew began to feel insecure of himself but the boy drew still closer and continued with rising intensity

"Would you hate and despise your son and never share any kind or gentle feelings with him? Would your only word be an unkind one or a curse? Would you break his spirit and make each of his childhood days a torment?"

"Why, of course not, now just …"

"Would you become an evil stranger to your son? Would your son lie hour after hour, night after night in eternal blackness too frozen by the cold sweat of fear even to cry out? Would your son know that no one, no one on earth would ever, ever answer his cries?"

"No, no."

"Would you make him feel sick with fear and then hit him with the back of your hand, or take away his toys and break them under your feet while he watched."

"Certainly not, has anyone beaten you?"

"Would you make his home a place of unnatural suffering; a place of endless dread; a symbol of hate; a place to return to secretly and with loathing. A place of eternal silences and eternal screaming."

"No."

"Would you steal your son's innocence; corrupt his joy and teach him to hate? Would you kill everything he loved and then kill love within him?"

Andrew's voice had now dropped to a whisper and then tailed off into nothingness. "No. No. No. No, no, no … no … no."

The child too paused, and then whispered.

"What … would … you … do?"

Andrew emitted a shuddering sigh, like a tree, suddenly grown old, bending to the wind. "I … I … would put my arms around him and tell him not to worry or ever be afraid. I would take him on my knee and softly brush back his hair and tell him that I loved him and that he need never be alone. I would sit at the bottom of his bed when he was sad and make the dark nights warm and comforting. I would smooth away his pain, turn his tears into laughter play his games with him, help him to brush his teeth and do up his tie. I would talk to him kindly about Jesus and the beauty and joy of life and I would kiss him to sleep. Oh … if I could; if I just could; oh God if only I could. If only I could take that sad, lonely, frightened child in my arms and make all things well."

"Yes, and you would take his hand in your hand?"

"Yes, his hand in mine … like this." Andrew became aware that he had been weeping silently for some time. He sank slowly to his knees and took the boy in his arms and kissed him softly on the cheek; he inhaled the warm scent of his hair and brushed away his tears. It was then that he began to take him home.

It was late when Andrew's Mercedes slipped into the hotel grounds. He parked by the tennis courts, some distance from Reception, where he could just see the occasional glint of lighted windows and the floodlit castellations of Victorian Gothic through a belt of swaying junipers. He turned off the ignition. The upholstery sighed and exhaled a scent of tanned hide as he stretched his stiff joints. The driver's window slid open as Andrew fetched a slim Havana from the glove compartment and a minute later there was a red pinpoint of light in the darkness. He let a serpent of smoke climb into the cool night sky and breathed long and deeply. Something in his left side, just beneath his heart was making him feel uncomfortable and, after a moments struggle with his waistcoat pocket he extracted a small, rectangular tin box about six inches long. It was an old cigarette box of a cheap, export brand he had bought in his student days in Jerusalem. It was, or had been, navy blue and the famous red-bearded sailor's head, framed by a white life belt, could still be seen in the top left-hand corner. At the bottom right, the words 'medium cig-arettes' were just discernible. Rust and wear had taken its toll of the tin-work. For as long as he could remember, he had kept his fishing flies in there, impaled on a piece of cork matting. Andrew switched on the map light and opened the box. That afternoon, the cork had become dislodged from the tin and fallen onto his lap. It had revealed to him then what he now took in his hand and held to the light. The creased photograph of a handsome, sandy-haired boy, of some eight or nine years, wearing a dark sweater, a couple of sizes too big, and grey wool trousers. Some time later he consigned the items to the glove compartment. He would go in and talk to James in due course. But not now, not just yet. When he was ready. So he sat watching the hotel lights twinkle through the trees, inhaling the cigar smoke and the scented night air. From time to time he heard the faint calls of plovers up on the hills, and he remembered.

Andrew was struggling to maintain the stability of his relationship with James. It provided a necessary equilibrium to his ambiguous life. He persuaded the night porter to ravish the sacred enclaves of his wine cellar for a cherished crusted pipe which was duly decanted with elaborate ceremony. He spied James in a corner of the lounge and saluted him with this ruby peace offering. "Blood of the Lamb?" he enquired, sitting down.

James almost smiled. "Andrew, the world lost a fine priest when you became a don."

"And Satan gained another sinner."

James narrowed his eyes. "You would be a lot happier if you just accepted your good fortune without the useless appendix of this constant ethical masturbation. The Cistercians inform us that Satan sends only one junior demon at each dusk to all the major cities in the world, and that this fiend sleeps at his post ... the battle against evil being lost long ago. Accept defeat gracefully, Andrew. I mean to set you an example by immediately and thoroughly abandoning myself to the pleasures of this truly excellent port."

"I don't believe you have ever truly abandoned yourself anywhere, except amongst the souks of Jerusalem."

"You underestimate me, Andrew. I talk not of the pleasures of the flesh. I may not wear my heart on my sleeve but I, too, have had my moments of spiritual flight."

James knew his friend well enough to realise at once that intimacy was not his métier; and although he smiled, his mental guard was raised. "Like you, I sometimes feel impelled by the need to confess, to share my burden."

"You do?"

"Why yes, and I would not presume to judge you for a like need. I dare say you have a special confidante of the soul." Here James paused, attempted to smile encouragingly and sipped his port. "Someone whom, in the sable darkness, eases the heavy cares from your shoulders until dawn."

Andrew exhaled a long, controlled, inaudible sigh. At once, he knew instinctively that he had failed forever to re-build that intangible bridge of confidence and trust which binds each friendship. When James smiled again his fleshy lips looked blood stained.

"My only confessor, as John MacDonald might have said, is my Maker."

"You were ever a canny man, Andrew."

"You say so, yet the penance from Him is like to be all the more deathly."

"Have it as you will, I'm too tired to argue."

"Something tells me, James, that you have not come here simply to talk to me. I know that the country bores you and I'm curious to know how you have been spending your time."

James smiled. "Just going to and fro in the world and walking up and down in it."

"Any particular part?"

"It may surprise you but I'm having a bit of a break and doing the tourist trail. I spent a few pleasant hours at a fine country house, mainly Jacobean, on my way here. You may know it, Drumelzie House."

That night, alone in his room, sleep did not come easily to Sir Andrew Farquharson. Around 3 am he woke for the third time from an uneasy, febrile slumber and groped for the bedside lamp. The wind was piping at his window like a demonic fife and somewhere up on the leads, some loose slates were tolling a mournful percussion. The table beside his tester bed swam brightly into view whilst the oak, linen fold panelling of the room faded out of reach beyond a crepuscular horizon. He got up and used the en–suite. An action that reminded him of how much wine he had drunk, but it was not port wine that was poisoning his slumber. Reading generally summoned drowsiness at such times. So, before returning to bed, he retrieved from his case an A4 sheaf of papers, bound with a slim black spine. As the minutes passed, Andrew turned the pages with increasing slowness and, after about 30 minutes, his head rolled back onto his pillow and his breathing became slow and regular. After a while, the document fell from his hand onto the counterpane. The cover page entitled, 'Post Mortem Examination Report' was clearly visible in the cold light of the bedside lamp. It was addressed to HM Coroner for Inverness & District and was signed by the Consultant Histopathologist for Raigmore Hospital. Under the Heading 'Name of Deceased' was entered 'Rev. John MacDonald'.

8

After a long drive, Charles Meldrum, Mary Dalbeith and Ronan
MacDonald reach Edinburgh. They stretch out on the grass at a vantage
point overlooking the City and the Firth of Forth. Later they visit
Deacon's Bar and Charles provides Ronan with a place to stay.

It was a bright, blue, blustery, cloud-strewn morning in early October. Tomorrow, the numbing haar could steal over the harbour walls and into the town with a lament of stifled fog-horns drifting with it from the Firth. The steel-grey sky clamped down on the horizon like a limpet. No room for even a sharpened knife blade to be slipped between the two to prize them apart. But today was typical of the sharp, eye-squintingly bright light which so often burnished this city by its northern sea. Picking its way through the flashing windshields, a black over maroon, 1947 Riley RME swung left at the Usher Hall and rolled in through the West Port of the city and down into the Grassmarket. A broad expanse of tarmac walled by ancient tenements. The driver remembered this place from his undergraduate days when at almost any hour he could be approached by sour-scented, crumbling grey-white men for a 'shullin fir a cup o' tea'. Rightful descendants of the cadies of old they may have been but no one entrusted these men with a confidence. Yet their mysterious bottles of burnt toast and blue liquid seem curiously innocent in retrospect. They are, as a minister once preached at the Tron, a shoemaker's paradox. On their uppers ... but still with souls intact. They at least represented no risk to the life or property of others. They just died quietly, if not always conveniently, in the unrelenting tenement closes

and wynds scoured by the winter winds. And today, well the old repro-
bate area has been rehabilitated. Yet its sad character somehow remains.
As the old car swung past the shouldering wine bars and antique shops
the driver smiled to see the Seamen's Mission still standing at Candle-
maker Row. He could have kissed the inebriate who dozed, like a mystic,
in its sunny doorway.

With all that remained of its 18 horse power the Riley cranked laboriously up West Bow and swept majestically into the Lawn Market.
Framed by the backdrop of the Castle, the car rumbled downhill over
the cobbles. Dwarfed by the oldest tenements in Europe, they passed
the 'Deacons'. "Time was you could park outside by the police station
and slip in for a quick dram to fend off the chill winds." The constraints
of traffic management and of his own liver now made this an unwise
proposition. Rumbling on into the High Street, St Giles and Parliament
Square slipped past. The driver looked over his shoulder; "You know, if
Jenny were to cast her stool at some clerics head today, in the middle of
divine service, it would probably still make the Evening News." The car
rode out of the Netherbow Port and on down, down into the Cannongate.
John Knox's Land. Again, addressed to the rear seats; "The bitter old
galley slave who gave every Morningside matron a reason for dying …
to have fulfilled a life of proselytising, religious intolerance, sexual guilt,
and cosmic arch-snobbery." The asthmatic old machine had summoned
up all its grace to drift its occupants, with near elegance, through the
gilded gates and into the Royal Sanctuary of Holyrood Park. The Palace
drifted by as the vehicle entered the Queen's Drive which circles that
most paradoxical bump, Arthur's Seat. The wild Scottish Highlands in
microcosm, complete with Highland lochs, carlin's wells, mystic stags
and haunted ruins, removed to the heart of this great city and offered
up for the recreation of its populace. This royal demesne still holds a
few surprises. First it is always more or less lonely of traffic; particularly
on its far perimeter by Duddingston Loch. Second, as you drive on the
sinuous ribbon of road as it cuts its way through sea deep lochs, green
terraces and red volcanic crags it is impossible not to feel grand or even

ennobled. And when you tread the springy sheep- and rabbit-cropped turves of the hill, it is impossible not to feel light-hearted.

The car slowed its forward momentum and, without the slightest air of impatience, swung smoothly into a small parking area beside Dunsappie Loch. It sighed as its ignition was extinguished and stretched its doors wide. Three people climbed out. They had driven a long way and were stiff in joint and muscle. A gentleman of middle years, who was Charles Meldrum, sat down stiffly on the long grass. His two young passengers, Mary Dalbeith and Ronan MacDonald stretched themselves full length at his side. Lying on the east side of the hill they had a panoramic view over the pretentiously named Portobello and Joppa regions of the city and the Firth of Forth. Dunsappie Loch, some way up the hill, gives a remarkable visual effect. The bank at the far side of the loch is almost level with its surface so that the waters of the loch appear to flow into those of the estuary some two miles distant.

"You know Mary, have you noticed ..."

"Yes, ... how the waters of the loch appear to flow into the North Sea. Don't pull such a face, Charles, Ronan and I have stoically endured Edinburgh mementoes from Messers Burke and Hare's recycling business and statistics on the construction of The Mound to Thomas de Quincey's impecunity and the gastric effects of the first time you imbibed strong waters in the Greyfriars Bobby."

Suddenly aware that, as usual, she had gone too far again, Mary blew Charles a kiss and instinctively followed it with a real one on his stubbly cheek to fully heal the wound between them. No longer offended, the defenceless Charles turned to face his two passengers with affected irony. "One day soon, you too will become an intolerable burden on society. So gather ye rosebuds whilst ye may. Clear off; and, whilst you still have wind and limb enough, climb yonder Seat, you idle scrimshankers, and leave me to enjoy the windswept autumn sunshine for an hour or so."

Mary clasped Charles hand. "Charles, dear, I ..."

"Go, I say, you academic siren, and if you are not back by noon I'll be off to the NB for lunch without you."

Charles laughed as Mary stuck out her tongue and then he turned towards the sea, as the two strode away up the hillside, dismissing their unseen and unseeing backs with an impatient wave of his hand.

The two young people walked together in silence. The way was steep and they pretended that they were too breathless to talk until, that is, they rested on a purple volcanic boulder growing from the green slope. The wind had been gradually rising during the morning and its power was accentuated by their rising altitude. Mary's hair swam in the wind like flame; an effect not lost on the young man. It was, as ever, Ronan who spoke first … something about the fine view.

"You are always first to break the silence, Ronan."

"And what of it?"

"Well, but you break the silence for your benefit not mine and, forgive me, you invariably tell me something I already know. You see, language should be used for communication, in all its different forms, and not as a displacement therapy, a way of managing personal neurosis."

"That's fine," Ronan rejoined, springing to his feet, "you walk on alone and I'll go back. That way you'll have a fine silence."

She took both his hands at that. "Oh, Ronan. I'm sorry, do sit down. You are such a handsome young man to walk arm in arm with, that no sane girl would want to walk on without you." They sat.

"Mary you play such a fiddler's reel on my emotions … no; don't laugh … on my emotions that I wonder at you. You are very, very judgemental. Why? And analytical. Why? And critical. Why? Do you not realise how you torture those that … those that …"

"Ronan …" whispering; covering his lips with her palm, "don't say it."

There was a silence between them for a long moment.

"Or, must it be said."

"Mary, I …"

"No, no you must not!" This said with a theatrical coyness. Then, laughing, she jumped up and half ran up the hill. He soon caught her up and hand in hand they walked up to the summit in silence. Ronan did

64

not smile as she did. It was uncertain whether they spoke, for the wind would have blown their words into the void.

On the hilltop, the city was laid out in the sunlight in all its Georgian and medieval beauty. Only people, in Edinburgh, are less than aesthetically pleasing. For all their creative pretensions, they remain a dour, unimaginative, cautious people. A town councillor was recently asked whether he thought that Edinburgh's Georgian 'New Town' had been a success. "Well, really, it's too early to tell," he was heard to reply.

The growing storm had kept walkers at home and they had the summit to themselves. The power of the wind surprised and exhilarated them. Edinburgh is the famous playground of the north-easterly. It blew them over and they rolled on the ground in breathless laughter. Eventually Ronan helped Mary to stand by holding her around her waist and leaning both of them into the wind. The air roared as it rose over the summit. It near deafened them and made their cheeks tingle. Struggling to keep their balance, like a couple of old winebibbers, they at once realised that they had braced themselves face to face. Holding on to each other there, as if lost. The wine-dark pupils of Mary's eyes seemed to be drowning him as he now gasped for air and now inhaled the scent of her warm skin and then, as in a dream, kissed her long and softly on the lips. He would always remember that moment. Mary's dress clung to her back and streamed in front of her into the wind. And then a powerful gust tore out the stitching of the hem, which flapped and cracked in the wind around her. The Earth ground on its axis, and moved on. He saw her gesturing to him to follow her to the leeward side of the hillock where they sat down on the grass.

Mary took up the hem of her dress and began to run it through agitated fingers. "Blast it. What a mess; I'll be no better than a tinker's child if we don't get out of this. And there are storm clouds coming in off the sea."

"Mary, I need to ask you …"

"Listen, Ronan, I'm not having an affair with you." Her laughter began anew. "A funny word, not sure it's the right one, sounds like something married people do. But you must get the point. You're lovely but you are too young, unformed, embryonic, and too good and far too nice. And, before you get angry, it is just that we really have met at the wrong time in my life, it's simply not the right moment for me. And also, you are far, far too serious."

This, it may be imagined, was the last thing our young lover expected to hear. But had he had even the slightest experience of womankind he might not have been so disappointed nor half as discouraged.

"Come on," she said, struggling to her feet, "I'm chilled to the bone and only one of Deacon Brodie's highland malts will save me." They both recognised how inappropriate this proposal was from Mary's lips, but, in the event, it was exactly what they did … and the best thing they could have done.

The sputum and wood shavings had gone the way of all flesh but the Deacon's was otherwise remarkably unchanged. The bar still cherished the most bewildering array of single malts in all Caledonia. And some of the windows of the 'public' were still bevelled and etched with the titles of long-forgotten distillations and blends. Thus reflected Charles Meldrum as he inhaled the sour scent of stale liquor as if it were sweet nectar. Best of all, there was not a gaming machine nor a pool table to be seen and, blessed inheritance, no musical wallpaper. If the old rogue, William Brodie, had toddled in from the Lawnmarket, his tail-coat flapping in the wind and one hand clasping his bag-wig in situ, he would have been very much at home. As was Charles, tucked up in a corner of the wall on an upholstered oak bench well away from the blustery swing door. Facing him, on the other side of a small marble-topped table sat Ronan, plunged in gloom. Charles seemed impervious to the other's mood, however, and discoursed amusingly enough about his recent career in the media. After a while though, he gradually fell silent. He sniffed his whisky, took a wee sip, smacked his lips, brought down his glass with a click and eyed his companion, as if for the first time.

"Well now young Ronan. Bye the bye, when you reach fifty it becomes legal to address everyone under the age of forty-five as 'young'. Well now, I have been talking at you almost non-stop for the half hour since Mary left us, and deil the word have you heard. Or, if you heard it, were as much moved as him over there," here indicating an old, tweed-bunetted worthy sonorously sleeping off his potations in the opposite corner. "The monosyllables, grunts and gestures you have made would probably constitute a challenging dialectic in a pre-lingual culture … but, today, they fall something short of stimulating debate."

Ronan's tumbler of scotch was rapidly replaced on the table. "I'm truly sorry, Charles … no, really I am. I didn't realise I was being so unresponsive … and after all your kindness too."

"Moribund, is the word I would use."

The two smiled, one more weakly than the other. Glasses were raised to lips again, and again, chinked on the table top. Charles sighed audibly and leant forward slightly, resting his chin on the knuckles of his left hand. He spoke with a tinge of mock irony.

"'And yet there's something in her gait gars ony dress look weel' … or something like that. Burns, of course."

"Aye, fine, but …"

"She's a pretty lass, Mary, is she not. Stepping straight out of a Burne Jones canvas with swirling skirts. I was her tutor for a term, before the bright lights lured me away. And I never knew the castle keep so fast or dungeon so deep and cold, that her smile could not storm and throw wide to the shining daylight."

"She is … most affecting. Although I hardly know her."

"Come now, Ronan, she has flattened your defences and no mistake."

"I think she finds me rather dull, you know."

"Well, she is three years older than you I believe, and in social terms, that makes a woman about ten years older. But in Mary's case, that makes her about one thousand, five hundred years older … and a million times harder to understand. Look, Ronan, in a few days time, having abjured the only worthy academic discipline, the history of the human race, you will be preparing yourself to follow the path of Hippocrates. Before you stretches a lifetime of sticking your forefinger up costive matrons' rectums and, if the undergraduates I sometime tutor are to be believed, of near infinite access to free fornication with a variety of genders. In a few weeks time, Mary will be in Stirling researching her doctorate. You will be in Edinburgh, immersed in anatomy, binge drinking and tearing the ears off those Jedburgh and Kelso gowks who ponce about with a rugby ball. Oh, yes, and probably fornicating, which brings us back to anatomy. Mary is a phase in your history. Like all things, it will pass. You must let it pass. Take my advice, don't dwell, only evil will come of it."

If possible, Ronan looked even more miserable. Nor was he comfortable with the robustness of Charles's vocabulary. "Is it that she has another ... involvement?"

"Mary has two loves only. Her studies and her faith. Work and pray. Come now, where are you staying in Auld Reekie, in Hall no doubt."

"I'm not exactly fixed up yet, I had rather underestimated the cost of things and I've arrived sooner than ..."

"You come to the city with no accommodation arranged? Or were you half hoping to ... never mind. In that case you will stay with me until you get fixed up, no, I insist. I have a small flat in the unfashionable end of the New Town. It would never do to have MacDonald of Dunlaith's son wandering the sinfu' streets."

"You know about my father?"

"Only something Mary said. Now do put on a more cheerful aspect, if only for my sake. Well, if it has come to this airt, only the cure will cure it. A *deoch an dorus* do *chaileag ruadh*. Did I get the pronunciation right, Ronan?"

"Like a hielan' coo wi croup, as father would have put it."

Late in the afternoon two men emerged from Darling's Hotel in Waterloo Place and began to stroll up the flank of the Calton Hill towards Regent Road. They had supped royally, although it had been a struggle for Charles to persuade Ronan to accept his hospitality. It was overcast and the wind had subsided but the two men appeared to make heavy weather of the ascent. They had also drunk deeply of *usquebath*, Scotland's anaesthetic of the soul and were bracing themselves at twenty-five degrees into an imaginary wind.

After about ten minutes of sinuous progress, the two branched off into Regent Terrace, where Charles had parked the Riley. The old car looked quite at home resting on the glistening cobbles, framed by Georgian facades. Charles ran his finger affectionately along her glistening bonnet and then stroked her rounded bottom. "I've spent more than was provident on this old girl and probably more than most men would spend on a mistress. But then, she is probably twice as reliable. We all need our little indulgences." He swung open the boot and held out Ronan's bag. Ronan gazed up at the imposing architecture.

"Is it here we are staying then?"

"It is here we're staying. Profligate I may be, but not profligate enough to risk monopolising residents' parking bays for four hours. I have the attic storeys of number sixteen."

When Charles had mentioned the 'unfashionable' end of the New Town, Ronan had imagined the periphery of Leith Walk or Inverleith. From the little he knew of Edinburgh, the ashlar stone houses on Regent Terrace with their twelve-foot high ceilings, eight-foot high Georgian windows with recessed shutters, pilasters, doric mouldings, two levels of basements and two layers of attics and their panoramic views over the Calton Valley were fashionable enough to be some of the most costly housing in the City. Charles's flat was just what Ronan had imagined. Book-lined, Kelim-rugged, leather-buttoned and oak-furnished. Both men were tired, and both had reached that point, which is always reached in even the most harmonious company, when they wished to be alone with their thoughts. Charles was teaching Ronan the intricacies of the espresso machine when the telephone rang. He took the call in his study. After a while Ronan, carrying two mugs of coffee, prised open the study door with his foot and eased himself sideways into the room. Charles was leaning against the empty fireplace intent on gently running his thumb along the blade of the most lethal *dirk* Ronan had ever seen.

Charles at once made to casually throw the weapon onto the mantelpiece, but in so doing he managed to slice the ball of his thumb with the blade. The knife fell short of the mantelpiece and fell to the oak floor, where the point embedded itself. The tapered edged blade and black, horn handle vibrated a second, then were still. Ronan observed the black haft, carved in Celtic knots for a better grip and the cruel mirror-like blade, clearly razor sharp. A single drop of ruby blood splashed on the floor and broke Ronan's astonishment. He laid down the mugs and proffered a grubby handkerchief. Charles was at once his old, urbane self.

"Thanks, but I'd rather risk catching bubonic plague from that old antique, than some vile scourge from your napkin. I'll just stick the old digit under a tap."

Charles returned a couple of minutes later, suitably sticking-plastered, to explain his passion for old, edged weapons. He then proceeded to show Ronan the several more-or-less pitted and dusty examples hanging above the mantle and on the windowsill. At some time during this tour the black knife had been removed and put away but Ronan could not remember the act. Charles gestured Ronan to a big armchair whilst he sat down on the edge of a desk.

"That was the delightful Freddie Goldberg on the telephone. Apoplectic as usual because my mobile has run out of juice. The fact is, the day after one of Freddie's people stuffed it into my breast pocket, it mysteriously fell off the Forth Bridge. But something's come up and Freddie is in a bit of a tizz and would like me to remove my bottom to Drumelzie House. He insists I bring you along, most unlike Freddie. But, look, why don't you come with me. You have a few days of freedom before you report to the Senatus. I can promise you that however emetic the media circus is, it can be most entertaining, and it means I can keep an eye on you."

The following morning, Ronan awoke to white sunlight, pastel-blue shutters and pale oak boards. An oak chest and a black, wrought iron bedstead were the only other furnishings. Prints by Matisse and Modigliani hung on the whitewashed walls. Ronan throwing on a white, towelling dressing gown, softly turned the brass latch of the French windows and stepped onto a small, cast iron balcony. Provence had come to Edinburgh. Something of the 'auld alliance', older far than her dalliance with stolid Anglo-Saxon culture, will always live on in Scotia. Full of strange, *recherché* visual experiences, Scotsmen or strangers will often be transfixed by sunlight welled in a medieval courtyard, or a town square in a Border town, a tree-lined avenue or broad, promenaded river drifting through a highland town. The stranger will think provincial France, the Scotsman with any sense will know of the debt of language, culture and spirituality which he owes to those other Gaels.

The balcony rail was slippery with melting frost and the broad tree-lined boulevard was dappled by autumn leaves heaped on the shimmering cobbles. Ronan's senses absorbed an intoxicating panorama. Over the tree-tops of the narrow gardens opposite, the eye travelled over Doric temples, across the valley where the great North Loch once lay to the medieval town and the sanctuary of Holyrood. The air was sharp and Ronan knew he had never felt more alive … in French provincial Edinburgh.

Fifteen minutes passed, then aware of the chill, Ronan returned to the bedroom. He tiptoed down the hallway to the marbled bathroom to wash and shave and tiptoed back. Slipping out of the dressing gown, he began vigorously to dry his hair with a hand towel when his attention was captured by a print of Gustav Moreau's St George and the Dragon. The damsel, in rich ruby brocades, appears to float atop an insurmountable precipice. St George, very young, slim, androgyne, fantastically dressed in art nouveau armour and silk, stands at the foot of the mountain staring into the jaws of unspeakable evil. The painting, in a carved oak frame, hung over the pine mantle of a tiny, cast iron fireplace. Ronan leant on the mantle to study the detail of the print and it was in this pose that Charles found him.

"Represents the power of youth and innocence to conquer evil," he said, placing a coffee mug on the mantelshelf.

Ronan smiled, "Or is it that youth is simply ignorant of evil?"

"It amounts to the same, evil enters the world through man. Besides, I'm far too hung over to theologise on this beautiful morning. *Carpe diem* and the older you become the more seizing you feel impelled to do. I'll to Drumelzie, follow who dares, to battle with the trendy enemy of mankind."

They talked for a few minutes and then Charles went off to pack. It was only when he began to towel his hair again that Ronan realised that he was naked. He paused, the towel held over his right shoulder and his left arm extended by his side. His long limbs and back were straight and well formed and the fine, boyish down and tight curls of his body hair were golden in the sunlight. After a moment he threw the towel over the bed end and began to dress. There is no reason in the world why the fact that he had not felt the least uncomfortable or self-conscious in Charles's presence should have disturbed him. But it did, and he felt, for the first time, a slight sensation of guilt. Then he pushed it to the back of his mind. There were too many other pleasant, new sensations to be savoured on this fine autumn day, which was as bright and as sharp as a keenly-honed blade.

9

*Whitby: David Garrett visits the church then takes a card from his
pocket. 'Look for the man who seeks jet' is what is written on it.
Mary Dalbeith arrives in the church and gives Garrett directions.
He meets a 'half-drowned' sailor who gives him a package. Garrett gets
rid of two men who have been lying in wait for him. He returns to Mary,
they share wine, then he vanishes into the darkness.*

To a seafaring man, there are few place names as deeply atmospheric
as Whitby. Ports as far flung as the Pool of London, Singapore and the
St Lawrence Seaway reverence the Prospect of Whitby in the names of
licensed houses, quayside thoroughfares and harbour districts. Today,
the haven is not quite a port, yet still more than a harbour. The best and
worst excesses of Victoria's reign saturate the town. Half close your eyes
and open your nostrils to find that 19th-century Whitby has not passed
away, not at all. Around each corner the vision of a drunken Lascar or
Dutchman yawing from an alehouse door, stumbling through a pungent
fog from the herring smokehouses. His feet still limping to the intermittent piping of an English concertina echoing from an open window as he
picks his way down the cobbled lanes. Clinging to the Yorkshire coast and
scoured by the freezing salt breath of an unrelenting sea, Whitby draws
its living from the sea and the rocks. Coal, jet, fish and seafaring. And
amongst the weft of this industry is woven a more obscure commerce. A
distributive trade only made possible by the unremarked and anonymous
ebb and flow of small vessels and nameless crew between Whitby and
the dockside warrens of continental Europe. Dark, glistening, strange,

secretive, this is no manicured toy poodle of a town. The National Trust
has not been here to remove its dockside ice factories and rusting trawl-
ers, the stink of tar and fish heads, foul-mouthed pot houses, gaudy fried
fish restaurants and incorrigible, disreputable old buildings. Whitby is a
serious, industrial place; and its industry is the sea. It lurks, ominously,
down by its shore under its rocks. In its fathomless, black, oily water.
More like a scaly sea creature than a place of human habitation.

For most visitors, blown in off the Yorkshire Moors, Whitby begins
with a cliff, and the stark Abbey Ruins, overlooking the town. So why
should Garrett be any exception to this rule as he parked his black Audi
estate car on the broad expanse of tarmac adjacent to St Hilda's church?
Early 19th-century St Hilda's, almost modern by comparison, waits
patiently as a supplicant outside the precincts of the Abbey which has
shouldered it to the very edge of the cliff. As he closed the driver's door,
Garrett looked uncomfortably at the car. He knew that his new life, since
it began a few weeks ago, was, like his self respect, simply on loan. It
still had to be paid for. And now he was to begin to earn what he knew
he could never, never lose again. His breath smoked as he turned up the
collar of his coat. Winter had come in earnest and it was freezing pite-
ously hard. The sun was low in the west and just beginning to turn cold
red as it filtered through the fretwork of sightless tracery and down the
knave of the extinct Abbey. In an hour or so the sun would sink into the
moors and the black shadow of the cliff would overwhelm this forgotten
town and plunge its inhabitants into oblivion.

Garrett walked slowly through the cliff top church yard where
drowned sailors moaned in their dreams, made restless by the vibra-
tion of the surf against the rocks beneath. He felt the sting of the cold
iron door handle as the oak gave way to the pressure of his arm. The
sombre interior was an unhappy space. Victorian etiquette had dressed
it for death and mourning. Not for this place the comfort of stained glass
sunlight spilling across mellow limestone tracery. Here, cast-iron pillars,
discreetly marbled, supported an oppressive gallery. Box pews, above
and below, wainscoting and ubiquitous dark oak panelling added to the

claustrophobia. Although designed for immense extinct congregations, the gathering twilight restricted Garrett's horizon to a few metres as he walked down the wooden floor of the nave towards the black marble altar. An intimidating two-tier Victorian Gothic pulpit with a vast canopy loomed out of the darkness as he passed. The altar rails forbade Garrett further progress, so he stood for a while in front of the sanctuary, alone in the musty silence. And yet it occurred to him, that in this house, he was not alone. Then he knelt and prayed. He had not done so for many years. He prayed quietly in his own mind. We will not enquire what passed; to eavesdrop on a private conversation with God, is death. Yet it was clear from the pressure of his bloodless fingers around the rail, that Garrett struggled. Then he relaxed and sighed, then stopped breathing. He had heard the faint noise of another mortal moving in the gallery above him. The sound of footsteps travelling across the boards. Then the sounds of someone heavily descending the staircase and beginning to walk slowly down the central aisle towards him. A man like Garrett does not turn around, nor speak, nor move away, but simply ensures that his mind and body are relaxed and poised. It is the art of the Zen patriarch, pulling the great bow a thousand times yet never releasing the arrow. The other visitor knelt beside him in the dusk. In these times it is rare to be disturbed in a church. It has thus become a more suitable place in which to commit a sin than seek redemption. More convenient, yet no less deathly. There was silence for about thirty seconds, then the other man got to his feet and left. A few minutes later Garrett also stood up and walked to the light of the leaded window. He removed a piece of white card from his left jacket pocket and read what was written thereon. It said simply, "Look for the man who seeks jet".

Garrett left the building and made his way through the blustery grass to the top of the hundred or so stone steps which coiled their way down into the town. The further he descended the more muted the offshore wind became and the quicker the remaining daylight faded, until he walked in a cold green glow and a murmuring silence. He was plunging into the depths of the ocean leaving a wake of dreams behind him.

Soon he found himself in a narrow lane amongst the curious collection of arcane shops, cafés and inns packed tightly along the foreshore. The shopkeepers were putting out their lamps as the innkeepers were lighting theirs. He was drawn to a tiny inn called the Captain Cook. It was between the smokehouses and a concrete slipway running down to the shore. Its maroon and gilt façade swallowed him in the dusk. Once Garrett had procured a pint of ale and a suspicious looking pie, he eased himself into a bench seat in a dim corner of the room. The smoky atmosphere and the low, nicotine-stained ceiling absorbed much of the ineffective light. In navy duffel, pullover and brown corduroys Garrett blended easily into the noisy crowd. Or so he thought. A vague scent of perfume, like the warm night air in a summer garden, was his first indication that a girl, in her mid twenties, had quietly sat down beside him. Garrett was trained to detect incongruity, a caution that had only failed him once when half a finger on his left hand had been lost to a parcel bomb in Beirut. Yet even a child could tell that there was nothing more out of place in this setting of harsh, uncomfortable masculinity than an attractive, unaccompanied young girl. The eyes of the crowd were beginning to be fixed on her and by proximity, and to Garrett's discomfiture, also on him. Her long slim legs in woolly black tights, beneath her very short velvety skirt, caused an electric discharge all around her. She smiled at Garrett and he knew that she was here, in some way, because of him. And such a smile, the distilled essence of all the life and joy that had passed Garrett by. She stood up and held out her hand to him. He took it and they left together as naturally as young lovers and as innocently as mother and son. Neither spoke, Garrett could not. He was, in a manner of speaking, forbidden by her pale beauty. She led him down through the narrow, cold alleyway where their breath billowed like smoke in the intermittent lamp-light. She was not his lover, nor his whore, the fact that she existed at all was improbable and ambiguous. Garrett guessed at her purpose, but vaguely. She led him up winding steps to the converted sail loft of what had once been a small, stone fisherman's warehouse. Inside, a fire burned in an immense stone hearth. There was no other light and the single room spread softly into darkness in all directions as if it had no walls or ceiling. Garrett was aware that there must be a large window, at one end, overlooking the harbour, as distant mooring lights shone like stars into the room. It made him feel tired and alienated ... as if he was standing alone in the midst of a swirling cosmos. He shivered and was drawn to the semi-circle of flickering fire-light and the need to be comforted. The only object illuminated by the fire was a mattress, smothered in a voluminous eiderdown quilt and a bundle of arctic furs. It was placed on the warm wooden floor boards in front of the fire. The girl took his hand and they sat down together. Garrett watched her as she undressed in a curiously artless and sexless way. She had kicked off her high heels and with a brief, unselfconscious arching movement was soon free of her tights and then her briefs, which she threw to the end of the mattress. She stood up and indicated the zip of her skirt. Garrett undid it and it whispered to the floor. He rested his hands on the girl's naked hips, to steady her whilst she struggled briefly to pull her sweater and T-shirt over her head. She stood naked for a moment in his hands. The moment could not be measured in time, only in beauty. Beauty so much more powerful to the human spirit than love or sex or knowledge. If Rodin had wasted a lifetime struggling to express such a nude in Carrera marble he would rejoice in smashing such apostasy to dust with his dying breath. With one final quick instinctive movement she undid the clasps in her gathered hair and shook her head. A cascade of shimmering hair uncoiled over her shoulders and dropped to her waist. Her hair was alive, dark and as rich as silk as it swung heavily against the gentle curvature of her back. Was it the glow from the fire which lent that warm red hue to her hair, or did her hair breathe life into the fire. Then, like a young otter, in an instant she had disappeared under the mound of eider feathers and arctic fox. The instincts of a young, warm-blooded animal of the Northern Hemisphere. Surviving, like all of us, in a hostile environment and seeking comfort where we may. She lay on her side and watched Garrett as he undressed and slipped in beside her. Soft, smooth, fresh-scented, warm, warm, warm, he experienced a delicious sense of falling as they lay together. Lay together through the winter's night like brother and sister. Once, vaguely, as in a dream, he had a powerful premonition that she might rend him, bloodily, in the night, like a wild beast. But the sensation brought him no fear, only release.

In the morning Garrett awoke to an abrasive winter sun scouring the room. His sleep, the morning chill and the white light refreshed him like a cold shower. When operating he had often slept on hard floors, deliberately, as he had been trained, so that his sleep would be shallow and his senses on stand by, half beneath the surface of consciousness. Today, he experienced the same exhilaration on waking … sharp, clear yet faintly light-headed. The embers still smoked within their stone prison, fingers of smoke scrabbling at the black walls, and above him immense roof trusses, like the hull timbers of ancient sailing vessels supported a roof of slates so small and thick as to be almost like cobbles. Chinks of daylight and an excoriating wind pierced these at intervals. A slight change in the light told him that someone had moved across the large window which had been placed where the loft doors used to be. He turned to see the girl sitting on the windowsill and as he did so her gaze shifted from the harbour to meet his own. They would both have traded their souls for an eternity of silence. But the World turns, the tide ebbs and flows, as do the seasons, poetry turns to prose, it could not be.

"Do you live here now?"

"Yes, for the moment."

"This is coincidence then?"

"It's more prosaic, I saw you in the town, and followed. But you know what Thomas à Kempis said about coincidences … when you stop praying, they stop happening."

"What did he say about forgiveness?"

"He said I should wash your feet and dry them with my hair."

They sat on opposite ends of the wooden windowsill facing each other, blank of expression, challenging each other. The girl wore an ankle-length grey corded velvet dress with a high buttoned collar and a wool cardigan; but her feet were bare. Her legs were drawn up close to her as she sat with her back against one of the deep baulks of oak, which formed the window sides. She folded her arms on top of her knees and then rested her chin on them. She studied Garrett through the pupils of her brown eyes. For years Garrett had not merely denied emotions, he had disconnected them. Weighted them with cold iron, cut them adrift and sank them thousands of fathoms down into the abyss. They were lost in depths beyond any salvage. Until he noticed that this girl's feet were almost blue with cold. Time and again some hidden mechanism began to activate his arms and hands to reach out and take those small, familiar feet in his lap and gently rub warmth back into them. But, each time, the impulse could not connect into action. He sat still, and looked at the small, perfect child's feet and felt pity like a pain deep in his skull. He pitied them both.

They sat until the sun climbed over the harbour wall and then began to scramble up the side of the cliff towards a row of grey, provincial Georgian houses, soon to become white. Then they ate some yeasty wholemeal bread and butter with a jar of fruit preserve. He broke the bread, she blessed it. The sun clock struck the top of the cliff and Garrett said, "Where can I find the man who seeks jet?"

"There is a Whitby man, a half-drowned sailor no good for the sea. You can find him around Wyke Beck Maw. About half a mile south of the town, where the Beck cuts through the cliff like a knife and opens it out to the sea."

At the threshold, he paused against the iron balustrading at the top of the steps. He took in the details of the harbour and riverside and the clusters of smoking, cottage roofs. He turned to face the girl and his breath condensed in the thin morning air.

"You have learned about this coast."

"Well, there is more to the world for a Scots queen than the herrin' fishing, Garrett."

Garrett forgot to smile, he forgot a lot of things and remembered too many others.

He was out of breath as he gained the abbey car park. He had climbed too fast, absorbed in his thoughts, abstracted and unconscious of his body. Very unusual and very unwise. He did not look in his rear view mirror as he left the car park. Thirty minutes later found him picking his way down the mixture of inclined earth paths and rustic steps which snaked their way down into the Maw. As he descended he could sometimes hear the ripple of the beck deep in the ravine to his left. There was no other sound except his own foot falls. No birds. No wind. The moorland vegetation was bleak and monotonous. There was no scent other than the borrowed fragrance that still embraced him. The frozen blue sky was glimpsed through the cleft of the defile and the stones in the path were slippery with ice in the shadows. Garrett turned up his collar, plunged his hands deep in his pockets and strode on. Before he knew it the path had turned to sand and the river had turned to sea. He had come out of the ravine where the beck fights its way out into the North Sea. The sea, in its fury, had hurled its flotsam deep into the mouth of the Beck. Plastic containers, pieces of hemp and nylon rope, wooden pallets, long strands of wrack and kelp, glass bottles, tin cans, fishing floats, milk crates and, eloquently, a pair of rubber sandals, lay strewn on the banks of the shallow river. Garrett awoke from his reverie and walked out onto the rocky beach, out of the shelter of the ravine. There was a stiff off-shore breeze blowing. Garrett brushed the hair from his eyes and squinted as he felt the sand powdering his face. The wind made his face ache. He looked back once and the cliffs had swallowed up the ravine. The waves sounded with a distant drumming but appeared to rise above him and threaten to overwhelm him. He had an uneasy feeling of being trapped between the sea and cliffs. He could feel the blown spindrift on his skin. After a while, Garrett realised how little thought he had given to his search. He had automatically turned to the right after the Maw, but could just as easily have turned to the left. He really had no idea where he was going and the shore was particularly devoid of landmarks to assist him. He had not prepared himself for the loneliness of the place. A hostile, featureless horizon on one side and grey, shale cliffs towering on the other. Garrett walked between high and low tide. A life-less strand which was neither in this world nor the next. No creature, not even a single white gull, had ventured into this uneasy, forlorn place. He strained his ears for the comforting cry but heard something else. Just on the threshold of hearing, blown to him in the wind, was an intermittent ringing sound, like the tolling of a small bell. Garrett was sure the sound was ahead of him so decided to press on through the shingley sand. As the shore swallowed him up the bell grew louder. At irregular intervals, the cliffs were indented by vast inlets where some moorland stream, high above, had caused the cliff face to collapse or where the North Sea had devoured millennia of the soft rock in the spring gales. Half an hour had passed since he left the Maw when, approaching one of these inlets, he spotted the source of the sound. There, dwarfish beside giant boulders, was the figure of a man. He was moving his hands in a slow, circular motion over the surface of the cliff. Like a blind man reading the secrets of a human face. As soon as Garrett put his next foot on the shingle the man turned to observe him. As Garrett drew nearer he saw the small steel hammer and narrow iron chisel which the man had tucked in the waistband of his coat. A full length, brown oilskin coat, a black woollen hat, fingerless gloves. This was his work-wear. Human voices were raised against the eternal sighing of wind and ocean.

"I believe you have something for me?"

"Aye, I've been expecting you. Follow me."

Ten minutes later, two men sat on upturned fish crates, facing each other across a smouldering driftwood fire. They sat in the mouth of a small cavity eaten into the cliff. These caves, many as much as 60 feet deep, are numerous along the coast. They are ephemeral shelters carved from a soft shale rock. The pitiless sea which gave them often takes them away on the next spring tide. Fresh water dripped onto the shingle floor at the back of the cave and the fire gave an occasional shower of sparks to the wind. A bottle of rum and two glass tumblers were set out on a third crate. Garrett was still trying to dispel his unease on finding two measures of the spirit already poured and waiting when they entered the cave. The sky grew wintry and a light shower of sleet was blown in front of the cave mouth. They drank before they spoke.

"You will be the man who seeks jet?"

"Yes, I am he but I'm not the one that you seek."

Garrett looked at his face, closely, for the first time. Here was the root of an ancient oak, salvaged from the tide. Bleached almost white in parts but mainly grey-brown grain and knots with deep furrows, shaded black. His hands also, pieces of dried and cracked sealskin. Eyes watery, pale blue with white pupils. Teeth, walrus tusks of antique ivory. Beard, a frond of grey seaweed. A half-drowned man. A faint, high, broken voice, like the call of a distant gull.

"No, it is not me that you are seeking," he grinned, "but you will find him soon enough, wickedness is never difficult to find." He stopped, and grinned up at Garrett, who betrayed no emotion but was inwardly driven to frustration by the pressures of time and task.

"But you are the one who seeks jet?"

"Men seek all sorts of things. Take these for example." Here he fished a round, heavy grey object from his coat and laid it in front of Garrett. It was a perfect Ammonite fossil. Garrett held the shiny weight of it in his hand for a minute, he ran his thumb over the sutures of the septa, where they bifurcated on the outer circumference of the coil of shell. Then he laid it down and rose to leave. The old man, for he bore many years, appeared not to notice. "There are endless numbers of these along the shore. The nuns from St Hilda's Abbey used to believe them to be serpents, agents of the wicked one, turned to stone. This," he gestured above him, "used to be the bed of the Rhine, one hundred and sixty million years ago. It ran across the North Sea to here and right across England to the Dorset coast."

Garrett began to turn to go.

"So you see, in prehistoric times, your man could have saved himself a sea voyage and simply floated his package down the Rhine." He smiled again and nodded amiably. Garrett sat down. The half-drowned sailor smiled and poured another two drinks. They drank.

Garrett said, "Go on."

"There is no beginning and no end; only the wheel of fortune, forever turning. Christ Pantocrator at its centre, formed by the six-pointed star of Solomon's Seal. The twelve Apostles are the first circle. The second carries the twenty-four elders of the Apocalypse, each bears a musical instrument and a phial of perfume containing the prayers of the saints. The Queen of Heaven sits at the apex of the wheel, weaving our fates. Forming the third circle are the prophets, martyrs and confessors of the faith. The final circle is a ring of angels and demons praising God. Faith, time, eternity, heaven, fate and the cosmos. And on the rim of this wheel, are you and I. We are drawn around the circumference. We are raised up by our power and riches only to be plunged again into poverty and misery. We descend into hell, thence to be resurrected. There are seven stages on the wheel and it revolves only seven times before we must face the judgement." The half-drowned sailor grinned encouragingly into Garrett's face.

"Tell me about the man who has been here, and the package. I have no time for riddles or theology old man."

"Are you so impatient to plunge your soul into the depths of hell? I have not always been half-drowned … and neither has your soul. I was once a chaplain to the Merchant Navy, if anyone remembers them or me, before my lungs were rotted with seawater. All vanity, just vanity in this transient world. Not so many yards from here, almost half a millennium ago, just before the time of Bede, so called the Venerable, Satan won a great victory which they called a Synod. Now don't get impatient my young friend, for it was all for political and military might; right up your street … eh? A power struggle, except only one side strove to win. Yet a pure light was almost extinguished. The Church of the Celts, which breathed the spirit of Christ. A church of self revelation and communion with God incarnate in nature. The simpler, sincere faith of the coenobite with too much humility to ride on horseback or to name himself anything other than a man. Here we had the like of Columba, striding the windswept moors, taking uncouth men by the shoulders and staring the gospel into their eyes and souls. Well … well, so it was overturned by a more sophisticated, materialist and politically powerful organisation. The Roman Church and all its wiles. And yet, all through the mire of medieval corruption, the Reformation and today's apostasy, something almost lost to the world still remains."

Here the old man grasped the other by the wrist and to Garrett's surprise it was like a steel, hydraulic grab tightening around the bone. "Young man, great power resides in stillness and in listening for the breathing of God."

Garrett was dismayed by his own confusion. He saw his left hand strangely white and bloodless against the sailor's dark skin. Garrett hated confusion and his past life. He lifted the ammonite high above the head of the half-drowned sailor no good for the sea. He spoke slowly, intensely.

"I don't want to send you to sea again old man, floating out on the ebb tide."

The sailor looked sad for the first time.

"So be it then. We each have our freewill."

Then releasing Garrett's wrist he rose slowly to rummage in some bleached fish crates at the back of the cave before returning to place a cardboard box, about the size of a shoebox, on the makeshift table. The dead sailor smiled and nodded his beard.

"All bought and paid for, I believe."

Garrett lifted the lid briefly, closed it and rose to go. He looked down on the half-drowned sailor, still seated by the fire.

"However pure your God is and however deeply you desire his reincarnation, how much have you and I really to be thankful for? His great mercy … or even his pity? And millions like us in sickness, pain or despair?"

"Jesus once sat and drew pictures in the sand, so do I … and even in your mind. Are those who commit evil wiser than God? Who were you before you were and where are you when you cease to be? Christ is not the source of evil. The enemy of mankind only enters the World by one gate and the gate to the human heart gets broader year by year. In the quiet wilderness of the World man used to hear the voice of God each day, as a father guiding his wayward sons and daughters. Then, by new testament times, only John, called the Baptist, Christ and the Apostle Paul spoke with God. Today, that voice is almost silent." He thrust out his arms, still, still in the fluttering wind, as in crucifixion. "Is this World? Is it Hell or is it Heaven? The heart of sinful man is very small but it is a miracle, for it is still big enough to contain God." The old man slowly placed his sealskin hands on the makeshift table and their eyes met as he looked up for the last time. "Ultimately, every question about God is a sin."

As Garrett left the cave, the wind raised a fountain of red sparks from the fire, flying around him like ministering spirits as he strode out onto the shore. The weak winter sun was now almost completely obscured by a filter of unbroken cloud. A chilling shadow had fallen across the sand.

When Garrett reached the foot of the Maw, he threw the cardboard box to join the collection of flotsam slowly eddying in the shallows, first slipping the contents, a heavy, oilskin parcel, into his coat pocket.

He walked steadily up the sandy path, into the jaws of the Maw. Half of his mind was distracted but, at a different level, part was alert. Alert enough to notice that the surface of the path, which had been smooth during his descent, now bore the imprint of two pairs of boots, both male. His mind cut over. His heart rate and adrenalin level imperceptibly increased, his breathing was slower and deeper and his pupils dilated slightly, increasing his visual acuity. He had reached a point where the path was hedged by a thicket of sea holly and gorse on one side and a sheer drop into the Maw beck on the other. The two sets of tracks were eloquent. They pointed downhill but one pair seemed to disappear about 60 feet above him and some 30 feet ahead of him the prints disappeared altogether. Garrett immediately crouched, then slithered into the undergrowth as quickly and silently as one of the several moorland adders that haunt the ravine. Foot by foot, he worked his way around until he could stand up, hidden behind some buckthorn, and survey the path. He was thankful for the wind, and that it was blowing north-westerly. He could see one man, crouching, concealed in the bushes which overhung the path. He held an unsheathed commando knife, with a thick, non-slip rubber haft and a cruel, pointed eight-inch blade with an oval cross section. The man, who was of medium height and heavily built was clothed in ex-army fatigues and was wearing a black, knitted balaclava. Garrett guessed correctly that his companion was similarly concealed further up the pathway. Their intention had clearly been to stop his advance and his retreat. And then, what? Garrett calculated that further information would be useful. The wind direction enabled him to crawl, still hidden to the casual glance, to within ten feet of the concealed man. At which point he threw a small stone high over the man's head onto the path. As the man tensed and craned his head towards the path Garrett, in one fluid, simultaneous movement, took the last three steps and struck his assailant heavily on the back of his neck with the side of his fist. His adversary had only time to sigh softly before falling on his face. The dull thuds, he calculated, might just have been heard above the wind. Lifting the man's eyelid briefly and then letting it close, Garrett picked up the knife and went systematically through his pockets. In one pocket he was almost startled when something alive shook and shivered like a small vole. When he drew it out he was looking at a phone. On it was the message, 'N E SIGN'. At once Garrett cancelled the message and keyed in 'NO – COMING TO JOIN U'. He pressed the callback button.

It was the work of moments for Garrett to don the combat jacket and balaclava of the unconscious man. Then he stood up and calmly walked through the undergrowth towards the point at which the other man lay hidden. As Garrett approached, the man stood up. He was wearing an Arctic Parka and his head was shaven. He had a stooping, simian appearance, a growth of unsightly stubble on his chin and a good crop of cold sores around his mouth. A gold crucifix hung incongruously from one ear. He cursed floridly as Garrett approached and glanced nervously from time to time down onto the path. Garrett waved and saw that the man was carrying a large, hardwood axe handle. When they were almost face to face, the dawning realisation of something amiss could just be seen in the man's eyes. It was then that Garrett tripped him and put the cold knife point to his throat. Mercifully for Garrett's soul, the man knew almost nothing. He had merely guessed the nature of the package when he saw it in his shipmate's locker and now wanted a pecuniary bonus to buy his silence. Garrett watched a ruby orb of blood, glowing in the sunlight, grow around the tip of the knife. The man realised that he was fathoms out of his depth with Garrett. He and his mate had booked a working passage on a coaster bound for Rotterdam in the morning, and Garrett had very little doubt that they would have been on it. The man smelt very bad and Garrett was glad to be rid of him. He breathed deeply as he continued up the pathway.

On the drive back along the coast, Garrett began to consider his ascent. He smiled grimly and shivered and thought, "From army officer to hired thug … or worse, or worse." He must not think about what he was doing … he just had to get on with it. It was only a process, just a process, too important to be undermined by ethical digressions. And the outcome, too precious to release from his grasp: self-esteem. As he parked in a side street near the old sail loft, he opened his fist and looked at the gold crucifix which lay in the palm of his hand. He closed his fist tight and put his hand in his pocket.

The sail loft was empty. He made himself a coffee that he couldn't drink, and sat by the window with a road map that he couldn't read spread out on the floor. He looked at the sun, which had no heat, and felt warmed. He had noticed the shadow which had fallen across the map for some seconds before he looked up into the girl's face. She was wearing brown stretch leggings, tucked into calf leather ankle boots, under a vast, brindled, fisherman's sweater. The effect, set off by her pale, cream complexion and glowing, auburn hair was an allegory of the queen of the autumn, straying too close to the king of the winter solstice. Garrett watched his life flickering across the pupils of her eyes. Then he became unaccountably calm and experienced a sense of falling into the pools of her liquid-brown eyes. So dark that he could not tell where the pupil ended and the iris began. Falling, tumbling, drowning as he went, spiralling down into the depths. When she spoke, it was as if the words were whispered, fondly, gently inside his head by his lover, the queen of heaven.

"You found what you were seeking?"

He heard himself give an evasive reply, and some time afterwards felt her arms around his shoulders. It was then that he noticed that his face was wet with tears, but whether they were his or hers was not important. He stood up and held the girl at arm's length the better to see into her eyes.

"What will you do now?"

"As much as any man does, begin again, work out his destiny. I can never go back of course."

"And I?"

Such a small question. How can she ask such a small question. And as Garrett said "You will leave me again", he had to grind his jaw to stop it from shaking.

She replied without any tone of protest or recrimination in her voice: "Leave you? Leave you? I never left you. But after you lost … your social position you changed."

"I lost everything, everything of value to a man."

"You always cared very much about the things of this world."

"Is honour a thing of this world?"

"Ah. That's a difficult one. Honour can be a false creature of pride and arrogance. But it can also be an inspiration of humility and truth. There is true honour which is love and false honour which is hate."

"And now I know neither love nor hate."

"You clamped down into a cold, bitter silence. I could not comprehend it. I was, am, young and I became isolated and afraid. You needed time."

"Three years?"

"You still need time. Can you talk about it? You never talked about it."

Garrett sat on the floor and she sat in front of him, holding his hand.

"Some of it. Some ... of ... it. It was Ulster. There were three of us in the 'Badlands', by the border. Bivied in a derelict croft house. We had been shadowing a terrorist cell in the area. But nothing was happening. It was often like that. Days passed, playing cards, observing the same monotonous horizon of barren moorland day and night, one always on guard by roster. Then, on the seventh day, the lads let me take the Land Rover and slip away in the night to an air base about 40 kilometres away. Two hours later, with just a brief hop across the Irish Channel, an RAF Sea King set me down in Kintyre on its way to Fort William. I knew one of the crew and, anyway, in special operations, regular troops hardly ask questions ... it's all a nod and a wink, so to speak. The paperwork follows ... or never follows. When I returned the next day ... the next day, when I got back ..."

He paused here and drew a long, long, breath. Then exhaled in a sigh which shuddered in his chest. "When I got back, the area had been sealed off by the RUC. The croft was smouldering and both of my unit were dead. With only two on the roster, one had got careless and fallen asleep. Provos. got in through a window. Shot one, tortured and shot the other. I never thought it could happen. You never do."

"Why did you go?"

"Why? To attend the funeral of John MacDonald at Dunlaith."

Garrett later thanked his cat-like reflexes that he was able to rise and support the girl, as she appeared to stumble and grasp at the sail loft window frame for support. A Pre-Raphaelite pallor had blanched her face, her breathing came shallow and fast and her lips were an open wound.

"Was it so gruesome a story? I should never have told you ... even for the sake of honesty. Are you all right ... here, sit down a while."

"No, no. I mean yes, I'm OK. Could you just repeat the last bit for me?"

"About John MacDonald, the old Minister of Dunlaith?"

"Aye, just so. I think I have heard of him."

"Another coincidence. Enough to make a man nervous. Though not so strange perhaps, given where you and I first met. My old brigadier, retired by then and in a wheelchair, asked me to represent the unit at the funeral. The message was passed on to me in one of the routine despatches. Obviously he had no way of knowing I was on opps. and at first I dismissed the idea. But the letter did say that he and old MacDonald had a special friendship. When the opportunity arose, for his sake and for honour, I became … dishonourable. The rest you know, or can guess …" searching her eyes, holding her at arm's length, "and you look much better."

"Sorry I tripped just now, I've been busy today and didn't get time to eat." Holding up her hand to stay his comment, "Very silly, I know. Was that the end of it?"

"It was the end of many things. But that is all there is to say about the events. Other than, for completeness, that the brigadier died two days after the funeral. I never kept his letter, so I never mentioned it. Didn't seem much point. It was more than John MacDonald that was buried at Dunlaith."

"Do you hate me?"

"Death is never a little thing, you see. Not then, not now. Can the sword pierce itself, even until death? Can I ever hate you?"

Garrett took a half full bottle of claret from the windowsill, a legacy of last night, and poured a glass.

The two, let us say, lovers, linked arms. Garrett smiled sadly: "Can you drink from the cup which I must drink?"

"Remember, you've not done anything wicked nor evil."

"No, not yet."

They shared that last glass. They looked at each other until their eyes grew dim. Then, Garrett turned quickly lest he should never go.

"I have to catch the fading light. My compass points north tonight. I'm sorry … I'm sorry …"

She placed her fingers on his lips, then he was gone. Yet all time swirled around him as he paused on the threshold. "Goodbye Mary."

10

Charles Meldrum and his fine kilt. Freddie Goldberg, Ronan and
Charles meet in a restaurant in Drumelzie. The fatal accident.
Ronan's discovery of a key.

Charles Meldrum couldn't remember when he had last seen such a fine kilt. In a full eight yards of the heaviest wool tartan it boasted a striking blend of red, blue and green pattern with a fine white band woven through. It was tailored in a military pleat, that is, pleated on the regular vertical white line in the pattern, rather than by random measurement. This made the back of the kilt look mostly white when stationary but aflame when on the move. This fine item of clothing was adorned with a chaste silver and horsehair piper's sporran of prodigious hirsuteness. Less happily, the regalia was topped by a black leather bomber jacket ... complete with bogus US Airforce insignia.

"What do you think, Charles, fantastic isn't it?" As he said this, Freddie Goldberg pirouetted like a ballerina in flying boots.

"A fine filibeg, Freddie."

"Huh?"

"From the gaelic *feileadh beag* ... little kilt."

"Little ... are you taking the piss, Charles, 'cause if you are you can ..."

"No, no, Freddie, it's the traditional description for that garment. It's a fine kilt, I don't recognise the tartan, though."

Freddie relaxed, smiled and winked. He beckoned Charles and Ronan to a nearby table and they all sat down. He leant towards them.

"Now, here's the clever part, Charles, you're not the only one who can do research. Just listen and see if you can follow. Now, this is Sinclair tartan. What does that tell you?"

Before answering, Charles shot Ronan a secret glance which said, 'For Heaven's sake don't laugh or we're both lost men'. "Well, Freddie, the Sinclairs are descendants of an ancient Norman family, St Clair, which in turn is descended from an even older Norse family. Some say the Clair or Clare in question, being a disciple of St Francis of Assisi, was so moved by his preaching that she formed an order of nuns or Minoresses known, I believe, as the Poor Clares."

"Yes, yes, go on … and …"

"Well, after her death she was sanctified of course …" At this point Freddie held his hands aloft to signal a theatrical silence wherein he completed Charles's sentence.

"… and recently nominated by the Vatican as the patron saint of television." Freddie was immensely pleased with himself. Charles did not have the heart to mention that there was an equally strong body of opinion which held that the family name hailed from a 10th-century youth who left his home in Rye in Kent to become a hermit in Normandy. The unfortunate young man had been beheaded.

The three were seated in a sometime threshing barn now converted into a restaurant. It formed part of Drumelzie Steading, a group of redundant farm buildings about one hundred yards from the house. One end of the barn housed a gift shop which offered scented candles with no aroma, unscented aromatherapy oils, a variety of votive stuffed toys in highland garb, a china Loch Ness monster in four sections, luminous presentation soaps, unspeakable polychrome woollen hats, CDs and DVDs of Scottish music performed by obscure amateurs, mini-curling-stone paperweights, a talking haggis, badges with inane mottos and cheap costume jewellery with fake Celtic motifs. In fact, nothing that any sane nor reasonable person would ever want to acquire. Yet even these items could not detract from the simplicity of the sublime stone walls and noble timbers of the great threshing barn in which they were housed.

"Ronan would probably prefer to look around the grounds while we run through the final screenplay, Freddie."

"Yeah, whatever, as long as he's not on the payroll."

"I think that means 'It's been a pleasure, Ronan.' I'll catch up with you back at the house. I've secured a couple of rooms for the night," with a glance at Freddie, "in the servants quarters, appropriately."

"We need something big, Charles, to bring the programme to a conclusion, and I think I've got it. Picture this; the pipe band are marching towards the camera, which is on the other side of the gates. Just when the viewer thinks they are going to walk into the gates, the Bonnie Prince strides into shot, lays his hand on the gates and they swing open as if by an unforeseen force. The band march through, following the camera and ..."

"But we're shooting tomorrow, Freddie, we don't have time to find a spot and build some replica gates."

"Not fake gates, the real ones, these." Freddie gestured vaguely towards the house driveway.

"Freddie! They've been closed for over 250 years. It's a family tradition, the earl would never agree to it."

Freddie showed one of his gold fillings. "But he has, my man, he has. Of course it put a dent in the budget. The band will not now be wearing Stewart tartan and I've had to substitute local majorettes in mini kilts for the Bonnie Prince. Who needs actors anyway, I can push the gates open, with the help of a couple of guys with ropes out of shot."

"I don't believe it, you're not serious?"

"I'm always serious about money, Charles. Always."

As he strolled past the rhododendron beds on the woodland walk, Ronan was lost to thought. He became aware of his growing disappointment with his visit to Drumelzie and began to wonder why he was there. Envisaging the filming and production team of a Hollywood epic he was downhearted to find a couple of Land Rovers, an American motor home of skyscraper proportions (Freddie's), some video equipment and a few technicians. Mary was gone. He kicked himself for not really knowing where and for accepting Charles's invitation. He made up his mind to return to Edinburgh and sort out lodgings as soon as practical. He would first ask Charles for her address. It was at this point in his deliberations that Ronan suddenly yelped with pain and shock. He was aware of falling and an impact which flattened his lungs. At first he thought he had walked into a wall. But when he managed to gulp some air into his chest he saw he had collided with another pedestrian and been knocked flat on his back. He lay gazing up at a tall, gaunt yet well-built man. He had a military hair cut and wore a navy duffel coat and brown corduroys. Before Ronan could speak the man had offered his hand and hoisted him to his feet. The man was profusely apologetic. Ronan rubbed the back of his head and after some other examinations professed himself in good order.

"I'm none the worse for the tumble," he assured the stranger. "It's my fault anyway, I was in a dream and didn't even see you. You just seemed to come from nowhere."

Some seventy-five yards from the accidental meeting stood the old estate granary, now redundant and appropriately converted into a small, specialist brewery. It produced enough beer to supply the needs of the estate and several free houses in the county. Visitors could also experience the brew first hand in a small bar which had been set up in an adjacent cart shed. The stranger had insisted on buying Ronan a drink, to show 'no hard feelings', and ten minutes later saw Ronan seated at a corner table with Garrett discussing the merits of small beer. They also discussed a number of things they appeared to have in common but Ronan observed that the man seemed most intrigued by John Macdonald's history and death. Somehow the man reminded Ronan of Mary, same interest in his father, and same ruthlessness. The two men would have made a good allegory for the Wheel of Fate. Seated on one side of the circular table, Ronan was in the ascendant, full of breathless anticipation for life and promise of a fine career in front of him. On the other side sat Garrett, bitter, disillusioned and inexorably slipping into perdition but desperately scrambling for a foothold. A light still burned in the soul of both men. Garrett was staying in an estate holiday cottage above the stables and on parting they arranged to meet for breakfast the following morning in the Barn Restaurant. When he reached the house, Ronan was dismissive of the fact that the man had really told him nothing at all about himself except his name, which he said was David Ramsey.

As Charles and Freddie entered the house they found Ronan seated in the main hall, in front of a very large tapestry depicting a hunting scene involving Venus and Adonis in a neo-classical landscape. Charles enquired briefly about Ronan's afternoon and then turned towards the practicalities. "Right, Ronan, we're in the servants' accommodation in the west wing I believe."

"... and I'm in one of the state bedrooms on the first floor," added Freddie. "See you sharp at 7 am, Charles." Then, as he turned to go, "Sleep well, Charles, and you Mr MacDonald."

Charles was deep in thought as he and Ronan walked along the vaulted service corridor which ran the length of the house. "Ronan, did you tell Freddie your surname was MacDonald?"

"No. I don't believe I did. Why do you ask?"

"Nothing really, it's just that I only ever remember introducing you as Ronan."

"Possibly just slipped out in conversation, does it matter?"

"It may do." They came to two adjacent, oak-boarded doors set into the whitewashed stone wall. "These are our rooms. I've put your luggage in the one on the right. Sleep well, I've got a long day tomorrow so I'm going to hit the hay now. Ronan, just do something for me, something important. Lock your door tonight. There have been some thefts here and it would be a wise precaution. You don't want any strangers wandering around your room."

"Sure, if you say so Charles. Goodnight."

As Ronan opened his door he turned to tell Charles about his breakfast appointment, but Charles had already closed his door. Well, it was of no moment, Charles was far too busy to bother and, he smiled, he was not a little boy to have to account for his movements.

Through the small Georgian window of his room, Ronan watched the pale wintry sun dip into the meadowland behind the house. A barn owl was quartering the meadow, floating like a ghost, hardly moving, all stillness and purity. Waiting. A sacred bird to the Celts his father had said and an ill omen if seen in daylight. The Celts, he knew, felt no need to distinguish between myth and reality and in their animistic faith all nature was possessed of an immortal soul. He thought of the Celts and the arcane Lachlan Mor. Of their pure, spiritual relationship with the world and that reverence for the natural world and the supernatural that is revealed in it. He thought of the purity of the alloy of Celtic values and the early Catholic faith. There was a power in the Celtic church which came from its belief in self revelation, visions and prophecy. So it seemed from the time of Joseph of Arimathea, evangel to the Celts, if reality or myth. In any event, he knew that no one now doubts that members of the Celtic Church arrived in Britain around 170 AD, via Asia Minor and Gaul, bringing with them the beliefs of St John the Divine. But the wheel turned and, strangely, within a few months of Columba's death, Pope Gregory's mission, led by Augustine, arrived in Thanet. He watched the brindled-white bird until it disappeared behind the trees guarding the river. Something almost lost to the world remained there.

The rectangular room had a bare-boarded ceiling and floor and a bedstead, washstand and single wardrobe in waxed pine. The light bulb lurked in the bowels of a glass jellyfish lamp shade. It was still relatively early and Ronan wanted to read. There was no bedside light and, as the room was cold, he did not relish relinquishing the comfort of his duvet to switch off the light and then negotiate his way back to bed in the dark. So he did what came naturally to him, as had become a habit since his early teens, he gently reached into his bag and took out the ancient brass candlestick. It felt heavy in his palm and the metal glowed warm. In his rather isolated life, it had become a source of comfort, even though his father sometimes chided him for it. On opening the base it became clear that the one inch stump of candle would not do much service. Instinctively he thought of the candle in the small, wooden chest bequeathed by his father. Somehow he felt sure the grubby candle could have no real significance, no doubt left there by mistake and forgotten, it was probably just the old box his father wanted him to have. What use could a length of candle be to anyone … except to shed a bit of light. Pausing just briefly for a second thought, Ronan nonetheless retrieved the candle from the casket. It fitted snugly into the holder. He had never polished the candlestick for fear of obliterating the inscription. 'Ego sum lux mundi qui sequitur me non ambulabit in tenebris sed habebit lucem vitae.' Ronan set it on the washstand by the bed and a few minutes saw him snuggled under the duvet in a pool of candle light being entertained by Mr Thomas Hardy. Fresh air, however, combined with new vistas, a long day, malted hops, a good book and a warm bed produces a powerful opiate. Before half an hour had passed Ronan found himself under the influence of Morpheus. Once more his recurrent dream flickered under his eyelids. His father, the casket and at last the blinding light played out their drama in his troubled subconscious.

Just when the light seemed at its most exquisite, Ronan awoke suddenly to a sharp metallic clatter. At once he sat up in bed. The candle still burned, brighter than before, but its length was half consumed. In the flickering light he could just discern that the door was still bolted. With a shrug he turned to blow out the candle and it was then that he saw it. A thin, metal object about two inches long lay on the washstand. It was white with candle wax in places and still warm when Ronan took it in his hand. He scraped off most of the wax with his thumb. It was a brass key, not very old and with a flat head about one inch square. It could only have come from the candle. A key, it had to have some meaning.

Forgetting the cold, his heart beating heavily against his rib cage, Ronan switched on the light and standing on the bed held the key close to the bulb. The metal was clearly stamped with a name, 'Sinclair WS', and a number, '68'. He knew little enough of his father's affairs but was able to recall his father's solicitors, Sinclair of Charlotte Square, Edinburgh and the partner who acted for him, Mr Sutherland. More excited than troubled, yet shivering with an apprehension he did not understand, Ronan once more wrapped himself in the duvet, but sleep was a stranger to him for much of the remaining night.

A grey dawn broke to find more than one wakeful soul in the strath of the Tweed. Andrew Farquharson was returning to Cambridge that morning. Last night he had retired to bed early, but spent a fitful night. At the hotel desk he discovered that James had yet to check out and as he approached the glass doors into the breakfast room he saw him seated by the window. He stopped for a moment with his hand on the handle peering at the faceted image produced by the bevelled glass. James was dining with a companion. Andrew made a fist of frustration with his free hand, he needed to talk to James alone, before his resolution bled away like the mist. In that moment of indecision, the wheel turned another notch. James's companion stood up, taking with him an object passed to him across the table. He was stocky, balding and bearded, wearing a leather jacket. Andrew had moved a few yards back from the doors by the time they opened to let the man through. James's breakfast companion barely glanced at Andrew as he thrust an envelope into the inside pocket of his black leather bomber jacket.

Andrew sensed that James had been slightly uncomfortable to find him at his table. But in a few seconds he had recovered enough to wave him expansively into a chair.

"I didn't recognise your companion."

"Just a media contact Andrew, one finds them everywhere."

"Did he get what he wanted?"

"How very cynical you have become. I was, however, able to advise him on an arts grant application."

"For services rendered, no doubt."

"I'm not sure I follow you dear chap. You obviously didn't sleep well last night. You should look after yourself more." James smiled, coldly, and picked up his newspaper. Andrew ordered a full English breakfast. The breakfast room had been a Victorian orangery, built when the hotel was still a private house. Since then it had been a TB hospital, a nursing home and now, a tolerably well-run hotel. Potted palms had replaced the oranges however. Andrew was carefully spreading some lime marmalade across a piece of toast when he next spoke.

"I've been reading the coroner's report on John MacDonald."

James looked at him over the top of, improbably enough, a copy of the *Guardian*. "Coroner's report, you should get out more."

"Oh, it was interesting enough."

"Well the document is a matter of supreme indifference to me. An annoying, bureaucratic formality. These days it seems to be applied to almost every death at home. In most cases it just causes unnecessary anxiety for the family."

"He did die within three days of the onset of his illness, and he was only 58."

James put down his newspaper. "And …?"

"As you know, last summer, John and I met up in the Languedoc. I was staying in a village in the Minervois and he was in Toulouse to research some Occitan documents. Toulouse University language faculty has a unique collection of source documents and the Occitan Culture Institute has excellent translation resources, as you may remember. On the morning I arrived to visit John in his hotel, he was sick in bed. He looked bad and was experiencing chest pains and shortage of breath. I quickly arranged for him to be admitted to the local hospital. Now, the French health service must be the best in Europe. I was quite impressed about how thorough they were. In addition to a general medical check up, they did an angiogram, full blood test, acoustic heart screening then injected a trace and scanned his coronary arteries. When he recovered, they even gave him a spirometry test and ECG on a treadmill. Of course, it was diagnosed as food poisoning from a salade niçoise John had enjoyed the previous evening. John was so acutely embarrassed by the whole thing that he made me promise never to tell anyone about it."

"And that's why you are telling me no doubt. Is there a point to this Andrew, I really would like to make a move before lunch is served?"

"The point is that the French cardiologist pronounced John's cardio-vascular system as unusually healthy. 'You have the heart and arteries of a young man', was the phrase I think he used. Yet, the pathologist gives the cause of John's death as 'myocardial infarction brought about by many years of undiagnosed and untreated coronary disease'. He records a long history of arterial disease, hypertrophy and a serious mitral valve problem."

James glared impassively into Andrew's eyes. "Hmmm. The moral here is never trust a French consultant."

"Or a British pathologist. The question is, how did John die or even why did he die?"

"Isn't it rather too late to worry about that now?"

"But I do worry about it, and I worry about your dinner guests."

"My dinner guests?"

"Yes, such as the Home Office pathologist you introduced me to at your London flat about a year ago. A nice young man and, as it happens, the author of John's post mortem report."

James's hand closed slowly and firmly around the neck of his folded newspaper. "A coincidence, and I'm not sure what, if anything, you are implying. I think you must be under some stress, Andrew. Perhaps this matter about John's son is making you too anxious. You're lonely perhaps, and with too much time on your hands. Have you spoken to anyone about this?"

"Not yet, I want to get back to Cambridge first and then think over my options."

"Exhumation?!"

"It's one option."

"Why are you telling *me* all this?"

"Insurance, old boy, I wanted you to know that this narrative, together with John's medical records from Toulouse, are safely deposited with instructions to be released in the event of my unnatural or violent death.

That's all for the moment, the rest is between me and my all too mortal soul."

Underneath the table, James's hand constricted his newspaper even tighter until the photograph of an innocent Archbishop on the front page was distorted with pain. "I would not talk about this fantasy to anyone if I were you. People would think you paranoid. And there's the boy to consider. I'm worried about you Andrew, you have so much to lose. You also have a febrile and over-active imagination. Be careful it doesn't get you into trouble."

Ronan's breakfast had been rather dull and uneventful. Garrett, he found quite sombre and unresponsive in conversation. Except when he told him the story of the key in the candle. "You see, David, although I had fallen out with my father I knew that he was involved in some important historical research. That kind of thing was his obsession. He spoke to me only once about it, after a dram or two, and it seems it was connected with the research his old friends were doing, right back when they were undergraduates. He travelled a lot in pursuit of documents, so it must have been important. He seemed to be on to something, and that's as much as I know. I'll be off to Edinburgh tomorrow to see what I can discover. You see, perhaps this key is something to do with it."

"Perhaps," said Garrett.

The demesne of Drumelzie rang to the strains of the Black Bear as the Melrose Pipes and Drums advanced down the drive. As they passed, Ronan felt the flams, rolls and paradiddles of the snare drummers pass through him like machine gun fire. One piper was having trouble with the reed in one of his drones and from time to time would place his finger in its end and draw it out to create a partial vacuum, fingering the chanter single-handed as he did it. It was not yet 9 am and a heavy mist, flowing down the valley, still lingered around the white spats of the pipers. He found Charles and Freddie in front of the famous Bear Gates. Amongst the small group of onlookers and technicians stood the old

Earl, in a tweed suit, overcoat, disreputable Homburg hat and Hunter wellingtons. He looked like a man attending his own funeral. His one secret hope was that afterwards he could convince the public that the gates had never in fact been opened at all, that some kind of replicas or trick photography had been used instead. His gillie had been instructed to keep as many people away as possible. Not sure how to do this exactly, the big, red-bearded man had taken an unloaded twelve gauge under his arm and circulated the perimeter growling and scowling ... which was actually most effective.

Had the real Young Pretender looked like Freddie Goldberg, Flora Macdonald might not have been so ready with the rowing boat. His dresser had done a magnificent job, but at a somewhat swarthy and hairy five foot five inches, and tipping the scales at 15 stone, a great deal of soft focus would have to be employed. After much discussion about historical accuracy, Charles had persuaded him to leave the basket-hilted broad sword in his trailer. This on the grounds that the tip of the scabbard dug into the ground as Freddie walked down the drive, leaving a wake of ploughed gravel behind it. By the time the final take came everyone was frozen but at last the ropes were in place, fixed to the bottom of the gates and hidden in the long grass on the far side. The hinges had been judiciously oiled and the Bonnie Prince bore down on the gates in stern resolution with the pipes skirling at his heels. The two teams of men braced themselves against the ropes as Freddie approached, then slowly began to pull. Nothing moved. Freddie, sensing trouble, slowed his pace to give the men a little more time. They heaved in real earnest. Nothing. The Young Pretender was now only ten paces from the gates. Then the men really put their backs into it. The two teams of four strained the ropes until they creaked. Their faces grew red with perspiration. The veins stood out on forearms and foreheads. Boots and brogues scrabbled for grip in the long grass. Finally, slowly, the gates began to move. But not as anyone had expected. The men had felt something give and this spurred them on to further efforts. What they did not know was that they had succeeded in pulling the rusty hinge pins out of the masonry supports. At first Freddie thought that he was experiencing an illusion of perspective caused by the gates opening. This gave him the impression of both gates falling inward.

Long after, witnesses would still say how chillingly fast the acceleration of the six tons of eighteen-foot-high ironwork was, as the gates fell. Freddie was killed instantly. His head was crushed like a walnut shell underfoot. The cast-iron family crest on the top of the gates came to rest a few inches from the Pipe Major's toes. In his statement, he would say that "If I hadnae stopped a wee tae clear that bluidy drone reed then the curse o' the gates wud hae plunged me intae Hell." No one had moved for several seconds, then all was confusion and the screaming of women. The gates, of course, remained firmly closed.

11

Charles stays on at Drumelzie to sort things out after the dramatic accident. Ronan and Garrett return to Edinburgh where Ronan seeks out his late father's solicitor, Archie Sutherland, at Sinclair's. Ronan uses the key to open a safe deposit box. Inside he finds an envelope addressed to him and sealed with wax.

Charles had to stay at Drumelzie and sort things out, all was chaos. To make matters worse, the beery police sergeant with the grey moustache had got it into his head that Freddie's mobile home had been ransacked. Charles told him of Freddie's apocryphal untidiness, but the police still had doubts. Although, if it had taken place it was surely unconnected with Freddie's death. No one could doubt that this was an accident. As soon as Ronan had given his brief statement, however, he was relieved to be able to accept an offer of a lift to Edinburgh. He had to go at once because his lift had an urgent appointment in town. Charles was nowhere to be found and the best Ronan could do was leave a note in his room. He felt guilty about not saying goodbye to Charles, but he would see him again, once he had sorted himself out. Ronan had made two phone calls that morning from the payphone in the restaurant. One to Sinclair's and one to the University Accommodation Officer. With all this excitement, it was not until mid day that Garrett's dark grey Audi rolled through the side gates of Drumelzie with Ronan in the front passenger's seat.

Garrett kept the car radio on for the journey, which mostly precluded conversation. Ronan had wanted to talk about the accident and find out more about David's life. Instead he resigned himself to watching the landscape slide past. The mist had given way to strong sunshine and with it a quietness settled on Ronan when he thought of death on such a day. He offered up an innocent prayer, under his breath, for Freddie's soul. Soon, leaving the glittering river behind, flickering conifers alternated with windswept moorland. From time to time he closed his eyes and dozed in the sunlight. Garrett looked straight ahead for the duration of the trip. That they were now approaching the city was evident from the oppressive roadside signage, police surveillance cameras posted every mile, the beer can-littered verges and a phalanx of wind turbines slicing across a hillside. Although he knew the city well, Ronan always felt vaguely threatened by it. It was as if the space for freedom, independence and privacy was getting smaller and smaller. Again he thought of Lachlan Mor and Mary Dalbeith and the croft house. There was power in that stillness, he thought, but here popularism, litigation, political correctness and so called democratic controls would squeeze the very life out of it. Well, he thought bleakly, enough injections of beer, television and the internet and everyone remains content, why buck a good system? He could just do with a pint himself, he thought.

They drove in by Liberton and Lothian Road and were fortunate to find a space almost immediately in King's Stables Road car park, huddled beneath the Castle Rock. Ronan never imagined he would see Garrett again. They would shake hands and go their separate paths and his first stop would be Mr Sutherland, of course. He was confused therefore when Garrett suggested they meet for a pint after Ronan's appointment. Ronan had unashamedly lost interest in Garrett but, as usual, he was too polite to negotiate a firm refusal.

"I don't know, David, I have to check into my new room in Residence before 6 pm."

"But you've made me so curious about the mysterious key. Just a quick pint, and then I can give you a lift to the University."

Ronan was already regretting having mentioned the key and he really wanted to shake Garrett off. He found him unsettling, very intense, yet mostly silent and shy of eye contact. Yet to his chagrin he heard himself agree to meet Garrett in a couple of hours in a pub called the White Cockade in Rose Street.

The wind blew Ronan's mop of blonde hair over his eyes as he crossed Princes Street and made his way into the formal squares, avenues, circuses and crescents of the Georgian New Town. Many solicitors had their practices here and, for a select few, their homes. Charlotte Square was really designed to be approached from George Street, the main thoroughfare of the New Town and fully a hundred feet wide. From that approach St George's Church dominates the Square and provides a striking vista. There is much stonework in Edinburgh which bears the name of George in one form or another. Mostly after George IV, of course, who visited the City in 1822, the monarch with whom Walter Scott claimed a 'special relationship'. He had been the first monarch to make a formal state visit to Scotland since the rebellion a generation earlier. At the time of the visit in fact he was still being petitioned in respect of Scottish titles and estates which had been sequestered after the '45. It was George's visit, and native financial and social ambition, that really began the cultural anglicisation of Scotland. The New Town had been a conscious statement of the new cosmopolitan image of Scotland and the King was duly impressed. Ronan made a humbler approach to the square from the west entrance, the one used by sedan chairmen up until the nineteenth century. He entered Edinburgh's commercial heart, and its heart was made of stone. Ronan located Sinclair's without difficulty. A varnished door to the side of a vast neo–classical façade. He had an unsatisfactory conversation with an entry phone and was asked to come up to the third floor reception. The big oak door swung on hinge pins let into the stone threshold and lintel. It opened with a groan and a breath of cold damp air. In semi gloom he climbed the echoing stone stairs between plaster walls painted a dark green gloss. The stairwell smelt of disinfectant. A brass plate on the third floor landing reassuringly confirmed Mr Sutherland as a partner of the firm. A fashionable young girl with steel-rimmed spectacles peered at Ronan through a glass screen as if he were a strange sea creature in the wrong aquarium. After grudgingly confirming that he did have an appointment but would have to wait, she paid him no further attention. Ronan suddenly began to be very unsure of himself. He was about to take up this important man's time to show him a small key. He needn't have worried. Archie Sutherland was warm and expansive, if only for Ronan's father's sake. They were both Highlanders and Royal High School FPs so the friendship went back a long way. Old Suthy, however, had long lost his highland tongue but had acquired a surprising amount of Middle Scotch and lowland dialect. The former from his romantic love of Border Ballads and the novels of Scott; the latter from his long espoused environment. Archie could slip from received English to broad Scotch at the drop of a hat, and frequently did. It was this habit and that of continually offering rambling and well-meaning advice that cemented his friend's affections. He was a small rounded man in a grey lounge suit. Almost completely bald, clean shaven and with twinkling blue-grey eyes. He was affable, clearly very comfortable with his position in life and Ronan warmed to him at once. Hands were firmly shaken and a tray of tea was called for. Archie left his desk, with its fine view over the dome of St George's, and the two sat down in leather arm chairs beside a low table. The lighting was soft in the plaster alcoves of the Robert Adam room, the upholstery was yielding and Ronan began to take courage. He was surprised by Mr Sutherland's clipped and almost nervous speech. But he should have known that those who charge by the minute are rarely brief.

"Aye, I remember when your faither and I were gytes thegither. A gyte ye ken is a new boy at the Royal High. That was when we first met all those years syne. But I'm that glad ye've cam tae see me. You will have heard the Will read by my agent in Inverness, and you will know by now that ye're no ill provided for. Now, if you'll forgive me, although it may seem like an unco sum at the moment, in fact John was not a wealthy man. You will need to invest that money well and even so you will still need to earn your corn, which is no bad thing. Take my advice and get straight down to your studies, the surest route to a rewarding career. Look at me, I could have retired years ago, probably should have if you listen to my partners, but I'm interested in the work you see. What else would I do but hang around in Edinburgh clubs boring innocent citizens into untimely graves like a latter day Dr Hornbrook. Well, there we are, what was it you wanted to ask me."

"Well ..."

"Oh, and bye the bye, I was very sorry aboot yer faither. He was a good, good man and to be taken so sudden like. Very sad. Sorry, I didnae get around to saying that at the funeral and I should have said it before now. Now what were we saying."

"I wanted to ask ..."

"Well, don't stand on ceremony, just come out with it. That's what we're here for after all."

Ronan took a deep breath, fished out the key and placed it on the table. With a glance at Ronan, Archie lifted the key to his eyes, turned it to catch the light from the big sash windows, rubbed it between finger and thumb then handed it back to Ronan.

"Aye, that's the key to John's document deposit box. No doubt you'll have found it amongst his effects."

"Yes, in a round about way."

"Sinclair's have been offering that service for generations. Long-standing clients can apply for their own key, which allows them to deposit, read or remove documents without bothering the partners. They have to give the girls at reception proof of identity and sign everything in and out of course, mind you most of our clients are known by sight, and we don't keep valuables in the boxes. I would have mentioned this to you in due course in my probate letter finalising the account. There are a number of minor legal and financial items still to be tied up. Although we do keep copies of all deeds on our own files as well, I still recommend you just leave all these documents with us for safe keeping. I don't know exactly what is in there without checking but if I remember rightly its just a wheen share certificates, title on the croft house, land registry maps, that kind of thing. I'll sort it out for you and confirm the contents in my letter of course. So that's that. Was there anything else? Ye didnae talk much at the funeral but I understand you are going to the University. Let me know your address by the way and if I can be of any help …"

"I'm sorry, but would it be possible to look at the documents?"

"Eh, look at them?"

"Yes, today if possible."

Archie was momentarily put a little off balance by this request, but eventually agreed readily enough. "Mind you you'll be sorely disappointed, all very dry. Dry as dust."

With much frenetic shaking of hands and more homespun advice, Ronan was left in charge of the perfectly-made-up girl in the steel rimmed spectacles. She put down her pen with a martyred expression and glared at Ronan with thinly-veiled resentment. Ronan felt that he had obviously asked her to do something beneath her dignity – like exhume a corpse for example. He smiled apologetically. Her glossy lips moved imperceptibly. "Follow me, Mr MacDonald."

The deed store was in a small, windowless office a few yards from the Reception desk. When Ronan offered the girl the key she merely pointed languidly to rows of grey painted metal boxes along two sides of the walls. He heard the clicking of her high heels growing fainter as she disappeared down the corridor. The girl made him think of the contrast with Mary Dalbeith's simple and natural beauty. And when he thought of it he experienced an unusual loneliness. He smiled at the idea of her striding through the heather in high heels, but the thought still brought a flush to his cheek. It took him a few minutes to locate deposit box 68 but it opened smoothly with the key. Archie Sutherland was mainly, but not wholly correct in his description of the contents. For underneath a pile of title deeds, maps and site plans and a few low-value debentures was a thick, brown envelope addressed to Mr Ronan MacDonald. It was A4 size and quarter of an inch thick. The flap of the envelope was sealed with a blob of sealing wax stamped with a Celtic cross emblem. He weighed it in his hand, turned it over and inspected it. The only written address was his name. The other side of the room held an oak table and chair under a fluorescent light. Ronan let the envelope flap down on the table as he sat down. He then looked at it for quite some time. Ronan had lived enough to know that things read can never be unread. Was there something in here he didn't want to know? Something which might change his memory of his dead father forever. It could be nothing, just a further example of his father's eccentricity in later years. Finally, he employed the following rationale. Whatever it is, it needs to be opened sometime. So it may as well be sooner rather than later. He opened the envelope and drew out the contents.

At about 3 pm, Charles had finally extricated himself from the police, the film crew, the production studio, a couple of local journalists, the Earl's secretary and a host of other people he never knew existed. Freddie, it turned out, had an older brother who was an insurance underwriter in Toronto. He was already at the airport waiting for a flight to Glasgow Prestwick. Freddie's secretary, now technically unemployed, had very kindly arranged to meet him and sort things out with the undertaker, once the body had been released. She would also put him in touch with Freddie's accountant and solicitor. On the phone, Freddie's brother had insisted on an orthodox Jewish burial in Kensal Green, as befitted such a devout adherent of the faith. Charles felt completely drained when he returned to his room to pack. In a funny way he had liked Freddie and his spirits were much depressed. Ronan's hastily-scribbled note was lying on top of Charles's suitcase, held in place by a bottle of his after-shave. With a pang of guilt, he realised he had given little thought to Ronan in the last five hours. The note read:

> Hello Charles,
> Sorry to leave so early but had to grab offer of lift into Edinburgh
> – a tourist I met at Drumelzie. Am going to see father's solicitor.
> Something strange has turned up. Hate to leave you in this mess
> but will visit you in town soon.
> Thanks for all your help,
> Ronan.

Charles did not move, other than to rest his forehead in the palm of his right hand. He exhaled a long, long slow breath. Ten minutes later saw him packed and standing at the payphone in the foyer of the estate restaurant. By contrast with the restored, white limewash plaster behind him, Charles's face was a shade more pallid.

In his hands, Ronan held a typescript document of some thirty pages. He was seated in a quiet corner of the White Cockade, almost empty at this hour, a coal fire smouldered in the grate and a pint of export beer sat by his side. He felt he deserved it having braved the wind-blown sleet driving along George Street like grape shot. He was glad to be able to dip down into the narrow, cobbled precinct of Rose Street and even more glad to see his pint being drawn. His interview with Auld Suthy had taken a lot less time than he had anticipated and he now had over an hour to kill before he met Garrett. This was one reason why he had persuaded the cool Miss Glossy Lips to let him remove the document. After much "I don't know if that would be permitted" and "I may have to ask what stage probate is at", the girl finally noticed that it was 2 pm and, this being her half day, she immediately lost interest. "Just sign here," she said. He had to agree that the document hardly seemed of much importance. The front page was blank but for the title; 'Archaeology of the Languedoc – The Templar Treasury'. It was dated about three months earlier. So that was all it was. His father's research and his wish to share it with him. He didn't know what he had expected but he was acutely disappointed. Without enthusiasm he turned the first page and began to read. As the outside world drifted past the small nicotine-stained panes of the White Cockade, Ronan became oblivious to that world as he entered another one and another time. It was certainly not what he had expected.

12

The envelope contains a thirty-page document from
Ronan's father, the late John MacDonald.

Archaeology of the Languedoc – The Templar Treasury.
John MacDonald
Dunlaith

With due respect for the reader of this research I have decided to summarise it in as digestible a form as possible. Those who want to dine on richer fare are referred to the detailed sources at the end of this document. What I have written is not an academic paper, but rather a letter from the past to the present. The future is up to the reader.

First let me take you back to the year 1118 anno domini. In that year, a group of nine noblemen, mostly knights, connected by family or feudal relationships founded La Milice du Christ, soon to become known as the Order of Knights Templar. They did so under the powerful patronage of the Count of Champagne and Bernard of Clairvaux, the Cistercians effectively becoming the monastic house of the Order. Indeed, Bernard's uncle was one of the nine, as were two Cistercian monks released from their vows. Their ostensible purpose was to keep the roads and highways safe for pilgrims. At the time this must have seemed an almost impossible dream, given the many hundreds of pilgrims who were robbed and/or murdered each year along the winding pilgrim routes from northern Europe to Outremer. Rationally, we must doubt that this was the main aim of these nine middle-aged noblemen, most of whom were unaccustomed to arms. And so it proved, for their first campaign was an archaeological one. Instead of throwing their efforts into protecting pilgrims in their dangerous passage through the Holy Land, the Order spent its first nine years almost wholly focused on the extensive excavations they were conducting under the remains of the Temple of Solomon on Temple Mount, Jerusalem. This right, and the right to be quartered there, they had readily obtained from the King and Patriarch of the Kingdom owing to their influential Frankish connections.

Now let us jump forward a little. In 1867, a Lieutenant Warren of the Royal Engineers conducted an excavation on the site. To his amazement he found that the Templars had driven an access shaft eighty feet deep into the solid rock. From this shaft, tunnels radiated horizontally beneath the Temple site. They were all empty of course, save for a few fragments of some Templar arms and armour. What had the Order found there? Perhaps nothing. From that time, however, the myth began to circulate that all sorts of precious articles had been found. Items as fantastic as The Ark of the Covenant, the Holy Grail, King Solomon's Treasure, the True Cross, the Crown of Thorns, the head of John the Baptist and even the head of Christ. There has certainly been more fantasy and nonsense circulated about the Order than almost any other historical movement, and most of it I believe can be discounted as such. Perhaps these rumours gained currency to explain the astronomical power and wealth obtained by the Order in such a surprisingly short time.

Well an undergraduate friend of mine, James Galbraith, and I had long been interested in the Order. We were both reading Archaeology and Ancient languages at St Andrews and had become aware of the strong Scottish connection with the Templars. Hugh de Payen, the first Grand Master of the Templars, was related to the Sinclair family. He visited Roslin, the then Sinclair seat, soon after the Jerusalem excavations were completed. The Lord of Roslin made him a grant of land at nearby Ballontrodoch, now known as the village of Temple, where he set up his Scottish headquarters. We also knew that Scotland had given refuge to many knights of the Order following their prescription by Pope Clement V and violent persecution by many crowned heads of Europe, principally King Philip le Belle of France. This persecution raged from 1307 to 1312 when the Pope dissolved the Order. Robert de Bruce, having been temporarily anathematised by the Pope at that period, was not minded to enact papal bulls and many refugee Templar knights came to his standard. They fought for him at Bannockburn and were influential in carrying the day. The battle took place on 24 June, the feast day of St John the Baptist, sacred to the Order. Templar graves can be found from the Borders up through Argyll and the Western seaboard. Often in lonely places, old Celtic burial sites and wooded islands in rivers, estuaries or lochs, and you will still find their stone grave effigies today. Mailed knights bearing the floriated cross or the barred Cross of Lorraine. So, when the first long vac. came around James proposed we spend the summer in Jerusalem and have a go at some fieldwork and some documentary research. We felt we had an almost personal interest in those old countrymen of ours. To our surprise our tutor agreed to arrange introductions for us and even join us out there for a time. It was 1959 and we were all optimistic, the war had been won and the austerities of rationing and shortages had, remarkably quickly, given way to relative prosperity. The state of Israel was still relatively young, the Suez fiasco had passed, the PLO was yet to be formed and, meantime, Arabs and Israelies held a grudging co-existence. So, off we went. Air travel was far beyond our means so we sailed steerage on a vessel out of Greenock. James had borrowed a white linen suit and Panama hat from his father. I remember he spent a lot of the voyage strolling around the deck puffing on filthy black Egyptian cigarettes. We docked at Haifa Port, which had been built by the British and was still being developed by us. An old American bus took us slowly down the coast road to Jaffa, where we stopped for almost an hour to pick up more passengers, and then on through semi-desert to Jerusalem. Until then, the impression was of intolerable heat, and a monochrome, pale grey landscape disappearing into dust. Nothing had prepared me for the evocative sights and sounds of the city as dusk stole upon us. The muzzeins calling believers to prayer and the setting sun drowning the buildings of the timeless city with blood. We had lodgings with a lecturer at the Hebrew University and it was there that we met Andrew Farquharson. A thin, wirey, likeable man, he was in his final year at Cambridge and had come to Jerusalem in the hope of learning more about the Dead Sea Scrolls. As the three of us were sharing one big room he soon became a firm friend. The room opened out onto a brick and stucco stairway to the roof, and most evenings found us lying under the stars, fuelled up on cheap wine, coffee or tobacco discussing the living history of the City of God. The whole academic community was still buzzing with excitement about the Scrolls. The archaeologists saw themselves in a race with the Bedouin to uncover any remaining fragments in the Qumran region. Rumour was rife at the university and some said that Kando, the Bethlehem antique dealer who traded several of the scrolls, had still others hidden away, waiting for the price to rise. John Allegro backed by Manchester University was trying to organise a dig near Qumran to excavate the treasure he believed was mentioned in the Copper Scroll. All more nonsense, a gross mistranslation of the Aramaic that was all. Well, let me get to the point. We were to join an existing small excavation in the temple's magnificent underground stables. We had quite a walk from our lodgings to the Old City, but for a historian – what a walk! Entering the city walls by the Damascus

Gate we passed through the Muslim quarter near the Arabic
Market or 'Shuk' as the Jews called it. On nearing the market we
would always be overwhelmed by groups of Armenian and Pales-
tinian children trying to sell us anything they could or just begging
for money. After a few days they left me alone but they always
seemed to hold a fascination for James, and he could never throw
them off. It was then that he started disappearing en route. On
some pretext he would disappear into the warren of covered alleys
around the market. He would often appear late at the excavation
site and, towards the end of the summer, sometimes in the
company of an attractive Arab boy. I was green as grass in those
days and it was some years later before I appreciated James's
unpleasant weakness. I think Andrew suspected something at that
time, just from the way he sometimes looked at James. Then
events took a more interesting turn. For it was at this period,
towards the end of our stay, that James showed us the vellum
parchment. According to his account he had been drinking coffee
in a room near the Souk when he was approached by an Arab boy
of about 14 or 15 years. Recognising James as someone engaged in
the excavation he immediately offered him a rolled up manuscript
which he insisted he had found, last year, in one of the passageways of the underground Stables of Solomon. In a jar in a wall,
was all he could make out from the boy and much of that from
hand gestures. It was very vague and James's Arabic was worse
than the boy's English, but he gave the lad a handful of coins and
stuffed the document inside his jacket. That evening as we sat on
the roof, cross-legged on straw mats, James unrolled the parchment and placed it before us. At first we thought it a fake, trying to
imitate the scrolls, but this was written on vellum, by pen and ink.
Then in the flickering candlelight, we could see that it was written
in a romance language, which looked to us like a mixture of Latin,
medieval French and Spanish. We could make very little of it but
Andrew, from a paper he had read at Cambridge recognised it at

once as Occitan, the ancient language of Southern France. From the material, the language and the script, Andrew had a pretty good idea, which proved to be correct, that the document was 13th-century. Of course I was all for handing it over to the Hebrew University but Andrew and James seemed to have come to an understanding that as a purchased artefact it was James's own property. I began to worry, as I do, about the ethics of this so I did something which was probably equally unethical. On the last evening of our visit, James had gone out as usual. So I quietly took the manuscript from his suitcase and made a fair copy of the text. There were only some dozen lines but even so it was not easy given the distortion and decay of the material and the fading of the ink. I never told anyone and in fact never looked at my copy again until two years ago. The unease I felt had been growing for some years. It was almost like being near bats foraging for insects in the evening lamp light, sounds you can't quite hear and shapes you can't quite see, but you know something dark and palpitating is near. What should have warned me at first was the abrupt and incredible alteration in the financial circumstances of Andrew and James. For a few years they tried to hide it but gradually, gaining in confidence, they began to exhibit all the external signs of con-siderable wealth. James had dropped out of university in his final year and whilst Andrew completed his degree, I never found any evidence that either of them ever took up gainful employment. Yet, by their early twenties, James had bought a large house in The Boultons and Andrew purchased a country estate in Cambridge-shire. Other houses, in Corsica and the Dordogne followed, domestic staff were hired, James began to travel the world and collect the rarest of antiques whilst Andrew began his now con-siderable collection of classic vintage wines and even had an Arab stallion in training. James, you must understand, came from a poor, working-class family in Leytonstone whilst Andrew had been fostered, having had a very unhappy childhood with an abusive, alcoholic father. His foster parents were an unexceptional working-class family living in Manchester where his foster father was a postman. Thus I could not look to inherited wealth as an explanation. If it was just the wealth I might not have pondered so deeply, but both men seemed to lead charmed lives as regards public careers, government honours and preferment. I almost began to wonder if the parchment, found all these years ago, had worked some occult charm on them. It was then I had the idea of seeking a translation, and the more I thought about it the more I wondered why I had never done it before.

Pleading overwork, which was true enough, I obtained some long leave from the Bishop, who arranged a locum priest. I took a flight to Toulouse. I had made telephone contact with the archivist at the Institut d'Estudis Occitans there and also a professor at the University. I checked in to a small hotel off the Rue de Metz and the following morning met the Institute archivist, M. Pascal Guillemard, at a nearby café. Pascal was a cheerful and likeable man, small with a goatee beard and lively, intelligent eyes. It was April but *la belle saison* had already arrived. I remember we sat outside in brilliant sunshine with a warm, dusty breeze from North Africa gently stirring the green canvas awning of the café. Pascal was fascinated by the copy of the parchment text. He turned to me beaming, hands gesturing wildly. "This is easier than you might imagine to translate, the language was surprisingly homogenous at that period. I would date this to the early part of the thirteenth century. It was only after the Albiginsien crusade against the Cathars of the Languedoc, which for the first time brought many, many Northerners into the region, that it becomes difficult. You see Occitan then got mixed up with regional French and split into a variety of forms, some almost like French dialect." He was so enthusiastic and excited and running on in all directions that I at last produced a sheet of paper and asked him to dictate a translation which I would write down. Propping his head in his hands he bent low over the text and began to translate, slowly but clearly word by word.

"OK, it begins; 'Peter de Montaigue, Grand Master of the Military Order of the Temple of Jerusalem sends his greetings to Armaund Gaudin, Knight Commander of the Temple Commanderie.' Then it goes on… 'We work in difficult times and you are to know that the Reserve Treasury of the Order has now been moved to the place we spoke of, la Cubertairata, where our knights keep vigil, even in death. In time of trouble it will remain there.' Then he says, 'This sent to you under my seal by a trusted knight. You are required to commit this to the fire as soon as you have read my words.' Then it finishes with a short prayer 'Mon Dius, fasetez-moi la gracia de plan vivre a de plan morir' 'C'est a dire, mon Dieu faites-moi la grace … pardon' 'My God bestow on me the grace to live decently and die decently'. That is all that is written here."

Pascal sat back in his chair and looked at me very strangely, but he was no more amazed than I.

"Alors, c'est drôle n'est-ce pas. Un bon mot pour rire, eh?"

"Only if the original document was a forgery, which I somehow doubt."

"Mon ami, but you know what this refers to, unless I am mistaken."

Pascal and I decided to stroll along the boulevard by the river. It was soft and sandy underfoot there in the shade of the plane trees with the warm scented breeze blowing coolness off the water. It was good to walk in the dappled sunshine together.

"You know, Pascal, there is a great deal of nonsense talked about the Templars … all except for one thing. The Templars, who gave civilisation much more than most realise … had princes and crowned heads throughout Europe in their debt. They were the international bankers of their day and invented the promissory note or bankers draft, the antecedent of cheques and credit cards.

They conducted direct money transfers by paper and the main Commanderies were effectively the clearing banks and merchant banks as well as farms and warehouses. They funded foreign wars, the raising of castles and the building of the great medieval cathedrals. There is no doubt that they were fantastically rich and that most of their riches were in property and in gold. Often this gold was never removed, like the modern Gold Standard, just to have it was enough to give value to the promissory note. They also had under direct ownership the forerunner of what we would call a merchant fleet, the largest trading fleet in northern Europe."

"This much I know, John, we are in the Languedoc, after all, the land of the Templars. What you are about to say, I think, is that when Philip IV prescribed and arrested the members of the Order he found not one bar of gold bullion nor one ship of the fleet, for it had already sailed."

"Yes, and since then everyone has assumed, as Philip's advisors did, that the bird had flown. The fleet had sailed from La Rochelle into the Western Ocean with several millions of Louis d'or never to return. Yet even under the torture of the Black Friars not one member of the Order could or would confirm this."

"And what, mon enfant, if the ships were all a deception. A – how do you say? – yes – decoy, to throw King Philip's men off the scent."

We had come to a small riverside garden with clipped rosemary hedging and an empty petanque pitch in the middle. We sat on one of the sun-bleached wooden benches.

"I still think that you are the victim of a hoax, John. A clever hoax, but still a hoax. It is clever, the way it has been written, the natural language of the Templars was Latin or the medieval French of the Île-de-France. So, if they wanted to hide the message from interpretation by the King's men, Occitan dialect would be a good code, yet readily understood by the Knight Commanders of southern France. But I still say a hoax. If it was real, why would anyone let you copy it? After all, it is the kind of information someone would kill for."

I thanked him for his trouble and walked with him back to his car parked beside the embankment. He opened the door of his Renault and leant on the window as we shook hands and chatted for a while about politics, rugby and the weather. Then just as he closed his door he stuck his head out of the window.

"Your hoax, it is very clever as I said."

"Why?"

"I now remember, 'Cubertairata', is the old Occitan name for la Couvertoirade, a fortified Templar village on the Causse de Lorzac, in Aveyron."

Like a true Frenchman, he then went on to extol the virtues of Aveyronais, a particularly delicious baguette baked in that Region. At last, with a wave of the hand he shot out into the traffic in a cloud of white dust, narrowly missing a Citroen camionnette which had to brake hard to avoid him.

Now, for a medievalist, where the Aveyron steals out across the Segala into the Languedoc is like passing out of this world into a dream. So, I made up my mind to spend a week there and just perhaps see if la Couvertoirade really existed. After visiting an old colleague at the university, I had a delicious supper at a seafood restaurant with a fine view of the Garonne. Returning to my hotel, the desk clerk handed me a message. When I read it, it took me several minutes to comprehend that it was from Andrew Farquharson. He would be in Toulouse the following morning and asked if we could meet. It was an astonishing coincidence, I hadn't seen him for over 15 years, and then only at an academic supper party. Now, I'll gloss over the next event pretty quickly. My seafood platter had given me a bad case of food poisoning and my meeting with Andrew ended up with him calling for an ambulance and me spending a couple of days in the local hospital. When I was well enough to leave, I was surprised to find Andrew still in Toulouse. Instead of taking me back to my hotel, he suggested I spend a week with him in a house he had in the Minervois to recuperate. I was very grateful and hadn't the strength to argue. I slumped in Andrew's hired Peugot like a sack of soft potatoes, but, as soon as the enceinte and turrets of Carcassonne rose over the horizon like a thunder storm my dark cloud lifted and my spirit flew.

Andrew came off the motorway so we could see la Cité still framed in low morning sunshine, then we turned east. His *maison de vacances* was near Minerve, so we began to cut our way through a patchwork of vineyards clinging to nearly every inch of the slopes. Countless columns of white sticks rising from pale stony earth, too desiccated to be alive yet just showing leaf, sucking in sweetness from the sun. A flash of brilliant turquoise as we crossed the Canal du Midi by an ancient hump backed bridge. The rows of plane trees and Corsican pines threw dark green shadows on the shimmering water. We paused now and then in small bastide-style villages sculptured in pale stone, each with its ancient Roman-esque church and occasionally a small abbey. At the centre of even the most unprepossessing town was to be found a medieval heart of jumbled streets and terraced stone houses. Tiny passageways, arches, vertigenous flights of steps, leading to secret flag-stoned courtyards with pots of geraniums. Bells tolling the hour, the sound drifting in the thyme-scented air. And in that air, all was stillness under the pastel-blue dome of the sky. It was the hours in the middle section of the day, when people seek quietness and solitude. In Pouzols, as we walked up to the fountain, an old monk gazed at us briefly from behind a wrought iron gate then disap-peared into his cloister. In the square a lean dog looked the other way and padded softly past. They were like apparitions. Some-thing almost lost to the world remained here. Every stone village seemed to bring contentment and peace to me, the breeze mixed spices from the Sahara with the scent of wild rosemary from the coastal marshes and dust from the vineyards. This pale incense dropped gently from the air and swirled warmly around our feet as we walked. Our footfalls, echoing up cobbled alleyways, were the only intrusion. I had forgotten to feel tired.

Andrew's house was in an undisciplined muddle of medieval buildings cascading from a rocky hilltop. Habitations huddled together for protection. We entered the village over a stone pack-horse bridge at the bottom of the hill. A pair of wild brown trout under the arch, lazily facing upstream in the afternoon sunshine, flashed for the water weeds as our shadow reproached them. The cobbled streets were on a human scale so we were compelled to leave the car in a square by the church. The sunlight etched every detail of the open wrought-iron belfry and the cream masonry of the Norman tower. We cut through the churchyard down a long line of tombs, like miniature stone houses. Each tomb had a photograph of the inhabitant, fixed to its gable, beside the family crucifix. Many were adorned with fresh flowers. The village seemed to borrow the architecture of an Escher landscape. Tall houses rose improbably from solid rock so that it was often impossible to tell where living rock ended and quarried stone began. Many had arched flights of steps to first floor rooms with the wooden doors of wine caves shadowy under the arch. Some three-storey houses were connected across alleyways by short, enclosed bridges with tiny arched windows, which also provided extra living space. As we climbed it was impossible to reconcile all the various levels. In one street we looked down to our right on the pantiled roof of a viticulturer's house only to find his ancient vineyard tractor parked at head height on our left. The houses did not have guttering. Instead their narrow, Roman roof tiles projected out over the walls casting long, serrated shadows on the masonry in the early afternoon sun. Andrew knew the village well and by a series of winding stone steps we came to his house. It was in a short row of three-storey houses straggling the rocky ridge. A large portion of the front was obscured by an old fig tree, competing jealously with the building for this narrow space. Only half of the top floor was roofed over the other half being left open to the sky as a terrace, floored with honey-coloured terracotta tiles. It was there we sat, watching for the dusk. Amongst the sandy-red roof tiles were patches of miniature green fields, invisible from the road. In one a donkey was standing patiently under the shade of an olive tree. We sat under a pergola where a grape vine in a vast green glazed pot was trying in vain to shade our meal. I gave thanks then took the bread and broke it and filled Andrew's cup with dark vin d'Oc. He whispered, "Agnus Dei, qui tollis peccata mundi, miserere nobis." Then smiled one of the saddest smiles I have known.

As dusk began to rise up around us, occasional pipistrelles flew in to catch moths in the lamplight and lights twinkled down the hillside. The air was still warm and fragrant. So was the wine. We had a lot of ground to cover. Andrew had never married and explained vaguely. At first, it was something to do with his own unhappy childhood and wanting to 'break the cycle of unhappiness'. Then, later, he had become middle-aged and set in his ways and it just fell off the agenda somehow. He confided that his one regret was that he had never had a son. As he felt this so bitterly, I never mentioned my own son; it seemed too unkind. The tragedy is, Andrew would have made an excellent father, much better than my own indifferent performance I suspect.

The conversation inevitably turned to the reason for my trip. I was quite open with Andrew. I even told him about copying the manuscript all those years ago and felt the catharsis of confession. I remember he stared blankly throughout my narrative and showed no emotion. His only question was, "does anyone else know this?"

"Only Pascal, he knows a bit, but doesn't believe any of it of course."

Andrew set his glass down on the table; "Do you believe any of it?"

"I'm not sure, but from what I remember of the document, it could be genuine, it had a seal bearing the Cross of Aquitaine."

"Well I can save you a lot of disappointment, it's a proven forgery."

I sat up so quickly that I spilled wine over my chest, in the dusk it looked like blood. Andrew passed me a napkin and as I wiped, he explained.

"James took it to an expert in Oxford you know, it was scientifically and academically dated to the present century. Just some poor Arabs trying to make a few shekels out of gullible young archaeologists I'm afraid. And you won't find anything in the graveyard at la Couvertoirade either, James and I actually dug there, just for interest really. We joined a French excavation there a year after we left Jerusalem. Nothing, not a thing; except a few shards of pottery and a lead Cathar cross. So the parchment was just an elaborate hoax, sorry to disappoint you."

I was quite willing to believe that there was nothing to find, or that the document was even misinterpreted. What I didn't believe was that it was a forgery, I'm not sure why. It just seemed so unlikely, when every academic in Jerusalem was searching for a papyrus scroll from the first millennium BC, why forge a vellum manuscript from the middle ages. But this would mean that Andrew had lied to me, something I had never known him do. Something else made me uneasy, Andrew had said 'you won't find anything in the graveyard' … yet the manuscript had not mentioned a graveyard.

The following morning I was woken by the ringtone of Andrew's mobile. At breakfast he announced that business matters meant he reluctantly had to go back to the UK for a few days. If I could drive him to Carcassonne airport after lunch, then I could have the car and the cottage until he returned. After I had dropped Andrew off, I spent a couple of hours walking around the fortifications of la Cité then drove back to the house for an early night.

At first light, I packed a map, some walnuts, dried fruit, bread and cheese into a rucksack and pointed the car east towards the Aveyron. I drove by way of Béziers and Lodève, the motorway from there climbing dramatically up the side of rocky escarpments and tunnelling through hillsides. Taking me ever upwards onto the bleak limestone Causses towards la Couvertoirade. Strangely, I was not really clear about what I intended to do when I got there. The Causses are a vast limestone plateau which forms the beginning of the Cévennes range. It is one of the least populated regions in Europe. Up on the Causses both vegetation and habitation are sparse. A relentless wind scours the plateau for many months of the year. It is the abode of goats and sheep and lonely shepherds who, in their hooded canvas capes, wander the scrubland and rocky outcrops like mendicants.

In this melancholy, rock-strewn wilderness la Couvertoirade appears as a dream to the visitor. At the end of a long straight track the pinnacles and machicolations of its fortified walls rise up out of the plateau like a vision from a lake. The area inside the walls was crammed with tiled roofs, square chimneys capped with stone slabs and a stone-arched belfry surmounting the church tower. The ancient skyline was seen in grey relief that day, framed against a rook-haunted wood on the slope behind. The sky was heavy, still and overcast as I approached. From somewhere in the village, a single ribbon of wood smoke climbed vertically into the cool air. Leaving the car I approached the final 200 metres on foot, like a pilgrim. The closer I came, the more forbidding la Couvertoirade became. This secret, brooding, hidden place on the very fringe of civilisation. Two giant, asymmetrical bastions flank and dwarf the portcullis archway which leads into the city. As I drew near they seemed about to crush the very soul out of the offending visitor. I almost tiptoed through the archway and held my breath. I was submerged in the kind of silence in which you can hear the air vibrate and the blood pulsing rhythmically in the inner ear. The main cobbled street lay before me, it was only about a bullock cart's width and even narrower streets snaked away in several directions. Some just wide enough for a pair of conspirators to walk hand in hand. I had stepped into the fourteenth century, or at least a sanitised version of it for surely there must have been careful restoration work here at sometime. There were no vehicles nor any other artifice of modern living. Every possible corner of the domain had been filled with perfect stone buildings. Some with timbered galleries and stairways and, through half-hidden archways, there were vignettes of secret, cobbled courtyards. I must have wandered as in a dream for about an hour without encountering any sign of life. Gradually, I realised that I was quite alone there, at that time of year the village must have been almost unoccupied. There was only the scent of wood smoke to remind me that the village was real.

A pointed archway brought me suddenly to the Templar church and its graveyard. The church had been built on a natural rock outcrop and a steep flight of steps led to the west door which, disappointingly, was locked. The churchyard had also been raised up, behind a massive retaining wall. Presumably to provide enough depth of soil in this rocky landscape. A flight of steps shaped like a bridge brought the visitor, and the resident, from this world to the next. I picked my way between the headstones sprouting from the damp grass. Many were round headed stones with Cathar symbols, others more rectangular or cruciform with the roseate cross of the Counts of Toulouse or the Cross of Aquitaine. Either there were no inscriptions or they had become illegible. Lichen, moss and ivy had encrusted most of the stonework. The dust of time settled everywhere, I shivered in the cool air and was reminded of an old Occitan poem Pascal had recited: 'You can turn your back on the wind, but you can't turn your back on time'. I was brought back to the moment by a faint noise. At first I thought it was the calling of one of the rooks circling over the wood. Then I recognised it as a person coughing, a regular dry cough. In a nearby doorway sat a man, or woman, on a wooden stool, leaning against the door frame. The door was held open by a lump of stone. My observer must have been there all the time, unseen by me. The cough turned to a croak and then a dry laugh as the figure gestured to me. I could not have described him, however, enveloped as he was by the traditional waxed canvas cape and hood of the Causses farmer. As I drew near, it became more clear that I was about to address a man of very mature years. He looked up with a toothless grin and said the most welcome word in the French language.

"Café?"

He got painfully to his feet with the aid of a long walking stick, laughing silently at his own stiffness as if time had played some hilarious practical joke on him. Gradually I realised he was inviting me to his fireside. The small room was dominated by a large fireplace of dressed stone with a wood-burning stove in the hearth. The room was lit through the open door and by a small, deeply-recessed window which looked out onto a cobbled yard. A stone sink was let into the sill. A flight of bare wooden steps ascended from this room to the bedrooms. Around the fire, some rugs were ineffectually being used to insulate against the cold which struck up through the tiled floor. We sat in threadbare arm chairs by the stove, which had no door on the firebox. A pile of unseasoned logs hissed inside. Taking a coffee pot, which had once been white enamelled, from the stove he poured out two cups of thick, black, Turkish coffee. This he sweetened generously with sugar from an old treacle tin. It was remarkable, with my high-school French and his limited English that between us we struck up a tolerable conversation. Once settled, he pulled back his hood revealing a weather-tanned face, corrugated with wrinkles, and a yellow-white moustache. He was wearing a woollen cap. His name was Fabien Morelle and for most of his life he had been a shepherd up on the Causses. He claimed to be 86 years old. After some heart trouble around 15 years ago, he had abandoned the Causses and had become a kind of caretaker for this place during the winter season. His wife had died eight years ago, and he had no immediate family. I had thought this room a cheerless place but, with its pungent reek of wood smoke, strong coffee and tobacco, it was couthy enough to someone whose manhood had been exhausted on the high Causses. He was much impressed with my Scottish name, the rural French always seem to have a kind of affinity with the Scots. Now, with unaffected directness he wished to know his guest's story.

"What are you doing at la Couvertoirade today, I saw you looking at the old graves?"

"Vraiment, je suis en vacances, but I am also interested in history and in Christianity."

"Eh, it is rare in France these days for anyone to be interested in Christ, are you a priest?"

I was rather taken aback. "Why, yes I am, in Scotland, does it show that much."

"Non, it is not obvious, but I know things about people, I am very old and have seen many things."

"My second love is archaeology."

"Pshaw! Digging in the earth?"

"That kind of thing, yes."

He took a pottery jar from the mantle, filled a wooden pipe with sticky black tobacco and took a spill from the stove to light it. A spasm of coughing ensued, culminating in a wet noise as he spat darkly into the heart of the hissing fire.

"Pardon, are you staying nearby?"

"Not really, I'm staying with a friend. He has another fine Scotch name, Andrew Farquharson."

Fabien inhaled deeply then blew a wreath of acrid tobacco smoke around them both.

"This is a very unusual name, but I have heard it before, many, many years ago. Let me think. Yes, I remember, not long after I came to the village he arrived, it was about this time of year. He was with an Englishman, James something. That is how I remember, Andrew and James, I used to call them the two Apostles."

"Are you sure, can you remember why they came, what they did?"

"It was a long time ago, is it important?"

"They are friends of mine and I would like to know."

He looked at me shrewdly. "Then, if they are your friends, why do you not ask them?"

There was no ready answer for that question. At my awkward silence he grinned his toothless grin and stabbed the air with the stem of his pipe as he spoke. "Monsieur, it is a struggle for me here, I am a very poor old man, with hardly a couple of sous for a mug of beer to comfort me." He winked.

I placed a 20-franc note in his gnarled hand and he pocketed it quickly as if it was something unpleasant.

"*Dieu vous benisse, Monsieur. Alors*, now I remember, they were digging, *une excavation archeologique*. They dug most of it themselves but on the last two days they were running out of time and needed some help. So, they asked me to dig for them. Paid good money too, yet the soil was surprisingly loose and easy to dig. They had a French girl with them, from the Government," he winked at me, "*une derrière superbe*, like a ripe peach." His laugh ended in a fit of coughing which brought tears to his eyes.

"What were they looking for, Monsieur Morelle?"

He shrugged: "How should I know. Bones, relics, turnips; whatever archaeologists dig for. But I can tell you that they didn't find anything. It was very strange. When they opened the graves, they were all empty. No one had been buried there. All that digging, a complete waste of time."

M Morelle could sense my disappointment, and he began to soften.

"There is something else, it may interest you. I have never told this to anyone but because you are a priest and I am going to die soon, I will tell you for a blessing." He sucked on his pipe, wiped his mouth with the back of his hand then slipped a hand under his cap to scratch his head.

"They did find one thing. Let me think, this is how it happened. In the grave I was excavating," here he made the sign of the cross, "we came to the remains of a coffin. All that remained was the lead lining and no traces of human remains. There was a hole in the lead through which we could see some dressed stone. So, the Englishman James and I, we lifted it out to get a better look. There was a bit more earth to scrape away before we saw a stone slab with an iron ring in it. Well, he was very keen to see under this slab. I don't think he would have been so keen had the French girl with the nice bottom been there, but she had not turned up that morning.

Eventually, using an iron rod as a lever, we managed to turn it over. *Nom de Dieu*, I got the fright of my life. I almost fell into a stone chamber underneath". He looked at me and nodded. "*Oui, c'est ca*, it was about five metres square and, he held his pipe aloft, 'completely empty'."

I could see that Fabien was really enjoying telling his tale. He looked at me again to gauge my disappointment, then leant over the arm of his chair towards me. The smell of ammonia and tobacco became uncomfortable.

"*Eh bien, c'est a dire*, we both thought it was empty, then the Englishman saw something lying in a corner of the chamber. He lowered himself down through the opening and slipped the item into his pocket as quickly as he could. I was supposed to be digging a neighbouring grave at the time and he thought I hadn't seen anything. But I did see, and saw something more."

Here he paused again for more dramatic effect. I thought I was certainly getting my money's worth. With the aid of his stick, old Morelle stood up and crossed to a small pine table near the sink and, leaning against the table for support, opened the drawer. He beckoned to me and I joined him next to the window. The drawer contained an assortment of life's detritus; odd pieces of bone handled cutlery, a large clasp knife, some cracked plates, a pair of broken spectacles, a bundle of letters, two pipes, a tangle of rubber bands, a pair of scissors, a tube of adhesive, a packet of sticking plasters, some ball point pens, a wrist watch without a strap, a few rusty kitchen utensils, a bottle of tablets and a dog-eared pack of playing cards. M Morelle scrabbled in the back of the drawer as he spoke. He put a forefinger against the side of his fleshy, Gallic nose:

"Yes, old Fabien noticed it all. The Englishman had found a small leather *porte-monnaie* … how you say, pouch or purse and slipped it into his pocket as quick as a cat. The leather was stiff with mould, it left a white mark around his trouser pocket. But, still pretending to be digging, I then saw something else. Something fell from the purse as he stuffed it into his trousers. Later, when the coast was clear, I found what had fallen in the long grass and brought it home."

He removed his hand from the drawer and dropped three items onto the table. They bounced and rolled metallically before coming to rest.

"Voila!"

I gathered the coins onto the palm of my hand and took them to the window. They were three pieces of Reichspfennigs. Two silver-coloured fifty-pfennig coins and one ten-pfennig coin. The silver coins were made from some light alloy, like aluminium, the ten-pfennig piece was dark grey, like pewter, and heavier, with white oxidisation around the rim. On one side the coins bore their denomination value and the word 'Reichspfennig' in Gothic print. On the other side, was the German spread eagle clasping a swastika in its talons and around it 'Deutsches Reich'. The coins bore the dates 1935, 1940 and 1942. Fabien lowered himself stiffly into his armchair with a sigh.

"You know what they are, *prêtre Ecossais?*"

"Yes, I know what they are. What happened next?"

"What happens next? Nothing, of course. The graves they are filled in and the turf replaced. And the archaeologists … The following day they are gone without even au revoir. But the question I ask myself is, how did a purse of Reichs money come to be sealed up in a grave from the middle ages, eh?"

The significance of this had not been lost on me, but the possible implications took a few minutes to sink in. When they did, my loins turned to jelly and I felt chilled and shaky. I asked M Morelle to remove his cap and as he sat by the fire I placed my right hand on his head and blessed him there.

I did not close the door on the way out.

The walk back to the car put but little heat back into me. It was a long drive to the house in the Minervois, the bed felt cold and I passed a troubled night.

The morning was mild and bright and I woke to a warm breeze stirring the lace curtains of my bedroom window. At first I felt feverish but I was much recovered after a gentle walk down to the village boulangerie. The warm croissants, fresh butter and apricot conserve washed down with hot, black coffee made me feel better still. Yet another kind of fever was still on me, a growing obsession to get at the truth of the bewildering events of that last week. My long-lost research skills, and not so long-lost contacts in the academic world came to my aid. I was careful, however, to provide the minimum of information about my requests. I telephoned a colleague in Cambridge and left him with a list of questions plus a general remit to find out anything relevant. I then made a call to the war archive at the MoD. Next was a call to Edinburgh University's Centre for Second World War Studies. Finally, I made calls to the mairies in Lodeve and Millau, the central library in Montpellier and the University in Toulouse. With each call and each discussion and reply, I refined my questions. A picture, a very clear picture was emerging.

That evening found me seated on the terrace in the lamplight with a pile of papers in front of me. It was perfectly still after the heat of the day and the stonework exhaled the sun's warmth. I read and re-read my notes to get it perfectly clear in my mind. Then, I took a fresh sheet of paper and summarised what I had discovered. This is what I wrote:

> In 1940 a German Division occupied the South in the area which was to become Vichy France, stretching from the Swiss Border to Bordeaux. Although their garrison HQ was in Bordeaux, they had garrisoned several other towns, including a motorised infantry unit of 7,000 men in Montpellier. In the summer of 1943, a small contingent of this unit, mostly officers, drove up to la Couvertoirade and evacuated the few residents still living there at the time. A recently discovered war diary kept by one of the residents records that the troops stayed there for some two weeks. At the end of which, a convoy of empty trucks was seen to arrive. The following day, the entire force departed but it was many months before the residents, mostly elderly, felt safe to return. The first to return was the elderly curé. He noted that the soil around the churchyard graves appeared

to have been disturbed but that no damage had been done to the church. With the rapid Allied advance in 1944, most of the German garrisons in Southern France found themselves trapped between the converging British and American forces coming from the north. As can be imagined this was a time of total chaos and confusion. The Germans were further threatened by the organised French resistance centred around Toulouse. The resistance was nominally organised by British SOE agents and supplied by the remnants of the Vichy Government, but in reality it was a fairly undisciplined force of armed vigilantes including many fanatical communists from the Maquis. The combined German force of about 25,000 gradually made its way towards the junction of the Loire and Allier rivers in the hope that they could break out towards Germany. In the event, a bold move by a British Army Captain and an SOE Intelligence Officer put an end to the attempt. They had rightly calculated that the German's biggest fear was the possibility of having to surrender to French irregulars. They believed that the French would shoot or hang most of the German officers. So the two British officers drove at breakneck speed across the German lines in a Red Cross car to negotiate a surrender. The German commander agreed to sign the surrender providing his men could remain armed until regular British or American soldiers could take charge of them. The following day, the first of the vanguard of General Patton's army arrived and arranged for the disarming and custody of the German troops.

Now we have to rely on the report filed by the SOE operative, which has recently become available in the Ministry of Defence war archive. The British Intelligence Officer recorded that the American disarmament was highly chaotic and poorly organised and that discipline was poor within the American advance unit. Most of the American troops were being recalled urgently for the Rhine offensive whilst others had their hands full trying to keep the German prisoners and the irregular French interior forces apart.

A couple of days after the surrender, the SOE Officer was sitting with some GIs outside a small bar-tabac in Bourges when a convoy of about six US Army trucks drew up. Steam was rising from the radiator of the leading vehicle and the driver had stopped at the nearby town pump to fill up with clean water. The British Officer at once recognised the passenger as an American Lieutenant who had been handling the disarming of the German prisoners. He strolled over to the passenger window and offered him a cigarette. As he did so, he passed the tailboard of the truck and noticed the tops of several wooden crates stencilled with the German eagle insignia. When he expressed his curiosity, he was told that during the disarming process the Americans had discovered what they believed to be a secret weapon and he was under orders to ship it back to the States for examination by American Government scientists as quickly as possible. He showed the Intelligence Officer an order which appeared to be signed by his Divisional Commander. He said he hoped to be in Normandy the following morning where a US ship was waiting. When the Officer asked what the Germans had said about these weapons he was told that all the Waffen SS officers in charge of the consignment had been shot by Maquis irregulars. The American was sorry for this and said that the US Army guard had been reinforced since the incident. As the British officer strolled back to the bar he was able to take another look at the crates. They also bore the name and number of the German unit. It was the 5th German Motorised Infantry Unit, which had been stationed in Montpellier.

These were the bare facts that I had pieced together. That night I stayed up late with a bottle of vin d'Oc for company. Over and over again I rearranged the pieces of the jigsaw in my mind, but I could only accept one way that the puzzle went together. The evidence was overwhelming that the contents of the ancient Templar treasury had been shipped back to the USA, either with or without the compliance of the American army command. It was allied treachery and international theft on a huge scale, whichever way you looked at it. I slept a thin sleep that night and kept bobbing up to the surface like a wine cork on a wake of fevered dreams.

It is always amazing what a hot shower and a crisp shave can do to rehabilitate a body. The following morning, seated on the terrace wrapped in a towelling dressing gown I traced a black Peugeot taxi as it dropped down off the main road onto the track which led to the village. It rattled over the bridge and disappeared amongst the houses. Fifteen minutes later I heard Andrew hailing me from the street and I stood up and waved to him. We sat in the lime-washed living room on the first floor in deep sofas covered in terracotta-coloured linen and drank coffee. His business in London had finished sooner than he had anticipated. Andrew was tired, reticent and withdrawn, but was trying hard to be affable. Inevitably, he asked what I had been up to whilst he had been away.

"Oh, just being a typical tourist. Relaxing and sight seeing."

"Anywhere in particular?"

That was a difficult one. I thought, how much does Andrew know and what has James told him? Finally, my conscience got the better of me.

"Here and there, I went up onto the Causses and had a look at La Couvertoirade."

Andrew gave me a thin smile. "I wondered if you would. And did you find the missing Treasury of the Templars?"

"No, Andrew, I can honestly say that I did not."

We both laughed. I left Andrew to relax with his newspaper and told him I was going to explore the footpath along the river. I would be back in a couple of hours bringing some lunch with me.

Near the river stood the abbey church. Its low walls of almost white limestone were huddled under a magnificent pantiled roof. Its Roman-style tiles came in every shade of pale ochre. The west front had simple, Norman blind arcading with a small rose window above. The nave windows were round-arched and instead of a chancel the east end was finished in an apse with three lancet windows. The tiles on the apse roof were flat and followed the contours like terracotta scales. The dust of the village square clung white to my shoes as I stepped inside. It was dark and half-panelled with a resinous wood which smelt damp. Threadbare pennants, crumbling into dust, hung over saints whose gilding glowed faintly in the false twilight. Traces of frescoes depicting the Stations of the Cross were barely discernible on the walls. As I made my way down the aisle the colours in the lancet windows flowed over me like moonlight filtering darkly downwards into a blue-green ocean. I came to a wooden sculpture of Our Lady also submerged in the flowing colours. Ave Stella Maris, star of the sea. Built in a corner of the west wall was a wooden confessional and a nearby sign indicated that it was the time allotted for the priest to hear confession.

After some hesitation I took the brass handle and opened the door. Inside I could make out a plain wooden chair and, in near darkness, I sat down. The green velvet curtain behind the oak tracery moved slightly as *le curé* drew nearer and cleared his throat.

"In nomine Patris et Filii et Spiritus Sancti. Amen."

I could sense his hand moving in the sign of the cross.

"Amen, Monsieur Le Curé."

After a brief pause. "*Êtes-vous anglais?*"

"*Oui, mon père.*"

"*Et êtes-vous confirmer dans la foi catholique?*"

"*Je suis un prêtre écossais dans l'église protestante.*"

"*Eh bien, eh bien … c'est le même Christ. Continuer.*"

"Bless me Father, it has been three months since I last sought the sacrament of confession."

"I am ready to receive your confession."

"I seek absolution for the sin of deceit … and I need your moral guidance."

"Go on."

Now that I had got to the very brink of unburdening myself, I began to feel confused, even silly. Given that the theft had happened, where precisely did Andrew and James fit in? It was possible, although unlikely, that Andrew knew nothing about what had happened in 1944. And how much did it really matter, after all these years. It wasn't as if it was a murder. So what I eventually said sounded very lame, even to me.

"I have discovered something dishonest, very dishonest that happened a long time ago, during the war. I don't know what to do about it. Part of me says, do nothing, but my conscience troubles me."

My confessor was clearly of advanced years. His voice was thin and trembled slightly, and he paused often to catch his breath. "My son, a great many terrible things happened during the war, especially here in France. Will anyone still living be harmed if you now make this thing known."

"There are two old friends of mine who could have done something about this, but instead may have chosen to hide that knowledge."

"You have not discussed it with them?"

"No, and I don't really know why not. Perhaps I should." I counted the long, rhythmical breaths, as the priest gulped life giving air into his lungs.

"My friend, I was a very young *curé* when the German occupying forces came to this region. I stood by and watched whilst those I held in pastoral care were evicted from their homes, imprisoned, beaten, deported or executed. I could do nothing … or rather, I did nothing. I said mass, I heard confession, I comforted, I pleaded, I gave the last unction and I buried. And finally, I forgave. I forgave myself for doing nothing and I forgave my enemy. After all these years, be sure whether it is God you serve or your own conscience, they are not the same thing."

"I understand, Father."

The *curé* paused once more and air whistled into his lungs several times before he spoke again. "One thing you can do is to bring your friends to the sacrament of reconciliation through mother church. God is the Father of mercies who has sent his Holy Spirit amongst us for the forgiveness of sins." A smile was in his tired voice when he said: "Let that be your penance, and your forgiveness. May God give you pardon and peace and absolve you from your sins."

I made what I hoped was a suitable act of contrition. Then we said a brief prayer together. As I left the confessional the door swung closed on its felt seal with a soft sigh.

Mediterranean light, reflected from the houses in the square, almost blinded me as I stumbled down towards the river. I did not glance back at the west elevation where carvings of the souls of men twisted and struggled around the circumference of the rose window. The wheel of fate was turning. Once by the river, my eyes were opened. I walked up stream for a couple of hundred metres to where a mill had once stood beside a weir, or barage, built across the river. Sitting on the wall of the mill race, water frothed and grumbled beneath my feet and the sound eventually soothed me. Warmed by the sunshine, with the clear turquoise water quickening the air, it became clear to me that the old priest was right, let the dead bury the dead. I stood up, brushed the lichen off my trousers and strode out for the village *boucherie*. For 60 francs, I bought the only chicken in the village and this important event was accompanied by a ritual plucking and dressing of the beast. Three village children and a dog peered through the shop doorway to mourn the passing of such an important member of the community. Declining, much to madame's amazement, the additional parcel containing the head and the feet, I carried the bird straight back to the house, as a peace offering. On the way uphill, I plucked some wild rosemary from the verge to add season to it.

The door was slightly ajar, as I must have left it, and I walked straight in without knocking. On entering the house I first had to pass my bedroom, on the ground floor, before reaching the stairs leading to the first floor kitchen. The bedroom door was open and something out of place made me glance in. Andrew was seated on my bed. In his lap was the pile of notes I had made the previous evening. The final sheet was held in his left hand. He made no attempt to disguise the matter, yet for a long time neither of us knew what to say. It was Andrew who spoke first, gathering up the sheets of paper as he did so.

"You have been a busy boy, John."

My first reaction was one of anger at the violation of my belongings and my trust. But it had to be short lived. I am a forgiving sort and perhaps always too ready to value the other fellow's point of view. An occupational hazard, being a professional listener. I was also aware of the improbability of sustaining righteous indignation in the bedroom of another man's house and with a dead chicken under your oxter. My next emotion was curiosity, I wanted to know what he would say about my research. I was quite unprepared for Andrew's anger however, and he clearly did not share my scruples about venting it.

"You damnable fool, John, I really thought I had given you a broad enough hint to leave all of this alone. Your wretched, morbid curiosity will be the end of you one day. I suppose that's why you became a priest, so you could scrape and scratch around on the dung heap of other people's lives like … a … a …"

"Chicken?" I ventured.

Andrew's red-faced, trembling anger gradually subsided into exasperation, tending to a wistful resignation. Yet I had never thought him capable of such anger. It made me wonder what else he might be capable of. I knew I had to get Andrew to talk to me before his emotion waxed cold.

"Look, Andrew, let's just sit down and talk about this now."

"Yes, we need to talk and I need a scotch, a large one. So will you."

"No thanks, I never indulge before lunch."

Andrew glared at me, his anger rising again.

"I'll still pour you a dram, I think you'll need it."

We sat on the terrace, far back against the wall, under the pergola. The vine seemed to have gained more leaves since my arrival. There was a cool wind stirring them. Three buzzards soared above a hilltop on the other side of the valley. I think the cool air whispering to us and the echoes of these birds of prey made us both mindful of our mortality. Andrew sat rolling his whisky tumbler between the palms of his hands, like a wheel turning, turning, turning.

"Suppose I tell you that I believe all the conclusions you have drawn are incorrect, that I know nothing about this discovery and that it is all uncorroborated hearsay and rumour. What would you do then?"

My all too recent confession was running around in my brain and thumping behind my eyes. I meant to honour it, but, I needed to know the truth. Whether it was morality or curiosity, in the worst tabloid sense, I did not know then and do not know now. But I presume I rationalised it as the former.

"Believe me Andrew, I do not mean any man, particularly you, any harm. This may best be forgotten, but I need to know the truth. All the evidence indicates that something of huge importance may have happened here. I can't simply bury it, if something, well, criminal has taken place. If you can't or won't help, then I will continue my research."

Andrew slammed his glass down on the coffee table and the contents slopped over his hand. "A typically sanctimonious sentiment, you should have been a Calvanist, John. Your moral high ground sits ill with the compulsory buggery so favoured by your fellow priests. And I should know."

"Andrew I hardly ..."

"You have never been poor, John. That is the only moral difference between us. You came from stable, loving, upper middle-class, professional parents. I don't blame you for that, but I do ask that you don't preach at me. You have always had choice. Choice of profession, choice of friends, choice of healthcare, choice of environment, choice of privacy and choice of security. Without money you have no choice in this society, I discovered that when I was very young and I never forgot it."

"Poverty is like death, it only has power if you believe it has power."

"And you don't fear death, I suppose."

"Time is like a river, Andrew, a fluid strand of life. The present, the future and the past. Life and death are identical. Different sides of the same coin. Time, with nature, was created by God, even Einstein knew that. We cannot escape its cycle, we fulfil our pre-ordained past and our future and cannot change them. It is the wheel of fate, it bridges every dimension of the universe and as it turns it generates time."

"You are a Calvanist, then!"

"No, my faith is that of the wheel-headed cross, the faith of the Celtic church."

"Well I believe in empirical knowledge. I follow the results of my own cold experience."

"You are not half as bitter as you pretend to be Andrew, I know you as a would-be *parfait*, a good man."

There was a long period of silence. All that could be heard was the bead curtain brushing the frame of the terrace door in the breeze. A rosary fingered by the wind. The stillness seemed to give Andrew the strength to make a painful decision. He drew his hand across his face and took two deep breaths before he spoke.

"What I am about to tell you, is known by only one other living person. It is most important that you understand the reason I am telling you. It is simply because I believe you may eventually discover the whole story yourself, or at least fill in the gaps with speculation. So, I will share the missing information with you, in the hope that it will save you from disaster. That you will finally be satisfied and have the sense to go back to your island home, praise God and keep your counsel close as death. At this point I suppose I should call for water and wash my hands."

"I think I understand, or will understand."

"I hope so, John, for the sake of both our souls. Let's start with the parchment. I apologise for misleading you, it is not a forgery, it's genuine. That was what the dating experts at Oxford confirmed. In the document it was the phrase, 'where the knights of our order guard the Treasury even in death' that gave us the idea to dig in the churchyard. James was very disappointed not to have found any gold, but I was very excited to learn of the underground chambers. They were direct evidence that the central Treasury could well have been hidden in La Couvertoirade. Like you, I was even more astounded when James showed me the pouch and explained where he had found it. We were seated in a café-bistro in Pezenas, wondering if we could afford anything on the menu, when James dropped the pouch on the table. 'Perhaps we can pay with these', he said. In addition to coins, there were Reichs documents identifying it as belonging to a soldier of the 5th German Motorised Infantry Unit, stationed in Montpelier. So, our subsequent research was a little easier than yours. We did of course wonder if the gold had already gone by the time the Germans had opened the graves. But the eyewitness accounts, many of whom we were able to interview in person, it being only fifteen years after the event, took that doubt from our minds.

We made two more discoveries that constituted irrefutable proof of the … theft. I can see, John, that you are about to ask me how the Germans knew the Treasury was there. In fact it was the war itself that caused the discovery. In 1940, when the Germans invaded Belgium and France, the then Grand Master of the *Ordo Templi* was living in Brussels. By this time the Order, as you know, had become a secular Order of Chivalry. Still, fearing the suppression of the Order, he arranged to transfer his Grand Mastership to a neutral, a Portuguese count, living in Lisbon. Of course, it was not simply the title he transferred. He also arranged for the remnants of the ancient Templar archive to be shipped to Portugal. Communications to the south through Germany and occupied France were far too risky. So he nominated a trusted member of the Order to take the boxes of documents in his car to Ostende, where he was to be met by the captain of a Portuguese coaster. It was dark and raining that night and a chill fog was drifting off the sea. The man was quite close to the perimeter fence before he discovered that the docks were guarded by German soldiers. Under the flood lights, dimmed by the mist into yellow globes, he could make out the Schmeisser 9mm machine guns slung over their shoulders and the insignia on the lapels of their great coats. Even those communicating with ships from neutral ports were under suspicion. The messenger managed to pass the main gate and customs house, telling the guard he was delivering a consignment of books for Portugal. However, when the man arrived at the quayside he found two soldiers waiting for him. He was forbidden to board the Portuguese vessel. Instead, he was ordered to leave his boxes in the adjacent warehouse and return to Brussels. The German soldiers would arrange for the consignment to be loaded and shipped. When the man protested, he suddenly found that he was talking to the business end of a Luger pistol. The messenger recorded that he had been informed that 'the Third Reich can be trusted to maintain order here, your consignment will be shipped safely, you are not permitted here. Please leave quickly.' Gestapo intelligence had apparently worked very well. To the relief of the old Grand Master, however, he received word from Lisbon two weeks later that the consignment had in fact been delivered intact and complete. What was not known at the time, was that researchers in medieval Latin at Berlin and Heidelberg universities had been asked to translate a coded document. The text had been encrypted in the thirteenth century. By a mixture of accident and elimination they found that the code was based on another document, a 12th-century epic Troubador poem, in Occitan. The only remaining copy of this poem just happened to be in the archives of the Berlin Museum. As the Grand Master, and his modern antecedents, had not known this, they had never been able to translate the text. It was James who discovered this fact. The two German researchers were soon able to break the code although, as they had been given half the document each, they never knew what their translations meant. It is important to appreciate that many of the officers in the new German army had been unemployed thugs in the depression of the 1930s. They had often made their way in the army, via the National Socialist Party, by means of their vicious and disingenuous natures. The clique of officers who found themselves in possession of the information about the Treasury retained many of the characteristics of the gangsterism that had spawned them. That they were mostly members of the German Motorised Infantry Division and that a unit of that Division was posted to Montpellier, was not a coincidence. In mitigation, they were only doing what very many Reich officers were doing. Acquiring what gold or art treasures they could from the occupied nations. Even today, the Foreign Office is running a large project to identify Nazi gold stolen from Jewish businessmen. Naturally, our conspirators did not trust one another, so they were all present with the consignment when their commander suddenly decided to surrender and deliver them into the hands of the US Army.

The second discovery was made wholly by James. He spent a month in the USA, mainly New York and Washington, trying to piece together whether there was any evidence of considerable wealth in unusual circumstances after 1945. He also did some digging in what US Army records he could get access to. Without going into detail, four US soldiers, who had been officers in the Division which had organised the surrender of the German Motorised Infantry Unit had remarkable subsequent careers. Two became Republican congressmen within four years, one of them the youngest ever appointed, one became a senator a few years later and the fourth a millionaire recluse in the West Indies. Although they had taken a number of modest precautions, there was still evidence that all had become very wealthy, in spite of coming from humble origins. There was considerable evidence that three of the four had funded most of Dwight Eisenhower's election campaign of 1953. Eisenhower was well-known, of course, in the European war theatre but was not a rich man and came from a very poor family. His campaign was the costliest ever staged, with widespread use of television for the first time. His election broke a 20-year Democrat supremacy. All of the four officers are now dead. The oldest died last year and his estate was estimated at 28 million dollars. James actually spoke to the man's two sons and both said that 'Pop had made neat investments on Wall Street'. Other than that, they had no idea how their father had accumulated his wealth."

Here Andrew paused to take a long drink from his whisky tumbler.

I was glad he did, for I was still assimilating what he had said. It spanned 700 years of human ambition, deceit, fanaticism, greed, violence and corruption … and was thus wholly credible. The cycle was almost complete, but not quite.

"Is there any more about this history I should know, Andrew, if only as a friend?"

He stood up, walked to the balcony and leant on the brickwork, steadying himself. Wrestling with himself. He shook his head and a great sigh shuddered through his rib cage. A small, green lizard scrambled down the wall and plunged into the shade of the fig tree. It was an hour after noon and the sun was beginning to cast short shadows on the empty streets. The whole village held its breath.

Andrew suddenly turned to face me, leaning back on the balcony. For a moment I had the awful feeling that he wanted to cast himself down to the street beneath. Instead he scrutinised my face as if divining my thoughts.

"A consummation devoutly to be wished, but not for me old chap. Rather I am about to test the apocryphal forgiveness and understanding of your creed and I hope it will not be found wanting."

"There is more joy in Heaven over one sinner who repenteth. And Heaven knows I am not your judge, Andrew, only your friend and counsellor. Do come and sit down, you're making me nervous." He sat down again and drained his glass.

"John, I have now confided the entire history to you. Believe me you now know as much as I do about the events and the evidence. What I must ask you, no beg you, to do for me is to now forget everything I have said. I have kept my promise, satisfied your curiosity and your moral scruples, I can do no more. It's not just for me I ask this favour."

"You are thinking of James?"

"No, I am thinking of you. As in Adam, knowledge is dangerous and, as in Adam, all men die."

"That's a bit melodramatic isn't it?"

"Perhaps, perhaps not. Enjoy your impending retirement, John, and be satisfied with what you have learned. Do this for me as a father would for a son."

My final decision was pre-ordained by the advice of my confessor. In such ways is our destiny decided. My pledge to honour the curé's penance, issued only that morning, weighed heavily upon me. If we can forgive our enemies how much more should we forgive our friends. I could not refuse him. "Yes, Andrew, I give you my word. As long as I live, this information will remain my deepest secret. More than that, you and I will never talk of it again."

The relief on Andrew's face was tangible. You could actually see his muscles relax and the darkness lift from him. In spite of myself, however, I could not resist having one last word. "Whilst I honour this promise, I will still often wonder what you and James did with this knowledge."

"What does any man do with knowledge?" Was all he said, and all he ever said on the subject. But from that sentence, I knew the wheel had not finished turning.

There is one final incident in my visit to the Languedoc that is worth recording, although even now I do not know how significant it was. The following day was my last full day in the region, I needed to get back to my parish the day after. I had always wanted to visit the abbey of St Marie d'Orbieu at Lagrasse and Andrew was glad to lend me the car for the day. He had work to do apparently and would be spending the day at home. As the journey was a couple of hours by car, I had a lazy morning and set off at around 10 am. Dropping gently down off the hills of the Minervois, the plain of the Corbières seemed very flat and featureless by contrast. I crossed the Canal du Midi at Homps. A few yards upstream from the bridge a huge German barge had grounded. I remember its glossy brown and black paint with gothic writing and copious amounts of brass fittings, it also had a superb container garden on the roof. The boat's powerful engines churned up a maelstrom of yellow water as she tried to pull herself back and forwards off the canal bed. A tall bearded man in a striped T-shirt shouted orders at his makeshift crew whilst a lock keeper on the bank gesticulated wildly with much incomprehensible French. The man replied with incomprehensible German at which the lock keeper shrugged and went off for a coffee. In my rear view mirror I finally saw the craft reversing up the river at full knots, its first mate having given up on the idea of lunch in Beziers. Two English girls in a twenty-foot motor boat which had been astern of the barge looked on with horror at this sudden change of direction. It can't be easy to reverse an eighty-foot barge and this might explain the impact of cast iron on fibreglass, the sound being clearly discernible over highly-strained English voices. By the time I stopped the car and went to see what I could do, everything seemed under control. Whether one of the English girls eventually married the German boy who pulled her from the water and lived with him in Munich where they had a son called Karl, after his father, I will never know.

At Fabrezan the road narrows and begins to climb into the Corbières hills, the first gentle signs of the folding of the landscape which becomes the mighty Pyrenees. Soon you notice that the River Orbieu is keeping you company though often lost from view in the deep, rocky gorge in which it runs. The further south-west I drove the hotter it became and the more intense the indigo blue sky. The heat was reflected mercilessly off the barren, rocky cliffs and escarpments of the Alaric hills. The sound of crickets like a hundred knifes being sharpened. Then, in sudden contrast to that unforgiving landscape, I crested a summit and found Lagrasse spread out below me in the broad, fertile valley of the Orbieu. Framed by a splendid 12th-century humped-back

bridge the river, which meanders past the town, draws the eye
to the abbey of Sainte-Marie d'Orbieu. The building, although
fairly unprepossessing externally, modestly hides its architectural
treasures within exquisite, hidden cloisters and courtyards. Its
only outward display of extravagance is the great octagonal tower,
soaring 360 feet into the sky, casting its shadow over the town.
Parking in a cobbled street that ran down to the river, I walked
between the 14th- and 15th-century houses towards the bridge. An
old lady dressed completely in black shyly wished me a whispered
'bonjour Monsieur' as she swept her door step. The opposite side
of the river is dominated by the abbey and I easily found my way
to the north entrance. Apart from a girl selling tickets and guides,
I did not meet another visitor as I wandered through the building.
Or buildings, I should say. For in St Marie d'Orbieu you can find
every type of architecture from 900 to 1800 AD and each style
seems self contained in a sequence of adjacent buildings. Norman
courtyards, lead on to medieval cloisters complete with wooden
galleries above, delicately carved from massive baulks of oak.
Finally opening out to larger Palladian/neo-classical courtyards,
arcades and formal, baroque walled gardens. Truly every vista
was a lesson in devotional architecture and how to blend styles to
uplift the spirits and turn men's eyes and minds towards what is
noblest. The contemplation of the creator of all such beauty. After
what seemed like a very long time, I found myself in the absolute
stillness of the abbey church. Stillness, but with a feeling of being
surrounded by the whispered echoes of human voices. Benedic-
tines murmuring their devotions or intoning a chant. The sound
rising from the stone floor like an invisible mist and filling the
high vaulted spaces, reaching for the light.

At the end of the south transept I found the doorway to the
tower. I had been told that those who are prepared to venture the
230 steps to its parapet are rewarded by one of the finest views in
all of France. As I drew near to the gothic door I became aware

of a low, continuous noise, occasionally changing pitch, like the unearthly moans of a troubled sleeper distressed by a recurrent nightmare. It was when I entered the base of the tower and began to climb the spiral stone stairway that I sensed an uncomfortable phenomenon. The hot, North African breeze blowing across the Corbières formed some kind of strong thermal current inside the tower. So great was the effect of the shaft of rushing air that my shirt flapped like a mainsail and my hair whipped across my eyes, blinding me from time to time. I had taken a small camera with me and I quickly stuffed this into my trouser pocket, took a deep breath and continued my climb. It was not the rush of air which concerned me but the distressing noise. It was like being trapped inside a giant, woodwind instrument. A thrumming, groaning, vibrating noise which, after the first 50 feet rose to a howl that vibrated the very walls of the tower and seemed to have penetrated my skull. At about that height the six-foot thick masonry of the rectangular base changed into the much finer stonework of the octagonal tower. At roughly 100 feet, the staircase came to a sort of landing which opened through a gothic door frame onto a small parapet. I use the word parapet because the French Department of Ancient Monuments has yet to succumb to the obsession with litigation and health and safety that bedevils our preserved, public buildings. Nowhere in the Languedoc had I found buildings encrusted with security cameras, warning signs, keep out notices, guard rails and designated viewing areas which so intrude on the visitors' reverie in England. In the abbey, as in most of Languedoc's medieval buildings, 'laissez faire' and common sense applied. This was how I found myself looking out onto a ledge with a low parapet and a strong wind trying to pluck me into oblivion. There was a window on the other side of the tower from the doorway allowing the wind to blast through the tower like a siren, sucking me upwards and making my world vibrate. The stones of the tower seemed to be swaying with every deafening rush of sound. I confess that I began to feel slightly sick and had almost decided to retrace my steps. It was then that the damnable Mac-Donald stubbornness surfaced. I had roughly another 250 feet to go to reach the main parapet and base of the clock tower. I knew I was out of breath and my heart was pounding but I also knew that these were mostly a reaction to the unsettling noise and the rushing of the wind. Reason told me I was perfectly safe although my instinct was to flee from that hellish place. The MacDonald who had fought beside the Bonnie Prince in '45 whispered in my ear. 'Why my wee mannie, you'll no be scared by a wheen bittock breeze.' A Carlyle-like reason also spoke to me of an opportunity missed. I blush to say I also experienced a brief vision of myself trying to explain my cowardice to Andrew. So, after a bit of a rest, I pressed on. Now, conventional open flights of stairs are one thing. But pressing on, ever upward, on a spiral staircase with a deafening wind howling between relentless stone walls is like a Sysyphean task. It is a treadmill from which you cannot escape. There were no more doorways opening to the outside world, just the relentless, drumming spiral. No landings or changes of features to relieve the sense of futility. No corners or bends, just one continuous spiral with each step identical to the one before. There was no way of knowing what progress was being made or when it would end. I just had to go on and on, hoping with every turn to see the light. Too numbed by the ceaseless howling to think, too battered by the wind even to breathe. Too exhausted to be tired. Too horrified to be afraid. Finally I was half scrambling, half crawling up the stairs, faster and faster wanting it all to be over.

This was how I fetched up sitting on the threshold of the top parapet, half suffocated, gasping for air like a beached fish my heart choking me by the throat. But clinging on for dear life to the stone doorway. When I could breathe again and my pulse had slowed a bit, I edged out onto the tower roof. Two compulsions drew me to my feet, first to be free of the incessant piping of the wind and, second, the mesmerising, compelling view. I was Aloysha from Karamatzov, who knows that one second in heaven is worth an eternity of purgatory. Here was a landscape of the Middle Ages. A patchwork of small, stone-walled grazing meadows and arable fields spread out from the abbey gardens along the west side of the river. Tiny stone field barns were dotted here and there. The river itself sparkled a turquoise blue deepening to purple under the ancient bridge. On the far side of the Orbieu, the sleepy medieval town clustered along the riverbank, some of the house walls forming the very embankment, and then rose gently up the side of the valley in a maze of cobbled streets and pantiled roofs. The vivid countryside buzzed and shimmered in the warm wind like a Pissaro landscape. When I could at last drag my eyes from the landscape, I found the roof of the tower very singular. A walkway ran for 360 degrees around the square top of the tower which supported a short spire. I took a sharp intake of breath when I saw that a parapet wall of no more than about a foot high separated the visitor from oblivion. At each of the four corners it was necessary to pass under an arch like a flying buttress. These four arches helped to support the belfry spire which continued upwards for another thirty feet, forming a pointed roof to the tower. Half way along the first parapet walk was a wrought iron gate leading to a flight of iron steps. The steps, fixed to the lead-covered spire, led upwards, at 45 degrees, to the flattened top of the spire where the bells hung in a wrought iron cage. The gate was unlocked but one look at this vertiginous ascent immediately convinced me that discretion was the better part of valour. However, my curiosity to see the view from the other side did compel me to begin to edge my way around the base of the spire, holding on to the low railings which formed the inside balustrade of the walkway. The more the wind beat its wings against me the more determined I became to complete the circuit. I got this strange and obsessive notion that if I did not do this I would concede some kind of triumph to the

Evil One and that a great catastrophe would happen. I kept my eyes fixed alternately on the distant horizon and the stone flags under my feet. To look over the edge at the 350-foot drop was to invite a sickening vertigo. Gradually, passing under the two buttress arches, I reached the other side of the tower. Looking down at the roof of the abbot's palace and the hostelry I saw a flock of collared doves fly far beneath me over the cloister and settle into the abbey garden. Suddenly they took off. A great noise thundered all around me. I swayed back and grabbed the railings behind me until the reverberations stopped. I had quite forgotten that the belfry is also a clock tower. Long after the great bell had stopped chiming the hour, the cool, clear sound still echoed between the walls, houses and cliffs of the still valley of the Orbieu. It was then that I decided I had feasted enough on great views and fine architecture and longed to find my feet back on terra firma. The wind had cooled and I began to shiver as I retraced my way back towards the spiral descent. I soon reached the furthest side of the tower, however, and began to edge towards the doorway, bracing myself once more to do battle with the infernal fluting of the wind. I think it was a sharp metallic noise that made me look upwards as I passed the gate to the belfry steps. Even on a windy day our ears can sometimes detect a small noise, out of place. Perhaps I can thank the many hours I have spent in stillness, listening, for this gift. For this power.

Immediately, I had the sickening impression of a slithering, clanging noise and a dark shape falling towards me. The next few seconds were of heart stopping horror. A bone-jarring impact on my left shoulder sent me reeling towards the parapet wall which only served to trip my ankles. I swayed on the very edge of the parapet as I fought for a foothold. Instinctively, my arms lashed out for something to grasp. First my fingers, then my arms, scrabbled wildly onto an object and held it tight. It was another human being. As we struggled I knew, even in my panic, that he was smaller than I. When he began to stumble I realised in dread that my weight was pulling him also over the edge. With a free hand he grasped for the railings and found the iron gate. For a split second the gate held, then flew open. My feet went over the edge. I slid down until I was stopped by my desperate grasp on the man's neck and shoulders. He was almost face down on the flagstones. My legs swung in mid air looking for a foothold. All they could find was the edge of a stone block where the mortar had fallen out. But this enabled me to take a little of the weight off my arms. The man was unable to push me off as he needed both hands to stop us spiralling into the void. By chance we had ended up face to face. I remember his smooth, olive skin and large brown eyes, wide with terror. He had no facial hair. He may have been a young, unemployed Arab, one of the many illegal immigrants who slip into Marseilles every year. I said, "Whatever you have done or will do now, I forgive you." I believed they were the last words I would ever say. Moments later I felt something warm on my forearm. A tear had run down his cheek. He opened his mouth to speak but never got the chance. With a dull metallic snap, one of the gate hinges broke. The gate skewed around until it was held by its one remaining hinge. The youth slid forward until his face now overhung the parapet edge. I knew that he was gazing down on the gravel car park, with the two cars like very small toys all that way beneath. I tightened my grip. Despite the frenzy of my racing brain I understood that my arms would not hold out much longer. I also knew that the only way back was for me to release the man's other arm which my grasp had partly pinioned to his side. That way, he could use the bars of the gate like a ladder and pull us both to safety. What made me trust him, I will never know. I simply nodded frantically to the gate and shouted "Ladder, ladder, climb up." Then I moved one arm so that he could free his. I waited in an agony of fear. But instead of pushing me to my death the youth bent his body slowly about his waist and, one arm after another, began to move his hands from bar to bar. With each grasp the remaining hinge groaned terribly but with each we moved nearer the railings. In a few terrible minutes we were both surprised to find ourselves lying on the paving stones of the walkway, leaning against the railings of the spire. I was too shocked to move. I just lay there, willing my heart to cease hammering and feeling, for the first time, the many bruises and sprains I had acquired. The other man got to his knees almost at once. Then bowed deeply to me, until his forehead touched the stone. He whispered, "The Prophet has preserved my soul this day." Then, before I could take in any of this, he jumped to his feet and ran off. I heard his steps growing fainter on the spiral staircase, soon to be lost in the mourning wind.

Back at the cottage in the Minervois, Andrew insisted on cleaning and bandaging my scraped shin. Considering my ordeal, I was surprised to find that, except for a few pulled muscles, I had sustained no injury. The wonders of adrenaline, perhaps. When Andrew asked me what I made of the incident I found it difficult to answer. Any explanation ranging from an accident, to the actions of a lunatic, to attempted murder seemed possible. It was just because it was all so uncertain, that I suggested we did not involve the Gendarmerie. I was slightly surprised when Andrew agreed. He seemed very withdrawn and introspective for the whole of that evening and the following morning as he drove me to the airport. As we shook hands in the terminal, Andrew once again advised me to go straight home and attend to, as he put it, 'pastoral good works'. He squeezed my hand very tightly as he did so. The only consequence of this incident was that I lost my camera. It could have been dropped at the top of the tower, or on the stairs or may have fallen over the parapet. I never found it, which is a pity as it contained all my photographs of the graves at La Couvertoirade. As this event was no less strange than the others which had befallen me that spring, I decided to record it here. Make of it what you will, dear reader.

The final page of John MacDonald's document was
in manuscript. Written in dark blue ink.

Well, Ronan, my very dear son. I have kept my word that I would do nothing whilst I lived. I honoured my confessional sacrament. It may seem strange to you that I did so to the end, but that honour is everything to me. Beside it the greatest wealth becomes as dust. I cannot, and should not, advise you what to do with this history. Perhaps all those involved are now dead. It was certainly my intention to do nothing in James's and Andrew's lifetime. You will now have grown to man's estate and you must decide. Remember, the work is not yet ended. You may wish to take it up where I demurred, or, you may decide to destroy this document in the flames. Either way you will have my blessing. Above all, rely on the good and powerful influences on this earth. Stillness, the Celtic church, its communicants and a father's love."

Ronan placed the document on the table and gazed absently into the embers of the fire. It was just because he was deep in thought that to be spoken to startled him so much.

"Hello, Ronan."

Garrett stood against the bar, not much more than three paces away. Ronan looked up blankly at this tall stranger.

13

At The White Cockade alehouse Garrett questions Ronan about
the document. Garrett returns to his hotel. Lying on the bed he has
an unsettling dream. He wakes with a start and takes
a heavy package out of his suitcase.

The White Cockade, as you might imagine, was an old Jacobin ale house. The tavern had found it difficult to cast off the cloak of its infamous history. In the nineteenth century it had been the haunt of radical poets, Whig reformers, impecunious romantic novelists, opium eaters, disgraced lawyers, failed medical students and unemployed catholic highlanders cleared from their land. By the early twentieth century its infamy reached a new low as it became the favoured meeting place of ladies of the night, who plied their trade along the then little-known thoroughfare of Rose Street. 'A business aye at its best when the Kirk General Assembly sit in session' was the scurrilous rumour spread by the landlord. As Ronan sat tucked in his corner listening to the sleet rattling the panes, the small inn was even more like the cosy parlour of a cave dweller.

Ronan had completely forgotten about Garrett and it was some seconds before recognition came back to him. How he had not heard the wind and noise of the city swirl in through the door when Garrett arrived and why he had not noticed him standing so close, surprised him. Garrett now approached with two brimming pints of what passed for 'best' on that premises. He gave Garrett an unenthusiastic smile. "How long have you been there, David." Garrett replied carefully in the character of his *nom de guerre*, the English tourist.

"Only a few minutes, you were so absorbed I didn't want to disturb you." Whilst James Galbraith would have exercised the subtlety of a serpent, gently stalking his prey, Garrett's approach was more direct. "How did you get on at the solicitors. Did you unravel the mystery of the key? I'm very interested in the outcome."

Ronan struggled between his natural openness and his instinct for discretion. His openness won, albeit grudgingly. He took a gulp from his new pint and wiped the froth from his mouth with the back of his hand. "Well, the key fits my father's safety deposit box at Sinclair's. In the box were some financial and property documents and a kind of letter to me." Ronan paused, slightly self-conscious, wondering if he might have said too much. The hesitation in Ronan's voice when he mentioned the letter was like the firing of a maroon to someone of Garrett's training. He spoke casually.

"Was the letter of any interest?"

"Not really, just some of my father's historical research. Nothing important."

"Really? But you told me at Drumelzie that you knew your father's research was very important." Garrett continued with a conspiratorial smile. "You're not going to disappoint me now, after I've brought you all this way."

Ronan could have kicked himself for telling Garrett so much at Drumelzie. Someone of maturer years would have realised that he was under no obligation to confide in a relative stranger and deftly put an end to this crude interrogation. Ronan, however, was simply experiencing a quite unnecessary guilt. He had been born and bred to be honest.

"To be honest, I still haven't digested it and don't quite know what to make of it yet. But I can tell you that my father did discover something important from his research, something ... that could seriously affect some high ranking people. That's all I think I can tell you, David."

That, however, was all Garrett wanted to know. He didn't want any more detail. In the company he was keeping he already understood that to know too much was as dangerous as knowing too little.

"Was that the document you were reading when I came in, Ronan?"

"Yes, I'd just finished it."

"Is it the only copy?"

"Yes, as far as I know. Why do you ask?"

"Just to remind you to take care of it."

"Oh I will, I will. I hope you're not too disappointed, David." And with that Ronan folded the letter lengthways and stuffed it into the inside pocket of his coat. Out of politeness, Ronan asked Garrett about his afternoon.

"Oh, I went to the Castle, like a good tourist."

"Were you impressed?"

"Only with the National War Memorial. I found that very moving. All those thousands of names of honourable men who did their duty well, who obeyed orders and stuck to their posts come what may. Heroes, each and every one. What it must be to earn the enduring respect of one's fellow countrymen, I can only imagine. How fortunate they are and what more can their loved ones ask of them. They had one opportunity in their lives for immortality and they treasured it. They grasped it firmly and didn't squander it."

Ronan had hardly heard Garrett say so much, or be so serious. To envy the dead, however, seemed a bleak philosophy to him. He reminded Garrett that he now needed to secure his accommodation in Hall. It had grown almost dark outside and gusts of sleet still swirled around the street lights. They drank up and turned their collars to the chilly night. Garrett had planned for a journey in darkness, the thing he was about to do needed no witnesses.

The halls of residence were in the south-west suburbs of the city. The city lights raked the dark interior of the car as they drove. Neither spoke until the campus came into view. Garrett drew up around the corner from the main lodge.

"I'll drop you here, Ronan, if you don't mind."

"No, that's fine. You've been very kind. I'll say goodbye then." They shook hands. As Ronan opened his door he said, "It's been a pleasure meeting you, David, enjoy the rest of your holiday," thankful that he had drawn a line under their acquaintance. It was not that he disliked Garrett, it was his brooding intensity, just beneath the veneer of affability, that unsettled him.

Garrett returned a wry smile that faded immediately. His lips moved with an almost inaudible "Goodbye."

Garrett watched Ronan, complete with tattered rucksack, disappear into an administration building. He had carefully moved his car so that he could observe without being seen. After a long time, Ronan emerged with a porter who showed him to his room in an adjacent low-rise block. Garrett noted the building and, when a light illuminated its window, the room.

Garrett had booked into the exclusive George Hotel in George Street. A porter in top hat and brown livery with cream piping carried his suitcase to a plush room overlooking St Andrew's Square. He took whisky and some ice from the mini bar and stood, drink in hand, feeling the warmth and softness of the deep wool carpet under his feet and gazing over the dramatic nocturnal skyline of the Old Town. The Castle and its War Memorial were floodlit. After a while he lay on the king-size bed, kicking his shoes to the floor and feeling the luxurious comfort easing into his bones. The delicious scent of fresh linen enveloped him. Yet peace did not come and his mind ran on feverishly. All that stood between him and this was one boy. An almost anonymous boy. Only one being amongst the hundreds of millions on this planet, living, loving, dying every hour of every day. In Africa, Asia and the Indian sub-continent, fate extinguished the being of thousands of men, women and children every week. Through disease, famine and atrocious violence. Why should this boy be any different? Had God marked him out for a beautiful future whilst he had prematurely cast millions of others into the pit? The answer to these rhetorical questions depended, Garrett knew, on whether or not one had a soul, or even, whether or not you believed in the soul. From his grammar school days he recalled that Aquinas reasoned that because we exist there must be a first cause. Then he remembered what the sailor no good for the sea had said about the souls of men. As his thoughts twisted and turned he knew there was one area of thought he must avoid at all costs. It was the portion of his soul labelled 'Mary Dalbeith'. He had met Mary whilst on leave in Argyll. The proud way she tossed her head and her soft voice with a Western Isles lilt was the best and finest thing in his troubled life. He remembered the way she looked at him, sitting by the fire brushing her long, red hair. His love for her had been a spiritual revelation, quite beyond the physical or intellectual experience. Lately he had been having a recurring, fitful dream. He had lost something infinitely precious and was running, running through a grey, wintry city, rushing down empty alleyways and along busy streets trying to find it. The dream always finished the same way. At the end of a long street of tall buildings he would come to some iron gates. They were locked and on the other side stood Mary. Try as he might he could not open the gates, pounding them with his fists until the blood ran. As he hung there, exhausted, crucified, Mary turned sadly away and walked into the distance. It was Garrett who was behind the iron bars and Mary who was free. All he understood was that there was no way back, the wheel had turned. Garrett jumped to his feet, then slowly sat on the edge of the bed. It was all too complicated. When he was in the army, life was much easier, simpler. There was no need to think, the primordial law of the jungle took over. You were either predator or prey. You fulfilled the prime law of nature, a predator killing to survive. Finishing his drink, Garrett removed a package from his suitcase. Unwrapping the heavy, oiled paper he carefully laid the heavy contents on his lap. He recognised the Russian VAL Avtomat Spetsialny. James had done well with Garrett's shopping list. Although this was a special forces rifle, he knew that it was readily available from the stock of former Soviet Union weapons now being traded in the black economy. It came with a clip of twenty 9mm AP rounds, a telescopic sight and a silenced barrel. This would cover all eventualities, Garrett had no intention of failing nor of being detected. The VAL would pierce sheet steel at 400 yards, was accurate at that distance and made no muzzle flash.

The AP cartridges and the gas ventilation for the silencer reduced the muzzle velocity to sub-sonic level. In use, the report, even from a short distance, could not be recognised as a discharge from a rifle. The cartridges were unusual enough to generate speculation, but by that time the weapon would no longer exist. Nor would the old Garrett. Pulling back the cocking handle he checked that the chamber was empty, then released the handle, pushed in the safety catch and pressed the trigger. With the stock folded and the sound suppresser removed, it was only 15 inches long and weighed about three kilograms, about the size of a newly-born baby.

14

*Ronan, hungover after an evening in the Canny Man, is visited
by Mary Dalbeith who invites him to a party that evening.
At the party he meets Susie.*

Fingers of sunlight played across the sleeping figure of Ronan. He had stayed up late sorting out his room, doing some late-night shopping and chatting with fellow students over dinner. Then he had been persuaded to partake of a nightcap at a local hostelry known as the Canny Man. Ronan rolled on his back and groaned. Rubbing the stubble on his face he winced at the light streaming through the thin curtains, turned on his chest and pulled the duvet over his head. A noise like a great bell, tolling for lost souls sounded in his head for a long time before he became dimly aware that someone was knocking on the door. Whoever it was did not seem disposed to give up easily. The banging continued relentlessly at regular intervals like the torture of the damned. When he could stand it no longer, Ronan crawled out of bed and stumbled to his feet. He was still half asleep. Someone seemed to have glued his eyelids together and they refused to open more than a few millimetres. His stomach lurched as if he was crossing the Bay of Biscay in a south-westerly and his mouth felt as if something had died in it. He had gone to bed in his boxers so he threw the duvet over his shoulders and gathered it around him under his chin. This necessitated a hunched posture. So, with this and his unshaven face, matted hair, and grey appearance he gave a fair impression of a homeless alcoholic who had been sleeping rough around the Cowgate for several years.

"Hold your noise please, I'm just coming now," he croaked. Ronan struggled with the catch for a while then threw open the door. It was just as well he was leaning on the door frame for support, for there stood Mary Dalbeith. Ronan gaped in stunned disbelief and could neither move nor speak. How had this happened? What witchcraft had conjured her up out of his sleeping visions? A gust of spring swept into the room with Mary's perfume. She was all youth, all beauty, all goodness, dressed in brown, woolly leggings and a cream Shetland sweater. Mary folded her arms and looked at Ronan in mock censure.

"Is this the Seamen's Mission, or have I got the wrong address?"

Ronan was too far gone to recognise the irony, but at last he found he could speak. Just. "Mary, it's yourself. It's me, Ronan MacDonald."

"Oh yes, thank you, Ronan, I recognise you now. Are you going to keep me talking on the doorstep like a Jehovah's Witness or invite me in?"

"Sorry, sorry Mary. Please, come in, I was in bed."

"You mean this isn't your normal mode of dress, Ronan?"

"No Mary, no. It's a duvet."

"And a very nice one. Do you mind if we open a window? It's a little close in here."

With that, Mary marched to the window, flung back the curtains and threw open the casements. It was roughly five degrees Celsius outside. Ronan winced at the light and clutched the duvet with more fervour.

"That's better, Ronan. Smells less like a brewery. Now I'm going to make you a nice cup of tea. Or rather, a cup of nice tea, to relate the participle. After all it's the tea I hope will be nice and not the cup." Ronan rubbed his hand across his face. He could think of many better times and places for a lesson in English syntax. Mary switched on the electric kettle then started to rummage noisily in cupboards for crockery and tea. The kettle seemed to roar in Ronan's ears like the discharge of a 12-pound cannon and his toes became decidedly nippy in the draught from the window. Yet he could still hear Mary's miraculous voice, so he knew that nothing else mattered.

"Is Typhoo Indian or Chinese do you think?"

"Eh … well … I'm sorry I really don't know, Mary."

She turned to look at him, eyes wide. "I can well see how your stand-ards have dropped, Ronan, when you no longer know nor care whether you drink Darjeeling or Lapsang Souchong." Whilst the leaves were infusing, she closed the window and pulled two upholstered chairs close to the radiator. "Now, we will sit down and catch up on all the gossip. What have you been up to?"

"Mary, it's just fine to see you, you look wonderful."

"Forgive me if I don't return the compliment until you are prop-erly dressed, Ronan MacDonald. I don't quite know if it's proper to be sitting here with you half naked." Here Ronan smiled in embarrass-ment. He was not quite the dashing figure he had hoped to portray when they next met. He looked at his feet and dearly wished that he had at least cut his toenails last night.

"If you step outside for a moment, Mary, I could just get washed and dressed." She gave him a reassuring smile. "Oh, I think my reputation can stand it and I can only stay a few minutes, so I'll soon be out of your way. And none of this is letting me know how you have been getting on."

Ronan first thought of his father's research. He wanted to talk about it to Mary but he had to acknowledge that his father had kept the secret until the grave. If his father could do this then so could he. It was almost like a dying man's final request, in a way. He knew if he mentioned it one thing would lead to another, so he resolved to say nothing at all. Thus they talked for a few minutes about Ronan's room and about the domestic arrangements and how he had spent his first night as an under-graduate. Ronan was keen to explain why she had found him in such a disreputable state at 11 am in the morning. After a pause, he dropped his voice slightly and leant closer.

"Have you heard about Mr Goldberg at Drumelzie, Mary?"

"I read about it in *The Scotsman* this morning."

"I was there when it happened. It was an awful thing. Charles had to stay and help sort things out and I took a lift from a friend so I could get here for the start of the term."

"Well, you do seem to be making friends. The question is, are they the right kind. It's important to keep focused on a course of study, Ronan, and not just fritter your time away in the Canny Man."

Blast her, thought Ronan, was she at it again. Talking at him as if he were a child and herself the mother, and him a grown man too. He felt himself go red in the face.

"Well perhaps you would like to choose my friends yourself, Mary Dalbeith?"

She smiled at him and held her head to one side so her chestnut hair tumbled onto her shoulder. That smile, warm and serious. "Perhaps I should. You need someone to look after you." Ronan smiled back hopelessly, he felt he could aspire to nothing better in this life than to be looked after by Mary. "Who was it gave you a lift to Edinburgh?"

"Just an acquaintance really. A young English chap called David. A batchelor, on holiday, doing the grand tour of Scotland. I met him at Drumelzie."

"Well, before I decide if he is a suitable companion, you must describe him to me."

Ronan laughed but went along with it. He provided Mary with a fairly well-observed description of Garrett, including an impression of his brooding melancholy.

"You know, Mary, I think that man has had a great disappointment in his life, but he would never talk about it. Is anything wrong, Mary?" Ronan had added the last sentence when he saw Mary suddenly become agitated. She gently wrung her hands and looked distractedly out of the window, but as soon as Ronan noticed this, she quickly tried to become her old self again. Still, Ronan felt he needed to reassure her.

"I don't suppose I'll see him again by the way."

"Sometimes just knowing someone is enough. Things are changed forever, whether you see them again or not."

Ronan thought this uncharacteristically pensive for Mary and tried to lighten the conversation. "And what have you been doing since you last met Charles and me?"

She looked less wistful. "I've been to Yorkshire, meeting up with an old friend. Nothing very interesting. Well now Ronan, it has been delightful but I must be going, I have my spinster's virtue to think of if nothing else." Ronan wanted so much to touch her, to press his lips to hers. But this ambition, he knew, could not be achieved wearing two day's of stubble, yesterday's underpants and a Paisley-pattern duvet. Mary got to her feet and placed her porcelain mug on the small desk.

"You had better be about your ablutions, Ronan, because you are going to a party tonight. At least I hope you are going, for my sake, I think you'll have fun." He could not refuse, so she wrote down the address and time. At the door she added, "Yes, you men certainly need looking after," and Ronan had the definite impression she was being serious.

The party was held at a large Victorian house in Marchmont, near The Meadows. In the 1960s various rooms had been amputated and made into rented flats. The building was occupied by medical students, a girl studying clinical psychology and a physicist working for his doctorate. It was dark and drizzling as Ronan pushed into the communal hallway. The noise guided him upstairs to the party. As he entered the flat the biological heat enveloped him. The lighting in the rooms was dim and a mist of cigarette and candle smoke mingled with wine fumes seemed to obscure the faces. There was a scrum of people trying to make themselves understood above the noise. The stereo was unequal to the task and had been set at full volume causing such a bizarre distortion of the music it might as well have been white noise. He navigated his way to the kitchen and deposited his entry fee, a bottle of Riesling, on the table, where it rubbed shoulders with several six packs of Tennants lager, an assortment of Spanish and Australian wines, a couple of bottles of spirits, a polypin of real ale and an unopened carton of fresh orange juice. By the sink a dumpy girl with bad acne, wearing a denim jacket and skirt, was trying to look busy with beer glasses but only succeeded in looking lonely. She gave Ronan a hopeful smile which propelled him into the middle of the lounge where two bearded men were stirring a bowl of hot wine punch. As Ronan's eyes adjusted he began to take in the furnishings. They were in the period 1955 to 1975 generally known as 'furniture no one else wanted.' At length he spotted Mary, behind a semi-circle of young men. She was wearing a dark green velvet dress which somehow complemented her hair perfectly. Green, thought Ronan, the colour of fairy folk. As soon as she saw him she made an excuse and came to his side. She had to half shout to make herself heard.

"I'm glad you could come. Give you a chance to meet some new people. Watch the punch, by the way, it's like aviation fuel."

Ronan knew he only wanted one friend, but she seemed as elusive as air. "You look smashing tonight, Mary."

"And so do you." Ronan looked at his fawn, moleskin trousers and brown, brushed cotton shirt, and wasn't fully convinced.

"Do you think so, I really didn't know what to put on. But you always know what to wear."

"I'm looking out for a Paisley-pattern duvet, actually, they tell me they're in fashion at the moment." Ronan thought that was typical of her, it seemed that every time he paid her a compliment she made something comical out of it. It was like trying to get hold of Scotch mist. Still, they both laughed. She looked at him sweetly.

"Ronan, would you be kind enough to get me a glass of white wine?"

When he returned, he found Mary talking with a group of about five people. He tried to engage her in conversation but instead ended up talking to a very earnest, whey-faced young man who was clearly looking for victims on which to test his theorem. His spectacle lenses flashed as he nodded to emphasise his words and his sallow complexion grew moist.

"I believe in anarchy to bring about the end of globalisation. Permanent revolution against faceless international corporations and the destruction of the world-wide capitalist economic system. The task is to set up a proletarian commune, directly accountable to the people. We would achieve this by civil disobedience and terrorism if necessary. Religion would wither away and proselytising would become a crime."

Ronan was rather scandalised by this. "Well, you're very hard on the priests, they provide a great deal of comfort and more, a spiritual understanding of life and the universe. What philosophy would you put in their place, apart from violence that is?"

The young man spoke in exasperation as if the answer was obvious to all.

"The philosophy of science, of course. The amount of human scientific knowledge now doubles every ten years. Just think what the earth will be like in a million years. We will have the answer to all the problems of the organism and the secrets of the universe."

"I grant you that in millennia to come we will eventually know how but knowing why may take a little longer. That is assuming mankind is still here of course, and hasn't been destroyed by anarchy and terrorism. Science doesn't have a philosophy, it's a tool surely, to be used for good or ill."

"A necessary tool, it will take us to other worlds, to other civilisations and other life forms when our own used-up solar system burns out. Why should we be so arrogant as to assume we are the only intelligent life in the universe?"

"Because there is a great deal of evidence to support that assumption."

"Your so called 'standard model' of the universe has ossified for decades and has nothing more to offer. But what if I were to say that there is a spirituality within science, within cosmology?"

"Such as?"

"How matter behaves at the quantum level. Even the simple, so-called, double slit interference experiment leaves me stunned by the jaw-dropping outcomes. I'm sure you must know about this experiment. Light or electrons or photons are projected on a box having two parallel slits. On the opposite inside face of the box, an interference pattern is formed of light and dark bands illustrating, we were told, that light/electrons behave in wave formation with peaks and troughs forming where the waves intersect. But things have changed a lot since then and the experiment has been developed a good deal."

"Is there a point to this?"

"When only one photon is released, you still get an interference pattern. One supposition is that the photon travels to every known co-ordinate thereby, somehow, interfering with itself. Now here comes the anthropic principal. When an observer attempts to measure the out-comes of the range of experiments the results disappear. They cannot be observed. It is said, that when measurement is attempted, it causes the wave to collapse back to a physical particle. Even attempting to collect data robotically does not fool the experiment. It is said that the results tell us that reality is a product of consciousness. It cannot work because, to put it simply, we become part of the mystery we are trying to solve."

"You know, I think you ought to be taking my science course instead of me. My tutor would love you."

Ronan felt not a little belligerent.

"How about I ask your tutor what dark matter is, given that it makes up the majority of the universe. Ditto, dark energy and gravity. All completely impenetrable to the scientific community. But this is merely scratching the surface, the real deal is of course Quantum Entangle-ment. An observer in, say, Australia, is observing the rotation of an elec-tron. When a colleague in Oxford intervenes to reverse the rotation of an electron under his observation, then at that instant the Australian electron reverses its spin too. You could say, that our consciousness is manipulating the universe across infinite distances."

Ronan began to feel more heated and slightly losing control. In his stomach two glasses of cheap red wine were fermenting with a pint of lager. This young man's nihilism had no understanding of spirituality, of poetry, or the still heartbeat inherent in organic nature.

"I'm not a physicist, but I maintain an interest and I do know that there is an infinite potential for life in an infinite universe. It has been scientifically estimated that there are at least 200 million planets in our own galaxy alone which are capable of supporting intelligent life. That equates to hundreds of billions in the known universe."

"There, you prove my point."

"Do I? Then why haven't we had an email from them?"

"Sorry ... I ..."

"For the past 50 years mankind has been broadcasting radio waves into space, rippling out in an expanding sphere to the end of the universe. It is inevitable that any advanced civilisations will do the same. Yet, we have detected nothing from any other solar system or galaxy. Since the early 1970s we have been systematically scanning the heavens with powerful radio dishes, looking for either radio waves or waste-heat signatures. Since then various earth stations have been scanning all star systems within a 200-light-year radius. Twelve years ago the USA set aside 100 million dollars to conduct a high resolution microwave survey. They named it SETI. Do you know what they detected?"

"No."

"Nothing. Not a trace. Soon all we will hear are the echoes of our own electromagnetic radiation in an empty universe."

The earnest student became uncomfortable but not discouraged.

"Science will give us immortality, is that not what everyone wants?"

"I believe we are already immortal, if we had eyes to see it. Don't you think that the fact that we are quite alone in the universe reveals a special purpose, a special value on each living soul? Each and every life on earth is infinitely rich and precious and each one makes an invaluable change to the current of time and the future. Your science and your anarchy is all very good but, ultimately, devalues us as human beings. People are not machines, they have a soul. I'm not saying a metaphysical soul but a perception of what is beautiful, good, honest and noble. They are also capable of love. Do you think the Prime Creator made the universe so that it could simply decay and be lost? Why would God do that if we are made in his own image? It simply makes no sense. Unless you can accept the anthropic principal, that the universe only exists when we intervene in it, then you have to accept that the only constant in the human condition is waste."

The youth began to smile nervously. "Sorry, didn't realise you were a born-again Christian. This is all getting a bit too primitive-superstitious for me. I'm going to find a beer." Ronan was so amazed and horrified by what the student had said that he did not even want to thump him, which would have been his normal, pacifist reaction. He thought, 'How dare he call me a Christian, I've already been there and done that. The spiritual side to our natures is a tenacious power for good even on a humanist level. It is enough, isn't it? Although, the more we unpeel our universe,' he reasoned, 'the faster humanism seems to run out of road. When you collide with the proposition that all time and matter in the universe was created in an infinitely small instant from an object smaller than the smallest known sub-atomic particle, containing an incomprehensible amount of energy, the breath of a creator seems to condense in the void.' But when his thoughts ran on they usually collided sooner or later with thoughts of Mary. He looked around and could not see her. The earnest youth passed with a glass of beer. Ronan caught him by the elbow.

"Do you know where the girl in the green dress is? I'm looking for her."

"Oh, she left about fifteen minutes ago. She waved to you at the door, but you were too involved in our conversation to notice." An involuntary spasm brought Ronan's powerful hands up towards the man's neck. Our young urban terrorist blanched and dodged behind a group of girls.

Ronan felt isolated and out of place in the room and was well aware that he did not possess the polished social skills required to make contacts in this environment. His feeling of alienation from this chance gathering did not improve with another drink, so he decided to leave. Two girls stood talking in the doorway of the room. As he approached, one of the girls giggled and left but the other continued to lean against the door frame. Ronan had not really noticed the girl until he was about to pass through the door.

"Excuse me," he said, "would you mind moving?"

"That depends how you want me to move."

Ronan supposed she was a little tipsy and emphasised his next words with pointing gestures towards the hallway. "No, sorry, really I just want to get through, to leave."

Ronan looked at her for the first time. He didn't recall having seen her before. Either she had just arrived or he had been too preoccupied with Mary to notice. The girl was not tall, and was very slightly built. Ronan's first impression was that she was like a scaled-down version of a fashion model, anatomically perfect, by the standards of present culture, yet slightly miniaturised. She had beautifully-shaped, long, Barbie-doll legs and a crinkly blonde perm which smothered her bare shoulders. Her silvery-fabric mini-dress seemed to have been tailored *in vivo*. It sparkled and clung to every pleasing curve. She was the sort of girl who tends to keep female or older male company at parties because young men are generally too intimidated by her desirability to approach her. Her blonde starburst of hair framed a childlike face which, as she turned to Ronan, was brightened by a mischievous smile. Her voice was bubbly and satin smooth. Like champagne.

"Well now, I am the official guardian of all comings and goings and all those that pass have to pay me a toll. Because you have had to endure such a truly awful party, I will take pity on you. You have clearly suffered enough, so if you would be kind enough to fetch me a G&T, I will grant you your freedom."

This made Ronan laugh. Just because it was such an awful party and he would never have dared say it himself. She followed him to look for ice and they both ended up standing in the kitchen, sharing their limited collection of gruesome party tales. The dumpy denim girl was still there but she soon left, shooting Ronan a miserable glance on the way out. The party had begun to thin out slightly and the music could now just about be heard. The stereo was playing a mushy ballad from the 60s or 70s. The girl took him by the hand. "Come on," she said, "let's dance."

Ronan's only experience of dancing hitherto had been the formal country dancing classes held at school. Initially, the boys had been seg-regated into two groups, one group taking the male lead and the other the female role and steps. Then they would swap roles. Then something Ronan never understood had apparently happened one afternoon in the showers after swimming. The next day the music master, presumably

175

because he was the one master who saw all the classes each week during his music periods in the great hall, spoke to the boys. His talk was all about the dangers of puberty. But because he was only slightly less embarrassed than his cringing audience and chose his vocabulary with such tortuous circumlocution, his point was lost on most of the boys, especially Ronan. After that day, however, sulky, smirking, girls were shipped in from Mary Erskine's Academy for the dancing classes. These stilted sessions were supervised by Ronan's form master, Mr Baillie, who always looked as if he would rather be playing golf, and frequently practised his driving when he thought he was unobserved. The girls were supervised by their music teacher, Miss Carmichael, a dry, middle-aged spinster with a passion for cats. The main task of these teachers was to ensure that the two groups never came into any physical contact unless it was absolutely unavoidable.

Ronan was thus understandably reluctant to dance at the party but when he looked at the other couples who had started dancing, it didn't look at all complicated. It seemed to just involve letting the girl hang around your neck whilst you held her around the waist. Then all you had to do was shuffle slowly from foot to foot, gradually circling around the floor. Ronan's self-consciousness at having to refuse in public outweighed his fear of trying a dance which appeared to have no known steps. That was how he found himself slow dancing with a perfumed delight called Susie, much to the obvious envy of the attendant young males.

The party noise still meant that Ronan was compelled to communicate by raising his voice and gesticulating. After their dance he led Susie to a partly occupied sofa and gestured that they sit down. Susie shook her head. "It's far too noisy to talk here. I've got some freshly-ground coffee back at my flat. Let's go there and talk, it's not far."

To anyone else but Ronan, such an invitation would have had a certain traditional meaning. To Ronan, however, a cup of coffee was a cup of coffee and a talk was a talk. "Oh aye," he said, "that would be fine."

The two talked freely as they walked between forlorn tenements over pavements which reflected the amber of sodium lighting in mirrors of puddles. Susie, it transpired, was a registered nurse at the Western General hospital.

"They don't like my hair, always complaining about it. I have to wear it tucked up under a cap, which takes hours to do. But I'm not going to have it cut. It's part of who I am and it's a kind of gesture of defiance anyway."

"What are you defying?"

"Being ground down by the system, having to be a wage slave. Having to grow old eventually."

"We all have to grow old, it can be quite dignified they tell me."

"You don't have to change incontinence pads and do bed washes. That might change your mind. I mean to enjoy as much of this life as I can before I end up old and stodgy."

It turned out that she was from Durham and that she had left home as soon as she was able. She had come to Edinburgh as a good place to study nursing and had stayed on. It was also a respectable distance from the influence of her parents who had christened her Janet Susan Williams. They had done this in deference to a wealthy aunt of the same name, half hoping that it would encourage the childless old lady to remember Susie in her will. When the aunt died they found out that she had bequeathed all her worldly goods to the Blue Cross Animal hospital in Newcastle. Susie had to make do with sharing her parent's limited means with her two older brothers and her dog. She never understood her parents' aversion to family pets until she learned of their fiscal disappointment shortly before she left home. When Susie was ten her mother had to begin working full time. She told Susie that her Border Terrier, Scamp, would have to go, as it was cruel to leave the animal unattended all day. Susie begged her mother all evening until her father got angry. When she came home from school next day, Scamp was gone. He had been given to an old lady in the next street. Apparently, the lady had been pestering Susie's mother for months to let her have him. So, sometimes when she went to school, Susie would see the old lady taking a miserable looking Scamp for a slow, uneventful walk on a new leash.

Soon she no longer saw Scamp and one evening her mother told her he was dead. The lady had taken him to the vet for a distemper immunisation to which the dog had taken a bad reaction and become paralysed in his hind legs. There was no alternative but to have him put down. Susie told Ronan that the first thing she would do when she bought a proper house with a garden was to buy a Border Terrier.

Susie shared her flat with another girl who was out for the evening. The accommodation had been squeezed into two rooms of a Victorian terraced house and comprised two bedrooms, a kitchen and a bathroom. They made coffee and took it to Susie's room. Ronan noticed that the room's ornate plaster cornice and intricately moulded skirting were both absent from one wall, where the room had been partitioned. A fact reinforced by the location of the ornamental ceiling rose only a few inches from the partition wall. The room was small to serve as both bedroom and sitting room. Two easy chairs sat in front of a fake coal-effect electric radiator and, opposite a bay window, a double, divan bed with no headboard was pushed against the wall. A ridiculously small white wool rug lay in front of the fire. A bookcase held a small number of nursing text books and several paperback novels. A large pictorial calendar printed by a pharmaceutical company hung on the wall. Each month advertised a different drug. An anti-depressant for the winter months, a statin for the spring and an H2 antagonist for the summer.

Susie sat on the bed and gestured to Ronan to sit beside her. As she sat down her dress rode up slightly revealing more of her elegant legs and there was an electric whisper of nylon as she slowly crossed them. As they spoke she moved closer to Ronan, her hair brushing his cheek and her scent filling his head. She made eye contact whenever Ronan spoke. When she spoke, she tossed her head coyly and smiled.

Sitting so close to Susie, Ronan suddenly became aware of a head-swimming physical arousal. When she slipped off her black velvet court shoes and drew her legs up onto the bed, Ronan felt his underpants becoming structurally challenged by a deep, pulsing urgency. His heart rate seemed very high, which he ascribed to the alcohol. Even more urgent was his confusion. The rules of engagement between couples had been clear and universally understood up until the 1960s. Since then, many young men have struggled to define what such situations demand of them. They strive to walk the correct line between being deplored as an exploitive, sexual predator on the one hand, or a bungling prude on the other. Ronan's somewhat sheltered upbringing had left him with a rather exalted view of womankind. As he looked at Susie he felt she was worthy of worship and almost too good to be true. He refused to interpret any of her advances as being sexual. He reasoned that the poor girl was naturally, innocently sensual and could have no idea what effect she was having on him. He was sure she would be horrified if he were to take advantage of the situation. It was his role to protect her from animal passions. Nor did he want to spoil the evening by making any advances. If he did that, he reasoned, he might never see her again. Well-brought-up girls, he believed, could never do anything like that on a first date.

Ronan continued to tell Susie about all the interesting gravestone inscriptions in Edinburgh churchyards. To his surprise he found she was deeply interested in this. So he then went on to tell her about the history and then the archaeology of the Western Highlands. She appeared less interested in that. She stretched her long legs like a cat and lay full length on the bed. Ronan found it less easy to talk to her in this position as he had to twist around on the edge of the bed where he remained seated. He averted his gaze when it came into contact with her legs. He had got on to the history of the Scottish Clans when Susie sat up and asked him to pass her handbag.

"I need to take my pill," she said.

"Oh dear, are you unwell? I'm sorry, I've probably given you a headache with all this talking."

"No my dear, I'm not ill, it's just a pill a girl takes."

This meant nothing to Ronan. He made to stand up. "Well, I'll just get you a glass of water from the kitchen." She put her slender fingers on his shoulder.

"No, it's OK, I don't need a glass of water."

"It won't take a minute."

"Look, I don't want a glass of water, OK?"

"Yes, fine, if you're sure, but you do look a little pale."

Ronan talked about the geology of the Hebrides until 2 am. He was enjoying Susie's company so much he just couldn't bear to stop. At 2.30 am Susie ran her fingers through her long blonde hair and stood up.

"Sorry, Ronan, I've got a shift early tomorrow morning. So I'm going to bed. I suddenly feel quite exhausted."

Ronan stood up too. "I really enjoyed this evening," he said. "I suppose all the buses will have stopped running, I hope I have enough for a taxi."

"You have been very … nice … Ronan. So I won't make you walk all the way back to Hall. You can sleep, and I mean *sleep*, with me."

As she spoke she had wriggled out of her glistening tights and then grabbing the hem of her dress she peeled it off with one lithe movement. Ronan saw a heart stopping female figure and a glimpse of tiny, white cotton pants as Susie slid into bed. Ronan hesitated.

"Hurry up, Ronan, I want to get to sleep as soon as possible."

She did not look at him as he undressed to his underpants and slid into the cold sheets beside her. Some instinct dimly began to dawn on him and he slowly extended an arm and gently put it around her shoulders. To his dismay it was grasped roughly and pushed away.

She said tersely, "When I said sleep, I meant sleep." Which, to Ronan, just confirmed his 'good girl' theory.

"I'm sorry, just cold," he said. "I hope we can meet again soon."

"I think I'm going to be busy at work for a few weeks."

"Oh, right. After that then."

She turned her back to him. "Can you turn out the light please?"

The rapid thumping in Ronan's chest, and his mental confusion kept him awake almost until dawn.

15

Garrett breaks into Ronan's study bedroom and is surprised to find Mary Dalbeith there alone in bed. They share explanations and Garrett leaves. Ronan, still in bed at Susie's, is visited by Mary who warns him that he is in danger and must leave with her immediately and go to Cambridge.

A dark grey shape slid silently into position in an unlit corner of the car park. The shape stayed there for two hours, crouching in the corner. Patient, like a predator waiting for its prey. One minute later, a door eased open just enough to permit a human being to slip into the night air. The interior light stayed out but, just for an instant, the weak moonlight revealed a man wearing a dark blue duffel coat, black corded trousers and thin leather gloves. Then he disappeared into the shadows cast by the buildings of the University Halls of Residence.

A slight scuffling, like the scurrying of a mouse, was all that was audible as Garrett eased through the window of Ronan's study bedroom. The bed mattress made a slight noise as the sleeper turned over. Garrett froze in the shadows, then removed a long, heavy shape from his coat. There was a metallic click. Then the bed spoke.

"There must be easier ways to get into bed with a girl."

The bedside light was switched on casting a pool of tungsten light over the head and shoulders of Mary Dalbeith. She was sitting up in bed as if she were a hospital patient receiving a visit from a concerned relative. Garrett's arms hung loose by his sides as his eyes and brain adjusted. Neither moved for several moments.

When Garrett still showed no inclination to move or speak, Mary got up very slowly and crossed the room to close the curtains. She took him by the arm and led him like a child to a chair. She placed a hand on the rifle. Garrett automatically pushed in the safety catch and then let her take it. It lay between them on the low coffee table as they sat. Mary knew that Garrett was trying to understand just how she came to be here. She smiled a nervous smile as she spoke and with a tremor in her voice.

"It seems that I have the element of surprise. Perhaps I should have joined the army."

Still Garrett did not speak. He looked like a man in shock, or someone who was concussed. After a long time he spoke, half to himself, "I very nearly killed you." Then he looked directly at Mary, rubbing his left temple. As he spoke his voice was dry and tense. "Can you tell me how you came to be here? I don't understand."

"Perhaps it's just a pleasant coincidence. I might ask, why are you here?"

Garrett's face flushed as he raised his voice. "This isn't a bloody game you know, I almost put two rounds through your skull." Then he immediately felt ashamed and whispered, "I think you know why I'm here. I don't believe in coincidences. I need to decide what to do now, I need to know what you know, how and why?"

Mary's mood became sombre and her voice sounded strained. "OK, I can tell you what I know, but I can't tell you how I know. If I tell you that it will put a friend in danger."

"Go on."

"I know that you want to kill Ronan."

"I don't 'want' to kill him, I need to kill him, it's my job. The only job I can do."

"I don't see the distinction, I'm afraid."

"Go on."

"There is no 'go on', that's it. That's all I know. I don't know why you 'need' to kill him. The person who told me simply informed me that you were going to try and kill Ronan and that he, or she, could not tell me why as it would put me in danger."

"And you believed this person?"

"Yes, absolutely. I know they would never lie about something like this. But I suppose it may still put me in danger. Are you going to kill me now?"

Garrett's eyes flashed then grew dim. "I would rather kill myself."

"Then give up on this. It's only money. What is money when weighed against a human life. The life of a boy who has done you no wrong."

Garrett sat up straight. "What is between you and this 'boy'; are you lovers perhaps?"

"No we are not lovers, only friends. But even if he was a complete stranger, do you think it would make any difference?"

"Have you told the police, Mary?"

"No."

"Why not?"

"To protect you and because I was asked not to."

"What did this person expect you to do?"

"To do what I am doing, I think, to try and persuade you to give it up. For love of me."

"For love! How would you like to live in a bedsit for the rest of your life, or an inner city housing estate. Or live off the charity of others and beg for your living. Or do menial, soul-destroying, low-paid jobs, touching the forelock to bosses you despise. To wake up every day without hope. To cringe and apologise your way through life, powerless to do anything about it. Yes, money is irrelevant, until you don't have it. You cannot love me without money."

Mary saw clearly, perhaps for the first time, how deeply Garrett's life experience had changed him. How bitter were his scars. It was a psychological burden, a demon to be exorcised. Whether he could or would ever recover she did not know. But as she stood looking at him, feeling his pain, she knew that she wanted him to. Love, after all, is also a kind of insanity. So, it was with more kindness when she next spoke. "What will you do now?"

Garrett stood up and slipped the rifle into an inside pocket, folding the stock as he did so. He paced about, speaking his thoughts out aloud. "This means that my cover is blown. At least two people know about the operation. However, neither of them will inform the authorities. If they had wanted to, they would have done so by now. It does mean I may need to plan for starting again in another country afterwards, just to be sure, but it does not mean I need to abandon the operation at present. I may need to refer back for …"

"For orders?" Mary said, "always orders."

"But not for much longer, not for much longer and then never again. And you should know, he who pays the piper …"

Mary moved close to him. "And will you tell your Mephistopheles about me?"

Garrett stopped. "No," he whispered, "I won't put you in danger."

"I hope he is paying you well. The price of a soul should not come cheap."

There was nothing more that could be said. Garrett stood by the window and looked at Mary, drinking in the memory. "When I do this thing, you will hate me forever." he said. Mary took his head in her hands and kissed him on the forehead. "I still pray that you will abandon this madness. You understand, I can't let it happen."

He turned away. "Whatever happens, Mary, for God's sake don't get involved."

Then he was gone, into the cold, dark night. And Mary wept.

*   *   *   *   *

Ronan had finally dozed off at around 5 am. Three hours later he was woken by the slamming of doors which shook the partition walls, and voices coming from the kitchen. Wakefulness did not come easily and it was some time before he could work out where he was and why. As soon as he remembered, he opened his eyes wide to find no trace of Susie other than several blonde hairs lying on her pillow. His head felt thick and when at last the mist began to clear a vague sense of guilt took its place. He was still wearing his watch which told him that he just had time to make his first lecture. Somehow, he would have to get to his room first to shave and collect his books. He sat up in bed and began to rub his throbbing head and neck. It was just at that moment that the bedroom door opened and Mary walked in. In his astonishment, Ronan grabbed the duvet and pulled it around his neck. Mary walked over to the window, opened the curtains and sat on the ledge.

"Well, Ronan, this is becoming a habit, isn't it. Although I must say that your taste in duvets is becoming more discreet."

Ronan's worst nightmares had all come to haunt him at once. His face was a mask of undiluted horror. It was bad enough that Mary should have seen him in Hall looking like an Edinburgh Corporation street scaffy but to find him naked, at eight in the morning, in another girl's bed was clearly not going to cultivate her affections towards him.

"Mary! What are you doing here?" was all he could think to say.

"Hmm. That is also becoming a habit," she murmured. "I often come here on the way to Uni. Susie and I are good friends. I didn't expect to find the late Rev. MacDonald's son in her bed though. This has come as quite a shock." Ronan closed his eyes and put his hands over them, at which point his duvet slipped down and he had to snatch it up again. Mary bit her hand to stop her laughing. Ronan stood up wearing the duvet and began to hop towards his clothes whilst talking to Mary over his shoulder.

"It's not at all what you think, Mary, I can explain everything. Or just ask Susie, nothing happened."

"Oh I can just imagine it, Ronan MacDonald. I suggest I leave you to dress and then we can have a strong coffee together in the kitchen." Ronan was sure he heard a girl's laugh as the bedroom door closed.

The small kitchen was dominated by a vast, wall-mounted, Sadia immersion heater that hovered over them like a Zeppelin. A plastic clothes dryer was festooned with nylon stockings of various colours, but mostly black. He gazed at them in a stupor and, when he noticed a pair of silvery tights hanging there, quickly turned his head away. The floor was covered with linoleum and a modern sink unit was wedged under the window. Mary closed the door behind them, then they sat at the plastic-topped table. Ronan had never seen Mary look so serious or anxious. His initial, sublime thought as he had come into the kitchen was that jealousy might be about to goad her into declaring her eternal love for him. But when he sat opposite her and saw the concern around her eyes he knew she was about to upbraid him for the lecherous lout that he undoubtedly was. He was slightly relieved when she leant forward and took both his hands in hers. His relief was not about to last.

"Ronan, you will find what I am about to say very strange but it is quite true nonetheless. I must get you away from here. Hide you somewhere. A man is trying to kill you. Unless we can get you away, hidden, he will succeed."

Ronan laughed, but unconvincingly. "Sorry, Mary, are you teasing me again. Is this some kind of joke." But when he looked in her face, he knew it was no joke.

"This is no joke, Ronan."

"But why on earth would anyone want to kill me? And, by the way, if they try anything I can look after myself". Then he added, "Goodness, it's not a boyfriend of Susie's is it, because nothing happened, I swear it."

"Ronan, listen, this man is a trained professional, a kind of mercenary if you like. There is no way you can stop him except by making sure he can't find you." Mary knew she couldn't risk naming Garrett.

"Mary, this is all madness. I have my studies, how could I possibly leave now. In the unlikely event that someone is trying to kill me, why don't we just tell the police. Also, you haven't explained how you know I'm under threat."

"I was told about the risk by a close family friend. I don't know how he knew, but I now know he was right. We can't tell the police for two reasons. First, I promised not to do so, it would put my friend at risk and, second, they would not be able to protect you against this man."

The conversation continued in this vein for some time with Ronan's incredulity gradually being worn down. It was when Mary told him that a recent attempt had already been made on his life that Ronan really began to worry. He knew that whatever happened in this maculate world, Mary would never tell him an untruth. It was the following conversation that finally persuaded him, however.

"Ronan, as long as you are with me, this man would never attempt anything. That is what we must do, we must go away secretly together and keep together until I can think of a solution to this." The thought of going away secretly with Mary seemed like an excellent idea to Ronan, whatever the reason. Suddenly his studies seemed to lose their importance.

"I'll tell the Dean of Studies I have to go away for medical reasons, or something," he said. Mary leant back in the dining chair, thinking and gazing, unseeing out of the window. Then she leant forward and held Ronan's hands again.

"Can you think of any reason why someone would want to kill you?"

"I've been wondering about that. I can't think of any reason … except … there is perhaps something. Yes, let me think, something in a letter my father wrote to me. Yes, I think the answer has to be in that letter."

"What we have to do now, Ronan, is think of a place to lie low for a while. I have a few ideas and I think I know someone who can help us."

"If we are going anywhere, we have to go to Cambridge first."

Mary looked surprised. "Why Cambridge?" she asked.

"Because there is someone in Cambridge who I believe may shed some light on all of this. Someone I need to talk to."

"O.K. If that's what it takes to get you to safety. And there's someone I need to talk to. I need some help from Charles Meldrum."

16

Charles Meldrum gives Mary and Ronan a lift to Cambridge and then on to a lonely cottage on the Norfolk coast. In Cambridge Ronan meets Andrew Farquharson. 'The terrible poison of greed and lust for power'.

The old Riley RME had been garaged for the winter in the corner of a friend's coach works in Silvermills. Today, Charles Meldrum was driving his workaday transport, a Peugeot Estate, and in the back seat were Ronan and Mary. They had left early that morning and, after an uneventful journey, were now rolling along the Huntingdon Road on their way into Cambridge. Charles had come up trumps. He knew of a lonely cottage on the Norfolk coast surrounded by reed beds, sand dunes and pastures that they could hire at a minimal rent until the start of the holiday season. If they dealt through him, no one would know who was living there. Mary had thanked him a hundred times for his kindness and selflessness. She had told him that Ronan was suffering from post-traumatic stress brought about by the death of his father and that he needed a secluded place to rest. She also emphasised the need for complete secrecy. At first she thought he would object to the whole idea and she was pleasantly surprised when he at once gave it his approval. 'Quite the best thing to do in the circumstances,' he had said. She bit her lip, however, when she thought how her plan to be alone with Ronan might be misconstrued. It was with resignation that she suffered this probable dent in her virtue. What she kept reminding herself was that it was not one man she was saving, but two. She had not fully decided what she would do when they got there. That, she told herself, could be worked out later once Ronan was out of harm's way. Mary had tried to persuade Charles to let her and Ronan make their own way from Cambridge, but he wouldn't hear of it. He insisted on driving them all the way to the cottage. 'Taxi drivers,' he rightly informed her, 'are probably the most garrulous of God's creations. It wouldn't take long for your secret to come out.' Charles would carry on to London after he left them, where he had some media business to transact.

Mary could barely conceal her frustration at Ronan's insistence on breaking their journey in Cambridge. Eventually he had convinced her that it would only be for an hour or two at the most. He would walk straight to his meeting and straight back and not draw attention to himself. She and Charles, he had said, could have a relaxed lunch in town and, by the time they had finished, he would be ready to travel on to the cottage.

Charles, who knew Cambridge, cut along The Backs by Queen's Road and across the Fen Causeway to Trumpington Road. There he managed to park in a small street near the Botanic Gardens. Nearby, Ronan left Charles and Mary at a trendy restaurant opposite the Fitzwilliam Museum. As he left, Mary was trying to look less cross, for Charles's sake.

"I'll save you a stuffed mushroom," she said. Charles added, "Don't worry, Ronan, nose us out in the Fitz. when you get back."

Yesterday Ronan had telephoned his contact's secretary and a meeting had been arranged for 2 pm. Ronan was to meet him in the church of St Andrew the Great at the junction of Bridge Street and St John's. As Ronan came out of St John's Street he saw the church at once. It occupied the corner between Church Street and Bridge Street and was set back from the road. The church was perfectly round with a low, tiled aisle roof out of which rose a high, circular clerestory bearing a cone shaped roof. It was one of the most redolently Norman buildings he had seen. The entrance was via a round arch with dog's tooth arcading and, at regular intervals around the building, small, round-arched windows gave coloured light to the interior. He crossed the busy street where buses duelled with taxis, belching their diesel dragon breath at each other, and pushed open the door. Inside, all was silence. The clerestory and roof were supported by cross-vaulting masonry resting on a circle of ponderous Norman pillars. Pale, glassy colours were projected onto the pillars. In the middle of the circle hung an iron candelabrum. The church appeared empty apart from a young Japanese couple, who left as soon as Ronan arrived. Ronan walked into the middle of the circle of stone giants and looked up at the ceiling. The central vault had been grandly conceived in perfect proportion and illuminated from every direction by the clerestory windows. The powerful daylight drew his eyes upwards. Gazing heavenwards Ronan had momentarily forgotten what was happening down on earth. He started slightly when someone spoke to him.

"Beautiful, isn't it?"

Ronan observed a healthy, wiry looking man in a brown, herringbone tweed suit. He vaguely remembered his face. The man held out his hand and Ronan shook it.

"I'm Andrew Farquharson, I don't expect you'll remember me. We spoke very briefly at your father's funeral."

"Yes, I do remember, you were very kind. Sorry, my mind was miles away."

Andrew's eyes were also drawn to the lofty ceiling. He gazed upon it as he spoke.

"I've always thought this is the most perfect Norman building in England. It's supposed to have been modelled on the Church of the Holy Sepulchre in Jerusalem. The design was brought back from the Holy Land in the twelfth century by the so called Confraternity of the Church of the Holy Sepulchre. A fraternity within the Order of Knights Templar. So it was built with Templar gold, like Temple Church in London. And here it stands on Bridge Street, like a bridge itself, connecting those Templars with us and an uncertain future."

"Rather like life then, full of ambiguity," said Ronan.

"Cambridge, like Jerusalem, is full of interesting juxtapositions, Ronan, where else would you have the central synagogue overlooking Jesus Green?"

They both smiled at this, then Ronan added, "It's not Cambridge I've come to talk about, Mr Farquharson, I rather hoped we might talk about you and my father."

"I gathered that much, but first you must do two things for me. You must tell me how much you know and you must call me Andrew. These days even my bank manager has stopped calling me Mr Farquharson."

They walked around the aisle until they found an oak bench and then sat down. Ronan gave Andrew a ten minute synopsis of his father's letter. Throughout, Andrew's face had been a mask. When Ronan came to the part about the attempt on his own life, however, Andrew turned to face him and gripped the arm of the bench until his hand whitened. There was a long pause before he spoke.

"Ronan, I had no idea this madness had gone so far. It has been a long and painful road for me, but I can follow it no longer. If I had only entered in at the 'strait gate' life would have been different but instead I chose, of my own free will, the wide road to destruction. All its paths and byways only lead to Hell."

Ronan was so dismayed by the other's hopelessness that he put a comforting hand on his arm. "I don't think my father believed in free will, only in the wheel of fate, turning. Recently, I'm seeing this in my own life. Preordination in all time since the cosmic millisecond in which it was created. What seem like critical, life changing decisions are only particles of a universal design."

Andrew looked at him. "Then where are repentance and salvation and the human capacity for good and evil in your philosophy?"

"Oh, they are there all right. But it is in our knowledge and rejection of them and in our repentance that the grace of Heaven is granted to us."

"Now, you sound like your father, Ronan."

"Heaven forbid!"

"He was a very good man, Ronan. And he had an obsession for natural justice and the truth. An obsession that would probably be classified as a human failing these days. I see you also have it and that it will either be your salvation or your destruction, preordained or not. You also have his power to make people look into their own souls." Andrew paused for a while, gazing through a high window, sighed, then continued. "I have a terrible weight on my conscience and I think you can guess at it. It is a burden I cannot carry any longer, it has become too heavy to bear. I did try to warn you, you know, that you might be in danger. Through a mutual family friend, Mary Dalbeith, I assume that's why you're here." Ronan started at this revelation. Andrew then continued, "Ah, I can see she kept my counsel close. So, it's purely your father's manuscript has brought you here. I can see now that there is no limit to this evil, this terrible poison of greed and lust for power." Andrew shook as he said this, but after a while he was able to speak again. "Because of those things I have done and those things I have left undone, I will complete John MacDonald's narrative for you. It will be a start."

So saying, Andrew stood up and crossed to the church door which he locked from the inside. Then he returned to the bench.

"Can you do that?" Ronan asked in surprise.

Andrew smiled, "I think, technically, my college owns this place. Let me first relate what happened when James and I returned from France what seems like an eternity ago. I will try and remember as accurately as I can."

"At Oxford, James had been introduced to a Whitehall mandarin in the Foreign Office. I don't know why he knew him, he was an Under Secretary I believe. When James suggested we meet this chap and another FO Official, an Assistant Secretary, it seemed a reasonable idea. If *the* major French archaeological heritage had been looted, the UK Government should know and the FO was a good place to start. We met these two 'men in grey suits' in an office off Whitehall. A girl wearing a twinset and tweed skirt met us at the security desk and showed us into a spartan office on the first floor. We sat around a plain wooden table on upright chairs. With the two officials came tea and digestive biscuits. A cast iron radiator with flaking paint tried unsuccessfully to heat the room. I remember it was February. Leaden, overcast with a chilling wind moaning along King Charles Street between the tall buildings. A scruffy, feral pigeon huddled on the window ledge, exploiting the opportunity for shelter. As the conversation got underway I was somewhat taken aback to realise that the FO officials had already been provided with a written brief by James, including some copies of his source documents. It was obvious that at first the two men were not fully convinced of our findings. However, sometime at about, say, an hour into our discussion I became aware that all doubts as to the accuracy of our research had been swept away and that they began to fully accept the evidence as proof of the looting. As they became more convinced their aspect grew gloomier. James was on excellent form, he was always very persuasive. After two hours more tea was called for and cigarettes were offered and declined. When the secretary knocked on the room door the officials suspended the conversation until she had poured the tea and closed the door behind her.

Up until that point, James and I had been doing most of the talking with the Assistant Secretary asking for clarification on certain points. The Deputy Secretary then entered the discussion. He removed his spectacles and pursed his lips.

'Gentlemen,' he said, 'of course Her Majesty's Government wishes to do the right thing but, frankly, I cannot conceive of a worse time in international relations for such information to have come to light. You have to appreciate the current world order. I wonder if you realise how thin the veneer of post-war peace really is. In fact, the world has never been a more dangerous place. I don't know if the journalistic phrase 'cold war' has any meaning for you but it is the prime influence on all foreign policy world wide. Khrushchev's regime is digging more deeply into Eastern Europe. They do not appear to have shrugged off the creed of world communism. Quite the contrary, they clearly have expansionist inclinations, not least in their puppet allies of North Korea, Vietnam and Cuba. We already have anti-communist riots in East Berlin and Nazi-style suppression by the Soviets. The USSR has had the atomic bomb for some eight years and has well developed delivery routes. Our US colleagues speculate about nuclear missile bases in Cuba and the Far East. The Americans have already sent several hundred military advisors to Vietnam and all out war there appears imminent. If that happens, we could find Europe slipping once more into Armageddon. In China, Mao is increasing his military war machine and already has nuclear capability. The only allies outside of Britain that the free world can rely upon are America and France and, to some extent, West Germany. Exactly the three countries seriously implicated in your report. You must understand that the 5th Republic has just been born in France and is not yet weaned. The 4th Republic was effectively dismantled by the Vichy regime and throughout the last 15 years there has been a very real threat of civil war in France. There is a very strong, unofficial communist party with a militant infrastructure. De Gaulle has been invited back to power, after the Algerian debacle, as the only man who can maintain order in this troubled time. The Republic remains fragile at a critical juncture. In the USA we have a weakening president. Eisenhower is rapidly losing public support and is in failing health. The only viable successors seem to be vice-president Nixon, and a young chap called Kennedy. Currently the FO does not have confidence that either of these candidates would be a safe pair of hands. The new world order is very much in a state of complete flux and we stand at the brink of disaster. The next five years will be critical. Thus, what I am saying, gentlemen, is that the best service you could give your country and allies would be to bury this information deep and not to communicate it to a living soul. I hope you understand. So, James, if you could make arrangements with my assistant to provide him with all copies of any ...'

It was then that James interrupted him. As if in a dream, I heard him say, 'I'm sorry, I don't think I can do that, Sir Nigel. This is just the sort of incident that needs to be brought into the public domain. The French must know what has happened to their heritage. I don't believe

I can cover it up, it's unjust. Surely we can't build a new world order on deceit.' I just couldn't believe what I was hearing and I was too astonished to do anything other than gape dumbly. In the 1950s when your Queen and country said jump all you said was 'How high?'

The two officials looked at each other then glared, perplexed, at James. This was outside their normal terms of reference and it took them some moments to adjust. The deputy secretary, Sir Nigel Farringdon, fingered his spectacles anxiously. When he next spoke it was loudly and indignantly.

'I don't think you quite understand, Mr Galbraith, this scandal involves a national treasure, a serious international dispute between allies, a war crime, murder, looting, religious desecration and a great deal of raw, unmarketed gold. I can only imagine what this information might do to the gold standard and the fragile European economies, but that would be trivial compared with the security impact. If your information is correct, it would give De Gaulle's and Eisenhower's internal opponents enough ammunition to easily topple them both from power. It would leave East Germany politically and militarily isolated and open up the way for communist expansion and, potentially, world war. I speak advisedly, I insist you keep this information most secret and hand over all your source documents. Is that quite clear?"'

At this point in his narrative, Andrew got up and walked into the centre of the church, standing in the aura of light from the clerestory. He turned to Ronan and shrugged his shoulders arms extended, hands palms uppermost in a gesture of hopelessness. Then he sat down again. "I'm sure you can almost work out the rest yourself. James, to my amazement stood his ground against the senior FO officials and, even more amazing in retrospect, adopted a high moral stance. The only concession he made was to do nothing until he had met Nigel Farringdon again. I remember I had said very little during this discussion. I was young, impressionable and was readily convinced by James's moral argument.

The next meeting was quite different. For a start it took place one evening in a private room in the Carlton Club in St James's. Instead of tea and digestives, it was port and cigars. A fire burned brightly in the grate as we sunk into old leather armchairs. Sir Nigel was there and another man whose name and rank I have now forgotten. I had a feeling he was someone senior from a branch of the intelligence services. James clearly loved the whole environment. He had a hunger for luxury and power over people, which has never left him. This time HMG were disposed to be more affable. We chatted, or rather James did mostly, about archaeology, college life and France in general. Then Sir Nigel put a hand on James's knee and said he felt he could persuade James to be more reasonable. Given what was ultimately at stake. James said he wanted to be cooperative if he could. To this day I don't exactly know how the conversation turned to the idea of placing James and me on some kind of government payroll. I heard Nigel Farringdon describe it as a reward for bringing such important information to the government and agreement to assist the Cabinet to ensure that the knowledge was managed correctly in the greater public interest. I won't pretend, Ronan, that I was too naïve to know what was going on. Even then I knew that they were buying our silence. It was as simple as that. The climate, I suppose, was ripe for that kind of approach. At that time the Government had got used to sanctioning the payments, inducements and direct aid that had been given to Spain, Greece, Iran and emerging countries in Africa and the Far East to maintain the balance of power in the nascent cold war. And, remember, those were in the days before the phrases 'investigative journalism' and 'public interest stories' were well-known. I suppose James and I were just one more political threat to be bribed into compliance.

In spite of everything I hadn't realised just how seriously our threat was taken until I noticed that James appeared to be negotiating with Sir Nigel regarding the amount to be agreed. After James and Nigel Farringdon had come to an accommodation the other man spoke for the first time. What he said, in spite of his circumspection, could not have been clearer. HMG would be keeping a close eye on us, for our protection. It was important, he said, that the information did not leak out as this would unquestionably lead to the destruction of our careers and even put us at personal risk. He smiled when he said, there are people who would kill for this kind of information. The message, however, was clear and palpable.

So, it was a carrot and stick approach. It was not until James and I spoke afterwards that I learned just how big a carrot James had negotiated. It was, and still is, a fantastic amount of money. We were sitting in a corner of the Nag's Head pub in Covent Garden when James told me. It was enough for us to live in modest luxury for the rest of our lives. To my amazement the 'reward for services to the Crown' also included an undertaking to give preferment for senior Government appointments where appropriate. James tried to convince me it was a legitimate payment to us as public servants, but that evening the realisation dawned on me that I had allowed myself to become a party to something ugly. I had been bought and sold for the price of my silence. But let's be clear, Ronan, I could have objected at any time in the proceedings, but I didn't. My only excuse was that I was young, unworldly and poor. The sums of money mentioned, seemed like an answer to a long and lonely prayer. In fact, I never knew exactly how much was paid. The money was transferred to James and he paid me a share, a very large share but I somehow guessed his was larger still. He told me he had given an undertaking to be responsible for my silence also. So, it seemed that it was James who was really buying my conscience. Still, I took a great deal of money and asked very few questions."

Andrew turned towards Ronan. "Ronan, I'm not proud of what I did. It was a chance to throw off the burden of poverty and the nightmares of my own brutal childhood, so I took it. I know this will sound sanctimonious, but I have always regretted it. However, there is something else I must tell you. To tell you this, Ronan, puts us at great risk and anyone you tell will also be put at risk. It is important to understand that point. This is a time for calm heads and close counsel. I need to warn you about the single-minded ruthlessness of James Galbraith. Once he had achieved his aspirations for wealth and high rank he meant to hold on to them. He became a self-styled keeper of the keys to the forbidden garden. He took it upon himself to build a discreet inner circle of power-ful acquaintances who, whilst they knew nothing about the events of 1959, were loyal in providing information and influence, for a price. Believe me, I never knew of this dark side to James until very recently. James and your father lost touch after they returned from Jerusalem. He never knew your father had a copy of the parchment and he never knew about you. I, however, remained in contact with James. Partners in crime you might say." Here Andrew stopped and seemed to be searching for a way to proceed. Ronan, held his arm.

"Go on Andrew, I'm sure there is not much more to tell, and what you do tell, what you have done, I will understand."

Andrew's voice shook, "Even if I have caused your father's death."

"What?! Andrew, surely ..."

"Let me speak now, Ronan, or I may never have the courage to say it again. When your father was staying with me in France, I took a couple of days out to fly to London, on business. Part of that business was to talk to James Galbraith. Foolishly, I think I must have given him an inkling of what John had discovered. James is clever and he was already suspicious about John's research. At no time did James say he would act upon it and at no time did I think him capable of violence or murder. I know him better now. Of course, we would struggle to prove anything I imagine. Yet the evidence points to him. I believe that James also knows that you could be a threat to him."

Ronan put his hands to his temples. "This is a lot to take in," he said.

Andrew had seemed to shrink inwards from the burden of his guilt. "You must hate me," he murmured. Ronan could see Andrew's burden, as corporal as a stone cross laid across his back. He placed a hand on Andrew's shoulder.

"Let us share this burden together, Andrew." They spoke for a few minutes. Ronan told him he would lie low for a while and they exchanged contact numbers.

"The knowledge is yours, Ronan, but remember, whatever you decide, you now have me to help protect you."

They agreed to leave separately, Ronan first. The sky had become overcast and it had grown dark in the church so that they could see the purple light from a vigil lamp suspended above the altar. They walked to the door and Andrew unlocked it. He embraced the building with a sweep of his left arm. "I've always loved this place. A sublime synthesis of a Templar preceptory and a Cistercian chapter house. Gaude Felix, Mater Cistercium. You know, I often wonder, whatever was or wasn't found by the Order in Jerusalem all those centuries ago, that a curse fell on them and all those who dealt with them, from that time forward. Superstitious nonsense, yet in spite of all their financial success, ultimately only evil came of it. Although, I will miss this still, peaceful place."

"You sound as if you are saying goodbye to it," said Ronan.

Ronan slipped out into the drizzly afternoon. After a few minutes, Andrew opened the door and stepped onto the pavement, closing the door behind him. Two American ladies who had been waiting to enter the church approached him. One of them, wearing a blue cagoule and carrying a very complicated video camera, stopped to talk to him.

"Say, is this church open?"

"Only for confession," Andrew replied.

17

Mary and Ronan stay at Charles Meldrum's cottage.
He takes them out in his boat to see the seals.

Mary was delighted with the cottage and, as soon as they arrived, disappeared inside to make tea. Charles helped Ronan with the suitcases. The wooden cottage stood at the end of a sandy farm track leading down from the coast road. It was weather-boarded and painted blue. Its frame had been constructed from massive wooden piles driven into the sandy soil behind the dunes and these raised the building slightly off the ground. A flight of steps led up to a veranda and the front door. The sea whispered its presence beyond the dunes. It had been overcast all day and an early dusk was setting in as they sat around a driftwood table for tea. Ronan was weary and occupied with his own thoughts and Mary was speaking earnestly to Charles.

"There is no way I can allow you to drive on to London tonight. It's getting late, Charles, you've driven a long way and you still have a long way to travel."

"Oh, don't worry about me, Mary, after a while the car drives itself, you know, I just hang on and make encouraging noises."

"Yes, like snoring at the wheel! I'm sorry, Charles, my mind's made up and you know what that means."

"Yes, it looks like I'm stopping here for the night and, to be honest, I'm beginning to feel my age a little."

Mary looked relieved and Charles was rewarded by a blissful smile. "I've finished my tea, so I'll go and sort out the sleeping arrangements.

I've brought plenty of linen. There's more tea in the pot." So saying, she swept down the corridor leading to the bedrooms where a distant rustling of sheets and complaining of mattresses could be heard. Charles passed Ronan a tuna sandwich.

"She's a marvellous girl, Ronan, and you're a very lucky man."

Ronan was a little taken aback. "I don't know what you mean, Charles, I think she feels sorry for me and is just trying to be helpful."

"You can't fool an old fool, young man. It looks pretty serious stuff to me, why else would Mary be so content to be alone with you here. Unless of course there is another reason you are here?"

Ronan thought immediately of what Andrew had said about loose talk putting friends at risk. "No Charles, you've got it wrong. It's all about my mental state. I've been overdoing it and Mary thinks I need a complete rest." Ronan was a hopeless deceiver, and he knew it.

"Have it your own way, I won't tell. But I must say, and nothing personal, I never envisaged you and Mary getting together."

Charles smiled infuriatingly, but Ronan knew, or at least hoped, that he was only teasing him. Ronan sighed and said nothing.

"How did your meeting in Cambridge go, was it a success?"

"Yes, I think so."

"Would I know the person?"

"I doubt it, an old family friend."

"A friend of your father's then?"

"Yes, that's right."

"An older man then? More my generation?"

"Ah … possibly."

"Did you meet somewhere nice for lunch?"

"We didn't actually have lunch, Charles, but if we had I'm sure you would like to know exactly what was on the menu."

"Ronan, dear boy, I am merely engaging in the art of polite conversation. But as you are so touchy I'll return to my copy of the yellow press."

"Sorry Charles, you have been extremely kind. I'm just tired. I don't know what we would have done without you."

"Don't mention it, dear fellow. It's been a pleasure actually."

* * * * *

It is a delicious feeling to wake drowsily from a deep sleep to the sound and scent of the sea. The distant beating of the surf and the faint calls of oyster catchers and black-headed gulls rocked Ronan awake to a bright autumn day. He stretched languidly and sniffed the iodine in the air. When he opened his eyes he found Charles sitting by his bed.

"I've brought you a cup of tea. Coffee's off the menu I'm afraid until you take some provisions aboard." Ronan sat up and gratefully accepted the drink. The old mahogany bed sat directly on the bleached, pine floorboards but for comfort's sake, a Turkish rug was spread by the bed. Charles sat on a Victorian dining chair which was much the worse from the predation of furniture beetle. As Ronan addressed his cup of Earl Grey, Charles told him of his idea.

"Look, I don't actually have to get to London until tomorrow. You and Mary are looking a little stressed and could do with some fun. So, I propose that I stay another night, if you'll have me, and that I take you out to see the seals."

"Seals?" enquired Ronan, "Do you mean the sea mammals type or the wax blobs that are fixed to documents?"

"I'm talking natural history here, young man. Don't you know that North Norfolk is famous for its seal colonies and the most important one is just off shore here on a small island? On fine days they pull themselves onto the sand by the hundred for a good scratching and a bit of sunbathing. You can't come here and not visit the seals." Half awake as he was, Ronan struggled to equate 'fun' with seal watching. Then he thought of something.

"How do we get to this island, Charles?"

"In my boat, of course."

"Your boat?"

"Ronan, I'm beginning to think there is an echo in this room. Now, you get up out of that pit of sloth whilst I tell you all about it. An excursion on the sea is just what you need." Ronan was at first uncomfortable about dressing in front of Charles but, as the other talked enthusiastically, he soon lost his awkwardness. Charles explained that he used this cottage so frequently that he had decided to buy a small, clinker-built day cruiser, converted from an old lifeboat, for pottering up and down the coast. It was moored in a muddy tidal creek nearby. "We'll need to wait for high tide, of course, before we can sail her out. That's in a couple of hours time, just long enough for a leisurely breakfast of toast and marmalade before we set sail."

Over breakfast Ronan found that Mary was equally enthusiastic about the trip. The window of the small lounge/dining room gave a view of the beach and although the sun shone bravely, a stiff breeze rattled the stalks of the marram grass clinging to the dunes. When Ronan took his crockery into the kitchen Mary whispered, "It'll be quite safe, Ronan, there is very rarely anyone about on the salt marshes apparently. It's an incredibly isolated spot, no one will see us." She seemed to think it was quite an adventure and of course, in Mary's eyes, anything Charles suggested had to be fine. These days, Mary saw little of her parents who had retired to Spain, and she had come to rely on Charles more than she would care to admit.

Dressed in jumpers and waterproofs the three figures made their way along a faint track behind the dunes until they reached the salt marshes. The marsh was thickly grown with cord grass, purslane, sea holly and thrift. In summer it would be an ever-changing carpet of yellow, pink and purple. At this season, however, its reed beds and tidal mud flats presented a much more melancholy aspect with some samphire, the 'poor man's asparagus', still visible on the tidal margins. Charles promised to pick some on the way back to complement their supper. Ronan asked him if that was a threat or an opportunity. Charles also spoke about the ornithology of the mud flats but by the time he had got to marsh harriers and migrating egrets, Ronan had forgotten to listen. Every so often they had to make a small detour around one of the narrow creeks which spread like muddy fingers across the marsh. Once or twice they crossed a small, makeshift bridge of salt-blasted timbers. From one of these Ronan threw a stone into the mud. The stone sank slowly with a sickly sucking sound. Beyond some stunted alders they came upon a substantial creek, full of brownish water. Overgrown paths led to a couple of wooden jetties, their timbers bleached and scoured by the weather. At the end of one jetty, Charles's boat rocked gently in the tidal swell. On the opposite bank the whitened ribs of a disintegrating yacht lay on a mud bank, like the ancient skeleton of a beached whale. The breeze sang mournfully as it blew through the rigging of Charles's boat and the flapping of the shrouds against the mast drifted across the marsh. The boat was not a thing of great beauty but, like all Charles's possessions, had a certain style, renovated with the addition of an inboard marine engine, a small day cabin and some decking. The hull had been painted dark green and the superstructure was varnished wood. The vessel looked a serious, seagoing proposition but was definitely overdue for some maintenance, if not some creative DIY. The hull had lost some paint and much of the varnish had turned white or flaked off. A row of small car tyres adorned her port side. She was moored fore and aft to the jetty by strong hemp ropes. The first task was to pull her towards the jetty. Charles explained that her moorings were kept slack so she could settle down on the mud at low tide. When they were all aboard and yellow RN surplus life jackets distributed, Charles slid back the hatch amidships to reveal a dark pit where the engine lurked. A pungent aroma of diesel fuel and oily brine suffused the boat. Charles's head disappeared into the pit as he knelt on the floor. Mary said what Ronan had been thinking.

"This is a side of your character that I've never seen before, Charles."

Charles's muffled voice boomed from the pit, "The sea is in every British man's blood, you know. We are an island nation, after all."

"Maybe, but I never had you down as the practical, nautical type."

"Well," Charles muttered, "I'll take that as a compliment. There's a lot you don't know about me, young lady."

With a waft of oily air the headless creature returned from the realms of the damned and smiled with satisfaction. "That should do it, let's give her a turn." They all congregated in the wheelhouse where Charles switched on the ignition, then, with his fingers crossed, pressed the starter button. The engine cranked over several times then fired once or twice and died. A respectable period elapsed before the starter was again pushed. This time she turned over six times, fired, then gradually came to life. The engine knocked unevenly for a while, but became more regular as she warmed up. The exhaust made hollow, watery popping noises. Ronan looked over the side to see water spurting out from the bilge, spreading an oily rainbow on the water.

The excursion turned out to be fun after all. The sky stayed cloudy-bright and once they reached open sea, the spray thumped over the prow as they lurched through the waves. Whilst Mary chatted to Charles, Ronan gazed over the stern at the frothy wake and diminishing coast-line. The old diesel engine chugged on reassuringly. Sometimes clumps of red or green seaweed drifted past, either floating or submerged at various levels in the water. At first, when they left the creek, the sea had been sandy-coloured and white with spume, then an azure blue. Now, in deeper water, it had turned a reptilian green and the once choppy waves had been ironed out into a long rolling swell. The breeze had stiffened into a brisk wind. Ronan began to feel just a little dizzy so, on Charles's advice, stared fixedly at the horizon. After a while he found that this trick had given him his sea legs and he no longer needed to do it. Eventually, Charles left Mary at the wheel and came aft to talk to Ronan.

"We should be there soon," he said. "We may have to wade ashore, depending on how close I can get."

"How long have we been motoring, Charles?"

"Oh, not an hour yet and we're only about a mile out from the shore. We've had an onshore wind all the way, you see. The old Morris engine is only about twenty-five horse power. Have you enjoyed it so far?"

"Yes it's been great. Just as you said, something to cheer me up. I feel splendid."

"Well you looked as though you needed it old chap. Look, I don't want to intrude, but what are you going to do about your course?"

205

Ronan came down to earth with a bump. "I'll go back as soon as I can, as soon as I can sort things out."

"Is there anything I can help with, a trouble shared you know. Mary and I have been discussing it, she told me everything. I hope you don't mind."

Ronan was horrified. "She told you about it?"

"Yes, but she asked me not to let you know we'd spoken. Are you sure this fellow you met in Cambridge can help you?"

"Yes, if anyone can, I think he can. I have no idea what to do next. I still think I should go to the police but Mary won't hear of it."

"Did this chap … um …"

"Andrew?"

"Of course, yes, Andrew Farquharson. Did he have any suggestions?"

"Not immediately, said he would phone me in a few days."

"Look, don't tell Mary I spoke to you dear chap, she likes to confide in me and I wouldn't want to break her confidence. I'm a sort of father surrogate, I think. Not very good for the old ego though, is it?"

Almost as soon as the island came in sight they could make out the black and grey torpedo shapes of the seals, lying in rows along the leeward side. Ronan reckoned that there were eighty or ninety of them. They didn't make much noise and mostly seemed to be sleeping. Occasionally a seal would turn over with a great flapping of flippers, the sand sticking to its wet underbelly. Or one would change position by arching its body and pushing with its tail. When adult males got too close for comfort they set up a discordant honking noise. So as not to disturb the colony, Charles moored the boat at the seaward side of the island. The shore here was steeper and he was able to anchor within four yards of dry sand. They dumped their life jackets in the boat and paddled through the water to the sand, Mary squealing and laughing. The island was about half a mile long and about 300 yards wide. It was completely covered in sand and bore no visible vegetation. They climbed laboriously in deep sand up to the low ridge overlooking the seal colony. In the wind, sand from the ridge blew away from them in a fine spray. A seal closest to them reared up on its front limbs, lifted its dog-like head and stared at them with large, liquid eyes. Then it closed its nostrils and its eyes and flopped back down onto the sand, resuming its blissful snooze. Ronan stood up on the ridge and looked around. The view was lonely, almost threatening, but uplifting. A very small dot on the eastern horizon, which could have been a gas platform, was all that was visible on the surface of the sea. The shore was a haze of browny-green in the distance. A flock of wading birds skimmed low over the water making for a safe haven. Ponderous white and grey clouds sailed across the arch of the heavens, driven by the wind. In the lapping of the waves, the sea seemed to be whispering something, but he couldn't quite hear it. Charles discovered a dip scalloped out from the leeward side where they could sit out of the wind. From Mary's rucksack came a bottle of buttery Sauterne, three tumblers, a pork pie and some cheese and pickle sandwiches. Ronan, who always had a healthy appetite, thought this nothing short of miraculous and said as much. Mary looked very pleased with herself.

"I made very good use of my time in Cambridge, Ronan, when you were gadding about with mysterious meetings." It was on the tip of his tongue to challenge her on how mysterious his meeting had now become, thanks to her. But for her sake and for Charles's, he held his peace. It was surprisingly warm out of the wind, with the weak sun reflected off the sea. Mary and Ronan made pillows from their jackets and stretched out in the sunlight. They were still somewhat worn out from anxiety and the previous days travelling. Charles stood up and a flurry of sparkling sand blew away from him. He sighed in exasperation. "Well, if you two are going to doze off, you must at least allow me to fetch my book from the boat. Although the art of conversation is now clearly dead, I can continue to improve my valuable mind."

Mary knew he wasn't really cross, then, before she knew what was happening, Charles knelt down on one knee and kissed her slowly on the cheek.

"I hope you can forgive me," he said.

"Don't worry, Charles, I know that the age of chivalry has died. You may desert me for a while, but hurry back." Ronan's even breathing told her that he was already dozing and, having watched Charles's retreating figure gradually disappear behind the sandy ridge, she very soon dozed off herself.

It was the cold that woke her. Shivering, Mary unrolled her jacket and pulled it on. It flapped wildly against her in the process, like a living thing. She felt disorientated as she gazed around. The seals were gone and so was the shoreline, the sea was much closer than it had been. The tide had obviously turned. The sky was now dark and threatening rain. Was it already blowing in the wind or was it drops of sea spray on her clothes? The change in the sky had altered everything. The sea was black and both the horizon and the mainland were hidden. A high wind was gusting across the sea which grumbled in discontent. A low, sullen roar all around her. Like a lion seeking whom he might devour. Some sense of her movement also woke Ronan, she crouched down beside him.

"Come on Ronan, we had better be going. The weather has turned and the tide is coming in." He rose stiffly to his feet, brushing the damp sand from his clothes.

"Where's Charles?" he asked. Mary shivered again and half smiled as she replied.

"If I know Charles, he's sitting in the cabin, with his nose into a good book, oblivious to everything." Ronan smiled back, "He probably wanted us to have some time alone together, he thinks that you and I are … you know …"

"I'd rather not know. Let's get back to the boat, I'm frozen."

As they breasted the low ridge leading to the windward side, they had to keep their heads tucked down, out of the driving sand. Before they were halfway down the slope they stopped, and stood and stared, uncomprehending. The boat had gone. Saying nothing, they ran to where it had been anchored. The waves lapped against the sand and all traces that humanity had ever been there had been erased by the time-less water. Mary was struggling to understand.

"He can't just have sailed off," she said. "Something must have happened to him. Perhaps he fell asleep and his anchor dragged." Ronan took her by the wrist, raising his voice above wind and sea.

"Yes, there must be an explanation, perhaps you're right. Perhaps he hasn't gone far. Look, let's check the sea all around. You follow the shore one way, I'll go the other. We'll meet on the leeward side of the island." He watched Mary turn and run off, her bare feet splashing on the wet sand.

On the other side of the island she came across Ronan sitting on the sand. Mary was so exhausted she dropped, almost fell, down beside him. He shook his head and made a thumbs down gesture. When she got her breath back she was determined to put a brave face on things.

"Well Ronan, I suspect that Charles will just come sailing back soon or failing that, it looks like a night on the island for us, Robinson Crusoe style. Is seal good to eat? I hope you can remember your boy scout training and at least build me a fire."

When this did not elicit any response from Ronan she turned and looked into his eyes and saw fear there. He took her by the hand.

"I'm a complete idiot, Mary. I guess I was just enjoying the day and my mind was kind of switched off."

"What do you mean?"

"Have you noticed anything strange about this island? Well I just have. For a start, there is no vegetation on it, not even any grass on the ridge. All there is on the sand is seaweed. No flotsam, pieces of rope or drift wood or the plastic containers that you normally find above the tide line. Not even any shells. And all the sand, even on the ridge, has regular wavy marks, wave marks. I noticed these patterns a dozen times but the significance didn't sink in." Mary gasped at him and gripped his hands tightly.

"What are you saying?"

"I'm saying that this isn't an island. It's a bloody sandbank, and at high tide it's under water. Twenty, thirty, forty feet of water for all we know."

A cold, loose-limbed nausea swept over them at the realisation. Fear made them light headed. Mary stood up and peered into the distance through the misty dusk that was creeping in over the waves. The sand bank had already been eaten away to half its size. The sea was stalking them like a ravenous beast, with infinite patience, knowing the inevitability of their end. She imagined she was looking down at this tiny spit of sand from a great height. There they were, two miles out into the North Sea, no more than two grains of sand in the cosmos, and completely alone. The earth turns and the moon pulls the mighty oceans back and forwards in their beds. Soon it would pull the sea over their heads, like a shroud. She had to sit down and think.

"There must be a solution, a way out. I just can't understand where Charles is. He must have had an accident."

Ronan looked at her. "It's nearly two miles to the coast, Mary. Two miles through a freezing, choppy sea with strong offshore currents."

"Charles may come back." Her teeth chattered as she spoke. After some time, Ronan felt the waves lapping at his feet like a thousand hungry tongues. Stiff with cold they stood up and moved to the highest part of the bank. Dusk was closing in fast and they both knew that even if Charles was somewhere out there it was unlikely he would ever find them. The human spirit, however, continues to hope. Ronan put his arm around Mary and she turned towards him. "Ronan, I'm sure you could swim to the shore. You could take it easy, a bit at a time. Then you could bring help."

"I ... uh ... never really progressed much in swimming. I got my Elementary Certificate at school in Edinburgh for swimming 25 yards, but kind of dropped it at that point. Field sports were more my thing. I'm sorry, Mary, truly sorry."

"No need to be," she smiled," I can't swim at all."

"Not at all?"

"No, I never liked water, other than a steaming bath tub with some lavender bath oil."

They held on to each other and couldn't speak. Although it had grown almost dark they could hear the sea flapping around them like vultures' wings. In the gathering gloom they estimated that the sand bar had now shrunk to an uneven circle about 15 yards wide. Ronan put his head in his hands, he had become angry.

"Damn Charles to hell. Why did he go off! This is all my fault, all my fault. You're only here because of me Mary and now you're going to … to …"

"Die," she said. "We may as well admit it, we are going to die, so no point in being sorry about anything. It doesn't help now and there's no need. And I'm not just here because of you Ronan. I'm also here for … for the man I love, or perhaps loved." Ronan threw her a look of deepening sorrow.

"I don't understand. Do I know this man?"

"Only indirectly," she replied, "he's the one who is trying to kill you."

She could sense Ronan's uncomprehending amazement even in the darkness. She went on; "I thought I could change his mind. I don't know who is employing him or why they are doing it. He has become vulnerable, suggestible and some of that may be my fault, or so he thinks."

"Is this why you told Charles about him," said Ronan.

"What? I never told Charles anything. We agreed not to, remember?"

"This is like a spider's web, Mary, but I think I have some of the answers, for what it's worth now". So, in the freezing dark and with his mouth close to her ear to block out the whistling wind, Ronan told her about his father's document and the meeting with Andrew. It only took a matter of moments for Mary to work out who was paying Garrett and why. "I didn't tell you before Mary, because it would have put you at risk."

"Thanks Ronan," she said flatly, "I'm very glad you didn't put me at risk."

Why Charles had lied and what it meant, ran feverishly around Ronan's brain. But he knew that even if he could work it out, it made no difference now.

Their legs were getting wet through with sea spray as they sat. The water had stealthily crept closer whilst they talked and they knew the end must be close. Ronan held Mary's hand tightly in his.

"You've been a great strength to me, Mary. I'm just like a leaf in an autumn gale, blowing this way and that; perhaps that's why you never could love me. But you have a stillness and power. You seem just to accept the inevitable, to welcome it even."

"What else can you do with the inevitable?" she said. "It is the wheel of life turning. Life is a journey and we all know its ending. Some arrive at their destination sooner than others, that's all. Life is a bridge in time, a blink of an eye which carries us from one state of being to another. You cannot take humanity out of nature and the cosmos out of time, they are all part of the wheel turning. So, don't be sad, Ronan. Grief and gladness, pain and pleasure, coming in and going out, it is all the same. Only good and evil, sin and redemption, and faith matter. These things matter."

"That might be my father speaking, Mary. He tried to make me understand about the Celtic Church. He used to say it had a simplicity and stillness in which resided pure power and revelation. He believed in prophecy, visions and angels, you know, a direct inheritance from the apostle John, he said, but above all in simplicity. He would say that other Christian churches were orphan children and that when they grew up they would return to their mother church. The proto-church of Christ. Return, he said, to the natural rhythms of the cosmos to walk hand in hand with the Creator. Out here, I almost see what he meant. Part of me fears the sea, but part of me will be glad to slip under the waves and let them show me dreams and visions, swept along by the eternal tide."

The fear, cold and exhaustion had a numbing effect on their senses so that Ronan and Mary were only vaguely aware of standing waist-deep in the chilling water. All their thought was put into the effort of constantly readjusting their footing as the sand gave beneath their weight and the sea currents tried to sweep them into deeper water. They still held hands. The darkness was almost total. The moon, having done its work, was ashamed to show its face on the water. By the time the water had reached their chests, they could no longer stand. The wind and currents had dragged them out of their depths. The cold and the shock had created a trance-like state in them both, but Ronan remembered holding Mary around the waist as he attempted to keep them both afloat.

He had no knowledge of how long he had been suspended in the sea, it could have been seconds or hours when he first became aware of a darker shape in the darkness. It drifted towards him with a slapping of water and oars. That was when two immensely powerful arms seized them one after the other, and lifted them up into the air. They appeared to float for an eternity before being laid down on the deck of a small fishing boat where they flapped about and spewed water, like a pair of flounders, before sinking into oblivion.

18

Mary and Ronan have been plucked from the sea.
They find themselves in an old fisherman's cottage.

Three figures sat around an oak kitchen table having breakfast. The table rested on a floor of red terracotta pamments in a small, smoky kitchen with an open fire and a cast-iron bread oven built into the red brick chimney breast. A rack of damp clothes steamed in front of the grate. A small window opposite gave a view of a cobbled yard and hand pump. The ceiling over the table was supported on soot-blackened oak beams salvaged from a 19th-century frigate wrecked on Gurney Point. They were in a flint and pantile fisherman's cottage located about two miles down the coast from where Ronan and Mary had been staying. Seated at the table were Ronan, Mary and Joe 'Cutty' Upcher, a local fisherman. A chubby, good-natured man, he was wagging a fleshy finger at the two figures wrapped in blankets as he spoke to them.

"Yewm be very lucky," he said. "Thas a high sea las noit and for yewm to be spotted in 'er ...why, is nothin' short o' a miracle."

Mary, in various layers of grey and brown blankets, a mug of steaming tarry tea cradled in her hands, spoke in a dreamy but steady voice.

"What we don't understand, Mr Upcher, is just exactly how we got here."

"Ahw, yew jus' call me Joe or Cutty, me young lady, everyone else do. Allus wantin' to know things you youngsters. Sometime is better nart to know things." Joe smiled and scratched thoroughly under his jumper before continuing. "Allus I know is that aroun' nine o'clock

214

there comes a mighty knocking on this 'ere dor. Fair made me jump, don't get many visitus in this lonely spat, now that the missus 'as passed over. So I opens the window and peeps out. Lorks amighty! There be a large fellow with one of you two under each armpit as limp and dripping as a pair of herring. 'Do you look ahter them two,' says he. 'They be swep away in the tide,' say he, 'and need lookin' ahter for the noit.' I says, 'Who be you and why be you not lookin' ahter them?' Then he stared at me long and hard and said 'cos I can't do no more'. Well it were funny, the way he looked. It made me feel strange like and I heard mesell say 'all right mister'. And there you are, and here you be."

Ronan put down his empty cup and shivered. His lungs were still inflamed with sea water and his voice rumbled as he spoke. "Mr ... eh ... Joe, what did this man look like, can you describe him?"

"Well now, that be the question. It were dark as pitch but oi did get a look at him in the loit from the window. He were a big man, verra big and tall, but the most 'markable thing was his hair. A huge, white mane of hair 'e had and a grizzled beard, full but cut short. And huge hands, loik reelway injuns they wus. Nort a fellow to be a messed with oi rekon. He were a seafairin' man too, of that I'm sure."

"Why do you say that?" Ronan asked.

"I knows. Jus' by the weather-blown look of um and his sea boots, rolled down at the top."

Mary said, "Thank you Joe. Did the sailor mention anyone else in the water?"

"Why no, he didn't. Was there anyone else in the sea?"

"No," said Mary, "not in the sea."

Joe turned his attention to Ronan. "Now me boy," he said, "you can now sartisfy my curiosity. How came you two to be a floatin' in the briney ahter dark on such a noit? Be you from a boat, you surely wasn't goin' a swimmin' fully dressed?"

Ronan and Mary smiled weakly. It was Mary who answered.

"We were out walking on the sands and got cut off in the tide."

"Well there do be some strange tides at this time o' year, all I can say again is that you 'ave been very, very lucky. It's a chance in a million that a sailor 'appened to be a passin' and seen you in the water. You must 'ave a good angel somewheres I reckon. Now I got to get me old crabber afloat and see to me pots. You two can set by the fire until you be ready to go. Just leave the door key under the big stone by the gate."

As the fisherman got up to go, Mary stood up and kissed him on the cheek and thanked him for all he had done. "It's little enough," was all he said. "Anything I can do to steal life away from that old bugger sea, I do. She have took many a one from my family over the years." He winked and smiled at Ronan as he went out; "You're a lucky lad," he said.

At first, Mary and Ronan just sat by the fire, too exhausted to speak. As the warmth came back to their bodies they felt restored, however. In fact they were both surprised at how well they felt considering their ordeal of the previous night. The events had temporarily masked the anxiety of their current plight, but both knew they would have to address the problem as soon as possible. Ronan was gazing into the red and yellow embers as Mary spoke. "Look, Ronan, there may be a very rational explanation for Charles's disappearance. It's probably obvious, we just haven't thought of it. What worries me is that he may have had some kind of accident or illness. Perhaps we should telephone the coastguard."

Ronan dragged himself from the fire and gathered his blankets closer around him. "If there is a rational explanation," he said, "then the last thing we want to do is alert people to our presence here, after all we have gone to great lengths to keep it a secret. There is something we can do fairly quickly. Joe said that there was a coastal path which ran from here to our cottage. I think that it will cross the creek where Charles's boat was moored, say about a mile from here. Let's go and see. If the boat is missing we call the coastguard. If it isn't, we walk on to the cottage and look for Charles there."

"OK, Ronan, I suppose things could be much worse. You could be wearing a duvet."

They reached the creek in under half an hour. There lay Charles's boat, rocking gently on an ebb tide. They both scrambled aboard and searched the small cabin and lockers. There was absolutely nothing to indicate the events of the previous night. They sat on the deck with their backs against the starboard gunwale, stunned by the autumn sun and the unreality of things.

"By rights, we ought not to be here," said Ronan. "This seems so unreal, we should be dead, drowned. Yet, it's like it never happened, as if time has been played backwards. Our hearts beat, we feel, we see, but are we alive?"

"Perhaps we dreamed it all, is that it?" said Mary.

"I hope it was a dream."

"Why?"

"Mary, don't laugh, but last night I was semi-conscious all the time. I remember being lifted aboard a boat and in the glimmer from the sea I saw who was doing the lifting."

"Well, that's great," said Mary, "we may be able to find and thank him."

"It was Lachlan Mor."

Mary started to smile, then stopped. "You mean Lachlan, the Ferryman, your father's friend? Och, it's a dream you've been having last night, Ronan, and who can blame you. Lachlan lives hundreds of miles away and has never been to England in his life."

"I have asked myself if it was a dream but it seemed so very real and he spoke to me."

"What did he say?"

"Well as he laid me down on the bottom of his boat I said, 'Lachlan, is it yourself?' and he replied 'Who else would be taking you across the sea now, but a Ferryman?"

Mary took his hand and his heart leapt as he saw his reflection in the dark pupils of her eyes. He wanted so much to close her eyelids with a kiss. "Life and dream are but one," she said. "Who can say what you saw? You were exhausted, half unconscious, half suffocated, chilled to the bone and it was dark. And have you thought that you may have misheard his reply in the blustering of the wind? Maybe the man will come forward and declare himself, or, and I'm sorry to sound so cynical, it may be that he would rather no one knew what he was doing out in a boat, so late, in the dark."

"Perhaps you're right. I did have a strange dream last night. I dreamed I was sleeping in an old water mill, in the bottom of a glen. Suddenly a shuddering and grinding of the mechanism woke me, it seemed like the whole building was being torn apart. I ran to the window overlooking the great water wheel, glistening wet and green in the moon light. There, up to his waist in the mill race stood Lachlan Mor with the river foaming around his body. His massive arms were stretched wide and his great hands clamped the wheel's rim. As I watched he gritted his teeth and, with chest and arm muscles straining, gradually, inch by inch, he turned the wheel backwards against the current. Then he held the wheel still against the pounding waters and, looking up at me, our eyes met. I knew in my dream that he was doing this for us but that it could not be forever."

"Nothing human is forever, Ronan MacDonald, dream or no dream," Mary whispered.

They walked on towards the cottage along the margin between the salt marsh and a stand of stunted, Corsican pines, resinous in the sunlight. With the ebbing tide the mud flats had dried to a honeycomb of shallow cracks. Wild seeds would be blown into these and in summer the marsh would be reborn in a blanket of pink thrift and sea lavender. The cottage appeared through clumps of marram as they climbed a slippery sand dune. Smoke from the wood-burning stove was rising almost vertically from the steel chimney. The building looked still, warm and welcoming. "Looks like someone's at home," said Mary when she had got her breath. "At last we'll have an answer." They both half tumbled down the dune but Ronan put a hand on Mary's arm as they started up the cottage path. Behind the cottage two cars were parked. Charles's Peugeot and another car which they did not recognise. Quietly Ronan turned the handle of the front door and pushed it open.

"This is a pleasant surprise," said Charles.

Charles was seated by the wood-burner in a cane arm chair. As they approached he put down his newspaper and smiled broadly. However, behind his candid eyes his mind was working quickly.

Ronan spoke with a mixture of anger and astonishment. "Is that all you've got to say? Where the hell did you get to last night, we almost drowned?"

"Onshore current, old chap," said Charles. "Fell asleep reading my book and next thing I knew I was being blown onto the shore, just managed to save her from being beached. There was no way I could get back that night so I decided to go and pick you up from the island this morning." Mary and Ronan looked at each other in disbelief.

"Charles," said Mary, also becoming angry, "none of that makes any sense. It's almost lunchtime and sitting by a fire eating toast and reading a newspaper hardly gives the impression of you scrambling to launch the life boats. Also, it's not an island, it's a sandbank, under water at high tide. I can't believe you didn't know that."

Charles laughed nervously.

"What are you implying, Mary, that I somehow deliberately marooned you there in the hope that you would perish?"

"But that's exactly what you did do, Charles, you just made such a bugger's muddle of it. Honesty, you know, is always the best policy and I'm getting bored with all this arguing." The three people by the wood-burner turned to face the man who had just spoken. In the bedroom doorway, attired in a crimson silk dressing gown, stood James Galbraith.

"Not going to introduce me, Charles?"

"Really, James, is this wise?"

"It makes no difference now. I am James Galbraith and you, I presume, are the young couple who can't mind their own bloody business."

"You're the one who's trying to kill us! Why?" said Mary.

James approached her. There was an intensity in his gaze and a sneer on his lips which bespoke menace. He stood about six feet from Mary and spoke over his left shoulder to Charles, still seated by the fire. "You said she didn't know about me. Not having much luck are we, Charles, old boy." He turned sharply to face Mary. "Charles is a very stupid man really, sorry Charles, honesty again, seem to have a taste for it today. However, I find I simply can't do without him. The flesh, I'm afraid, has always been rather weak with me but it is, after all, my only weakness. As to why I need you and the delicious Ronan to die, I'm sure that must be obvious. You can't expect a man in my position, if you pardon the expression, to return to the seething mass of humanity that are the common people. That would not do."

Mary turned furiously to Charles. "Charles, do you know this man, really?"

"Er … only in the Old Testament sense, Mary. Sorry, but I did try to warn you. Both of you."

Ronan was amazed at how difficult he found it to be angry. He was surprised to discover that curiosity about the human soul, his father's weakness, was his most prominent emotion. So when he spoke to James Galbraith it was without rancour.

"You are really prepared to kill two innocent people for money, or is it the secret of the Templar treasury and the gold that's behind it. I know you are a freemason."

James exploded with laughter. A cruel, mocking, chilling laugh but still so intense that it caused him to splutter and grow red faced. Eventually, he just held his sides and gasped for breath but was finally able to turn and reply to Ronan. "It's you who will be the death of me, my dear holy fool," he smiled. "There is no gold, there never has been, it was all an illusion. A tale told by an idiot for idiots."

Ronan was incredulous. "I don't understand. There is my father's research," he said, "and the documentary and witness records. Then the Templar parchment and the Nazi coins, the evidence is overwhelming."

"Overwhelming crap," spluttered James. "I had the parchment made, dear boy, and yes I dropped the Nazi coins, having planted them a few moments earlier. Thank you, by the way, for bringing John's report with you dear boy, most convenient. If you read his report, as I have just done, you will find that most of the important evidence came from me. In fact almost all the incidents really happened, just one or two didn't and that made all the difference. It was subtle, bold and well planned, even Andrew never realised the truth. And it was effective. It produced the results I wanted. It put the fear of God into the British government, like lambs to the slaughter really."

At this point Charles finally abandoned his newspaper and stood up. He put a hand on James's shoulder as he spoke to him. "In the interests of honesty, and immodesty, which seem to be the order of the day, I must point out that you appear to have overlooked my contribution." James shrugged, clearly annoyed, but Charles continued. "You see, I developed the idea with James. I was a successful student reading medieval history at the time. It was I who created the excellent parchment and advised James on historical accuracy."

James smiled his cold, indifferent smile again. "A successful student and a successful lover, you have been a great support to me *mon cher* not least in dealing with that blood-sucking parasite Goldberg."

Charles reddened, "James, you go too far there really is no need ..."

"Now don't be modest, Charles, it was one of your better plans and ran like clockwork ... to be honest."

Instinctively, Mary backed away from the two men. "You killed Freddie Goldberg?" she asked, her voice heavy with horror.

"Only a little bit," said James. "He loosened the hinge pins and made sure the ropes were positioned correctly. That unknown force, gravity, did the rest. I wouldn't shed too many tears my dear, he was blackmailing me. So there you have it. You can see why defrauding the British Government is not a tit bit I would wish to give to the tabloid press. It's all rather sordid, isn't it. It's a strange thing about the human condition, people would rather believe a powerful myth than a prosaic reality. All one has to do is to create an environment where a willingness to believe in the extraordinary exists. Then feed that hunger. I suppose that was the basis of poor John MacDonald's new age religion. I rather follow the philosophy of Job's wife, 'curse God and die'". James looked at his watch, "Well no more time for philosophy I'm afraid, I have much to do."

"Wait!" Ronan shouted and all turned to face him. His hands were clenched into white fists by his side and the muscles in his neck strained like cords of rope. "Did you murder my father?"

"Oh come now, my boy, you already know the answer to that," smiled James.

The next two seconds were a blur of violent activity and then all was immediately still. Ronan had lunged across the room at James but before he could reach him, with split second timing, a sharp pointed piece of metal was at Mary's throat. Mary's back was to the wall. Ronan froze, immobile where he stood. In James's hand was a steel blade, it's cruel point was pressing against the soft white skin of Mary's neck. The object had been hidden in the folds of James's dressing gown all the time and no one had noticed it. James gave Ronan a gloating look.

"You may recognise this from your school days my dear Ronan. It's an épée, a duelling sword. This one, however, is not for games, it's the genuine article. Rather splendid, isn't it? Made in the early nineteenth century in Cadiz, from tempered Spanish steel. The triangular cross section of the blade ensures that it will not flex when I drive it through your young friend's neck. It was last used to impale le Compte Felix du Muy, who was not so felix on that occasion, in a duel fought in Mont-martre in 1841. Our collection of edged weapons gives us a great deal of pleasure, does it not Charles? But the point, if you excuse the pun, is that one more move from you young man and this beautiful smooth throat will be impaled like a piece of sausage meat."

Charles had moved to James's side and Ronan was told to stand near Mary, 'where he could be seen'. Ronan stood with his back to the east wall, speechless with anger.

James then felt secure enough to taunt his victims with a sardonic smile. "Rather like being checked at chess don't you think, except I think you will discover this is checkmate. I expect you are wondering why I have been disposed to be so free and sharing of information with you this morning. Well let me enlighten you. Some fifteen minutes ago an employee of mine, a very special employee, telephoned to say that he would be arriving here in about twenty minutes. When he does arrive he will, shall we say, immediately get to work fulfilling his employment contract. In the meantime, you will just have to enjoy the pleasure of my company."

Mary was having trouble breathing, so painful was the sharp point of the duelling sword. But every time Ronan tried to edge closer, the point was pressed a fraction more so that he was forced to back off again, grinding his teeth and tasting blood in his mouth. Charles was finding the sight so uncomfortable that he had gone to the north window, over-looking the sea, where he stood and bit his lip. As he looked over the cold grey waves something on the dunes caught his attention. It was a small column of smoke. He turned to James.

"James, someone's lit a fire on the beach about 80 yards away."

James turned to look. In that split second there was a faint plink-ing noise from the window and a loud thump in the room. A 9mm AP round from an automatic rifle had entered James's mouth, shattering his cervical spine and removing a small portion of his skull. He fell dead at Mary's feet, the sword still in his hand. As Charles turned and ran towards James, scrabbling for the sword, a second round entered his back and ripped diagonally upwards and out through his chest, shredding vital organs in its path. He fell on James's body in an embrace of death.

All was stillness. Even the wind had ceased. Then the sound of three light footsteps on the veranda were heard and Garrett entered the cottage.

But Ronan and Mary had already left.

Garrett checked all the rooms and drew the curtains. As he drew the last pair of curtains, on the north window, he looked long and hard at the North Sea, far away to the horizon meeting the grey-blue sky and becoming one with it. First he looked for the two rounds he had fired and after much careful searching was able to dig them out of the wood-work with a clasp knife. He put them with the two cartridges, warm in his pocket. Then he began the slow, laborious process of undressing the two bodies and dragging them to the bed. After he had washed the floors, and himself, he took an antique oil lamp from the table and threw it onto the carpet in front of the wood stove. From his pocket he took a two-litre bottle of lamp oil and poured it over some adjacent soft furnishings, the floor boards and the rugs. If forensic found petrol they would at once be suspicious but traces of lamp oil, if found, were to be expected. He had parked a long distance away, leaving no tyre tracks near the cottage. Just before throwing the lighted match, Garrett had taken two bottles of whisky, emptied the contents onto the beds and placed the empty bottles on the driftwood coffee table with a couple of glass tumblers.

From the empty dunes Garrett watched the white smoke rising from the cottage windows and the red flames consuming all within. A few minutes more and the inferno began to roar like the fires of hell. The sun was once more breaking through the cloud layers, lightening the sky and making the smoke difficult to see from a distance. He knew that had this been a conventional house, getting rid of the evidence would have been very difficult. But, being built of timber, a great deal of timber, the cottage would act as a funeral pyre, reducing all organic matter to dust. In a few brief years, with erosion, the action of rain, of neap tides and wind-blown sand, all traces of the cottage would have ceased to exist. The ancient spirit of the natural world would have washed the stain from this place. If not from the human soul.

19

*Andrew Farquharson and David Garrett meet and walk by a bridge
over the Stiffkey River. Later, Garrett visits Walsingham.*

A late summer breeze blew dreamily over the land. The barley fields
rippled in green waves and the winter-sown wheat rustled yellow in the
breeze. Two men walked slowly down the sunken lanes of North Norfolk
wandering through the rolling farmland. Cow parsley and wild fennel
crowded the verges and the field banks blushed red, blue and yellow with
corn poppy, speedwell, scabious and tufted vetch. Once, as they passed
through a hollow, they smelled wild garlic, shaded under ash and oak.
Around the corner, a small, elderly combine was working an eight-acre
field, bringing in the first of the corn. An aromatic dust blew along the
lane as the wheat was separated from the chaff. A boy with a gun followed the combine, whistling silently and waiting for a plump rabbit to
break cover.

Eventually, one of the two men grew weary and they made for a
dank, shady spot where a cast-iron pedestrian bridge crosses the Stiffkey
River. The river runs slowly, in no great hurry to reach the salt marshes
and tidal creaks where its journey ends and begins. The two men, one
young, one not so young, sat on the open triangle of grass by the bridge.
The iron sections of the bridge had been cast in a neighbouring village.
Strange for an East Anglian village to have had an iron foundry, in a
land where coal and iron ore are conspicuously absent. Yet this was a
typically British solution to the unemployment faced by artillerymen
returning home from the Crimea. All they knew, apart from the art

of death, was how to cast and maintain the King's Ordnance. So they used those skills to fashion the various farm implements and architectural ironwork needed by the local community. A form of turning their weapons into ploughshares. The allegory had not been lost on Garrett as he sat contemplating the drifting current. It was Andrew Farquharson who drew his attention to the name cast on the rails of the bridge, it read 'J. Cornish – Walsingham.'

It had been Andrew's idea to come to Walsingham, to the shrine of Mary, Mother of God. Pilgrims had been making their way there for almost one thousand years. Leaving their shoes in the Slipper Chapel a mile or two from the village and walking barefoot, in penance, to the mysterious holy well to take the spring water into their bodies that they might be cleansed. Or their hands washed clean of blood. Palmers on their return from Jerusalem or those with the scallop shell of Compostela in their hats. The shrine had always drawn those with a heavy heart and tortured soul, those who had sundered God's and man's commandments, men and women who woke to their own cries and feverish remorse in the dead of night, a cold anguished sweat leaden on their brows. Every soul received a precious gift from Our Lady of Walsingham. Something not definable by language. Peace, stillness, forgiveness, reconciliation, healing. Even today, in a world of lost innocence and forgotten values, an intangible spirituality pervades the very molecules of the place. On reaching the Slipper Chapel the pilgrim seems to pass through a veil out of this world of confusion and into one of childlike simplicity. Something almost lost to the world remains there.

The two men sat mainly in silence, each in his own reverie. Their voices told of the effort required to overcome their despondency. Andrew sat with his back against a stanchion of the bridge, the dappled sunlight masking his eyes, and watched Garrett for a long time before he spoke.

"Did you read all of John's letter?"

"Yes, I did. Before it burned."

"I'd gladly make this whole cesspool of deceit public property. I feel the thread of my life has been unravelled, right to the last fibre."

"No, Andrew. No, don't do that. No point now, it would simply blacken the memory of those senior Government officials who were involved. There is nothing to be gained now, best to leave it for everyone's sake."

"Perhaps you're right. Sorry to ask, but, was I ... was I next on James's list."

Garrett's eyes flickered restlessly over the other man's face before he replied. "No, he never mentioned you. I never knew you existed until I read John's document. So many lives bound up and spun together like cloth, and me to tear them apart."

"Garrett, I'm so sorry, I should never have mentioned it. But remember this, you were never a force for evil in this, merely a victim. What happened would have happened, men can be instruments of good or instruments of evil. Sometimes we climb up to reach perfection only to overreach and be cast down to destruction. Satan enters into the human heart when it is angry or lustful or broken in spirit. Do not ask too much of yourself or blame yourself for the inevitable. There is nothing you could or can do about it, other than pray." He smiled slightly, "Here endeth the first, and last, lesson."

Garrett threw a flower head into the river and it floated under the bridge where the sun reflected from the water made glassy ripples of light in the darkness. "I had free will, Andrew, I had a choice and I took the wrong path. It was insane, bitter, obsessive, I can see that now. I may be free from my obsession but I stay bound and naked in the flames of the inferno. The inferno of my guilt and self loathing. What a creature is man, who brings evil into the world. Who breeds hatred out of love."

"Garrett, Garrett, who can say that any man has freewill in this blinding cosmos of time and place. This momentary life, this speck of dust. Focus on the small and simple things in the natural world. Nature can always heal itself, like you can."

The medieval Slipper Chapel was built of dressed limestone and flint. It was a small, unpretentious building close by the pilgrim road from Houghton St Giles to Walsingham. Garrett had to push his dark thoughts through the dense incense of tranquillity which surrounded the place. The effort slowed him down and made him almost want to weep with exhaustion. Andrew had shaken his hand in the chapel cloister. He would have liked to have embraced Garrett, but the Italian Minoresses from the Convent of the Poor Clares, seated around the fountain, made him too self conscious. Andrew would walk into the village, to the Anglican Shrine. He hoped they would meet for lunch later in the day and he named a meeting place. Then the two men parted.

Garrett entered the chapel. It was empty and he sat alone on a wooden chair near the altar rails. His gaze rested on the statue of Our Lady of Sorrows. The place was completely still. Gradually, his thoughts ceased to race and words from his childhood drifted back to him; 'Agnus Dei, qui tollis peccata mundi, miserere nobis.' He had not prayed since he was that child and had forgotten how. All he knew was the Paternoster. How could he have the arrogance to even think of praying in this holy place. If he opened his mouth the miasma of his sins would choke the very air with poison. But at last he knew it was all he could do. Garrett knelt slowly by his chair and then began to whisper, "Our Father who art in Heaven …" Immediately, unnoticed at first, a dark cloud stifled the sun. The sky grew black and a stygian, velvet darkness fell within the chapel. It grew chill and Garrett shivered as he spoke, "Hallowed be Thy name …" A strong wind rattled the windows and the chapel door blew open with a flap and a bang, extinguishing the vigil lamp. "Thy kingdom come…" The wind grew in intensity so that Garrett had to raise his voice for his prayer to be heard above the storm. The chapel became too dark to see, the air too cold to breathe. His syllables condensed in the frost-bitten air. "Thy will be done in earth …" With a fearful noise the furious wind fired hail against the glass, like shot, until Garrett's ears ached. The deafening storm raged around. Garrett felt the pressure of a cloven hoof on his heart and knew that if he did not finish the prayer the enemy outside would instantly shatter the windows and roof and tear the chapel stone from stone never to be rebuilt. He had to strain for his voice to be heard, "… as it is in Heaven. Give us this day our daily bread." His throat grew dry and he began to choke with guilt. The horned beast clattered on the slates and howled blasphemy at the door. Suddenly, he felt himself spring to his feet and shout his prayer at the rafters, "And forgive us our sins …" Then, his voice died within him and he was suffocated by a dread fear. But it was then that he heard another voice. Mary, reading with him. Her voice bold and peaceful but soaring above the tempest like a bird, "… as we forgive them that sin against us." They completed the prayer together. "Lead us not into temptation but deliver us from evil. Amen." Almost instantly the chapel was flooded with warm sunlight as the storm passed. Seen through the south window, in the ice-blue sky a hawk drummed its wings but its head was immovable, frozen. Power and the breathing of the infinite reside in stillness. Before he left, Garrett lit two candles in the nave. Their flames burned bravely in the purple-blue glass. Finally he was able to leave. Outside, everything looked the same. Such flash storms are not unheard of in Norfolk at the end of summer, it was just a coincidence.

Garrett took off his shoes, stuffing his socks inside, and left them in the porch of the chapel. He removed his wallet and car keys and placed them in the alms box. Then he began to walk.

20

Andrew Farquharson back in Cambridge makes plans for the future.

The President's rooms at St John's looked deserted. It was early autumn and wind blown vortexes of brown leaves swirled across the quad. Summer had played its last drowsy act and a cool, damp air quickened the city. Evening was drawing in and lights were going on in the porter's lodge, tutorial rooms and halls. It was the Monday market and desultory groups of undergraduates dug through piles of faded dinner jackets, starched evening shirts and cream dress waistcoats on the stalls. Soon they departed, drifting away to their rooms or to pubs and coffee bars to discuss the cost of education and housing, their career prospects and the latest fashions. Third millennium college life, a hot bed of conformity. Darkness settled over the city; over the empty market stalls, their striped awnings fluttering; on the Backs where the Cam glistened; over the spires of college chapels; over cattle grazing by the Fen Causeway; over the few cyclists and pedestrians still making their way home from work, bicycles leaning into the wind; over the streaming glasshouses in the Botanical Gardens, the noble Georgian houses on Madingley Road and the yellow brick back-to-back terraces on the city's east side. Lights were being lit all over the city but still the President's rooms remained dark.

Andrew sat in almost perfect darkness, watching the lights of the city playing across the ceiling. Feeling the tide of humanity turning. Preparing for the evening and for whatever unknown pain or pleasure it might portend. On a nearby table was an untouched tumbler of malt whisky.

In his hand, held between finger and thumb, was a dog-eared photo-graph of a slight, sandy-haired boy, tall for his nine years and wearing an oversize, blue jumper and grey trousers. For the first time that evening Andrew gave voice to his thoughts. Some conversations we have with ourselves are not pleasant, particularly those in darkened rooms. "I can't go back and make everything all right for this boy, this boy who is now a man, or at least a man's shadow. I can't turn back time and erase the gothic horror that was his childhood. I can't even punish nor redeem his parents, both now dead. Either I can continue to turn on the spit of my torment for all eternity or ... or do something. Do something right. To pay their debt for them, and to purge mine. And to redress the balance of suffering in the world. I can just place my foot on the scales and lighten the load. James was wrong, the battle against evil is never wholly lost. Each of us has their own demon to fight. It's time to buckle on my tin plate armour, mount my hobby horse, draw my wooden sword and do battle."

That night was the genesis of the St John's Trust. A registered charity based in Cambridge. Within a few months, it was operational. Its main benefactor was one Andrew Farquharson who, if truth be known, invested the majority of his wealth in it. The charity's terms of reference and prime objective was to support children who have suffered parental abuse, social exclusion, violent crime or extreme poverty. Towards this aim his small committed team would work tirelessly. They specialised in inter-agency working with other charities, government departments, local authorities and those companies who believe that a social con-science is good business.

They built homes and refuges, started an independent fostering agency and a team to support and integrate young adults into society, assisting with employment, drug addiction, alcoholism, mental health issues and accommodation.

Andrew employed a marketing manager and kept a low profile himself. Yet it was his new found energy which drove the organisation to success. In years to come, those who had been St John's beneficiaries but had now grown to man's estate, would occasionally visit Andrew to share with him their joys and their problems. Some scars never heal, as Andrew knew. But he was never judgmental nor hypocritical, how could he be. The old man took especial pleasure when visited by the few children who had been fortunate enough to accompany him on a fishing trip to the River Tweed. On those misty occasions, they birled the bottle far into the night and spun yarns of heroic endeavours with rod and line.

21

David Garrett lays flowers on two graves in Dunlaith Kirkyard.

Over the green and purple braes of Ramasey the lonely figure of a man was moving with the motion of the sun to the west of the island. At last he began to climb steadily up a marshy hillside rising to the moors. It was still before noon and this day the island fulfilled its agnomen 'eilean flodigarry', the floating island, rising out of the fading mist, floating above the world. The Minch, an oftimes fickle and treacherous mistress, was china blue and smooth as stretched silk. Holding the island still and breathless with sunlight in her embrace. The man stopped once to rest and remove his pullover, tying it around his waist. The brief Hebridean summer had faded to purple autumn and such days were now a rare and cherished gift. Yet the man was oblivious to the beauty of the views from the moorside. His mind was on other matters for he was going to meet the girl he loved. He had promised her a posy of wild flowers, which he knew she adored, and was intent on gathering them. Even if he needed to scour the entire island. As he crested the moor and began to skirt his way along an old sheep track, he spotted a tiny lochan, like an eye gazing at the heavens. The man made his way down to it through the chest high bracken. It was a perfect sun trap, tucked away in a cranny of the hillside. One end of the pool was still crowded with water lilies, their blooms faded, but the banks around provided his needs. From between the roots of a stunted rowan, the eyeless skull of a ram watched him as he worked. Within a half hour he had furnished himself with stems of marsh marigold, lady's mantle, cranesbill, marsh violet, water mint and purple loosestrife, all tied with a blue ribbon. He had wanted more colour to the posy, but this would please her just fine. The man knew she loved the subtle colours of the moors. He could hardly wait to talk to her again. On the way back to the trackway, he came across a tumbled sheep fank and added some honeysuckle to the posy, for scent. Before long he saw his destination in the distance and hurried his pace. He kept the place in view continuously from now on. It was meat and drink for his tired eyes.

At long last he arrived at the black, iron gate set in the whinstone wall. Passing through, he walked up the short path a way and then turned off to the left. Side by side, two dressed stones were set in the grass. The man cradled the flowers in his hands as he read the familiar inscriptions:

IN LOVING MEMORY OF

MARY DALBEITH

OF GLENELG

DROWNED OFF THE NORFOLK COAST

4TH OCTOBER 2004

AGED 22 YEARS

HERE LIE THE EARTHLY REMAINS OF

RONAN MACDONALD

OF DUNLAITH

DROWNED AT SEA

4TH OCTOBER 2004 AGED 19 YEARS

'THE SEA SHALL GIVE UP HER DEAD

AND THE CORRUPTIBLE BODIES

OF THOSE WHO SLEEP IN HER'

Garrett knelt to place the flowers by Mary's grave. The two stones were freshly carved and stood out whitely beside the weathered moss- and lichen-covered memorials of Dunlaith Kirkyard. Garrett had no more tears to shed. He often interrupted his restless wanderings and directed his feet towards the island. He was a man grown old before his time, with prematurely greying hair, worn long and generally unbrushed, and a grizzled beard. His cheeks were sallow and his eyes sunken and lifeless. These days, he spoke even less than before, except when he came to the kirkyard. His habit was to avoid the company of others. Today, however, he had put on clean clothes and brushed his hair. These visits to Mary were the closest his life came to endurability. Once he was content with the arrangement he sat down cross-legged on the grass and began to talk. Very quietly as befits the whispered confidences of lovers. When Garrett judged that Mary was growing tired of his conversation, he said an ardent farewell, 'until my next visit', and slowly made his way down the hill. The miniature blooms, and the ends of the blue ribbon, fluttered in the breeze. The only sound in that still and peaceful place.

Mid afternoon brought Garrett to the jetty where islanders took the ferry to the mainland. He couldn't have called it a pier let alone harbour, nor warehouse let alone a ferry terminal. Just a concrete and wood jetty with a rusting steel tender, bearing a central wheelhouse, rocking at the end of its moorings. A tin shed with one door missing was the only nearby building. If the ferry was berthed here, Garrett knew it was just a matter of time before its master arrived to nurse the evil-looking brute over to the other side. He sat on the jetty with legs dangling over the clear cold water. As ever in these situations, an almost irresistible desire seized him. A desire for oblivion, an end to everything. Just to slip slowly into the crystal liquid and let it drag him down, down to where even sunlight dare not intrude. He had left his rucksack near the jetty and, as he had yet to eat that day, he took from it some bread and cheese and an onion. These he sliced with a clasp knife and ate absently, mechanically, just to keep going. As he chewed, he remembered the crossing from the mainland. The same as last time. The Ferryman standing by the wheelhouse, one hand on the wheel, looking at him. Scrutinising him up and down and through and through. Neither man saying anything. Lachlan Mor his name was and there he stood, each and every time, like some great eagle owl staring at his prey. Quiet. Still. Poised to strike, or so it seemed. The first time Garrett had taken the ferry it had been even more unsettling. As he disembarked, Lachlan had barred his way with a mighty arm and then given him directions to Mary, without Garrett having asked for them. They were the only words spoken between the two.

A shadow fell across the water and Garrett looked over his shoulder as the Ferryman walked onto the jetty. He stood up, put the remains of the food into his bag and stood by the tender, shoulders hunched, absently waiting to board. The Ferryman still stood at the other end of the jetty, hands on his hips, pale grey eyes consuming Garrett. White mane streaming in the wind. More mythical beast than man.

The voice of all sorrows spoke to him. "Aye you're an arrogant enough chiel for a bloody murderer. Sitting there eating and soaking up the sunshine while others are stiff and cold beneath the mould."

Garrett snapped upright and swung to face the man. Had his ears played tricks on him. Yet the red flame that had leapt out of his eyes just as quickly faded. He had drunk his fill of that fire and it sickened him. He opened his mouth to speak, then said nothing. Lachlan Mor walked slowly up to him and put a hand on his rucksack. As Garrett held the bag, Lachlan ripped it away from him, leaving the broken straps in Garrett's bleeding hands. In the bag, were some keepsakes from Garrett's old life. Regimental stuff, family keepsakes and his only photographs of Mary. Almost without pause, the Ferryman swung the bag around his head like a sling and threw it far out into the channel. Garrett watched it float for a few seconds then sink under the waves deep into the hungry sea. He took two steps towards Lachlan, teeth bared, spitting saliva. The two men's faces were so close that their foreheads clamped together and they could smell each other's sweat. Massively powerful as Lachlan was, Garrett knew he could kill him, he knew where and how. But his hands hung limply by his side. The Ferryman spat at him; "Why you're not worth a drunken tinker's damn, as far as I can see. Murderer," and then he turned his back on him. Garrett didn't move. He had no argument with what had been said, he knew what he was, what he had done, what could never be undone. Seconds later he sprawled on the jetty. Lachlan had swung around and dealt him a scythe like blow with the back of his hand. The blood flowed from Garrett's mouth and he felt his face tighten with swelling tissue. As the Ferryman stood over him, shaking his fist, he spoke again with even more venom in his voice, "She never loved you, never. You just amused her, it was the other she really loved. She hated you."

Garrett tripped the big man with a scissors movement of his legs. Lachlan fell heavily to his knees. Two quick sounds drifted across the bay. They were like those a slaughterman makes when he cleaves a carcass. Garrett rubbed his hands in anguish as he stood with Lachlan immobile at his feet. The Ferryman, however, was not dead, nor even near it. After a couple of minutes he began to breathe heavily and then rolled on his side clutching at his neck. When he opened his eyes they were heavy with pain. Garrett relaxed enough to speak with relative calm as he lifted Lachlan to his feet.

"The pain will soon pass, old man, but in the morning you'll have the mother of all headaches. Assuming you live long enough to see it, you evil-mouthed bastard."

The Ferryman's legs seemed disinclined to support his weight. He gestured towards a circular structure of rough whinstone under a thatched roof and Garrett knew this was the man's home. Garrett bent his back and heaved Lachlan onto it. Bent almost double he half carried half dragged the old man up the hill. Every so often, Garrett stopped to catch his breath. The fifth time they stopped he heard the Ferryman gasp out faintly, "Only another nine stations to go." Their painful ascent brought them at last to the house. Its site had been well chosen on a flat step of the hill overlooking the bay with a shelter belt of stunted pine and oak to windward. Nearby, a snow-cold stream cascaded over its rocky bed impatient for the sea. Two cheviot ewes ran from the overgrown garden as they approached. As he pushed open the door with his foot, Garrett was unprepared for how primitive the dwelling was inside. It comprised one large room only and the stone of its walls, or rather wall, were neither dressed nor plastered. Its circle of rafters converged in a central point about fifteen feet above the paved floor. The roof had been close boarded with oak planks and it was on these that the thatch had been laid. An assortment of timeworn rugs covered the floor and light was provided by an opposed pair of round-topped lancet windows at ninety degrees to the door. Under one of the windows was a brown glazed stoneware sink. In front of the other one a large, deal table and two chairs rested. At the back of the cottage were two high cupboards serving as headboard and footboard for a low, box bed. The rafters were supported in the centre by a column of mortared stone. This pillar was hollow and also served as flue for the small iron stove behind it. Around the wall the floor had been worn smooth by its use as an ambulatory. In some places, the remains of a stone entablature, or wall seat, like the stalls of a chapter house, remained. Whilst, to the left of the door, an aumbry, held a lighted candle. The construction of the place was simple and strong and timeless.

Garrett manoeuvred the Ferryman towards the bed, then paused in disbelief. The box bed was a plain, unvarnished coffin. It contained what looked like a straw filled mattress and the lid, complete with engraved plate, stood propped against the adjacent wall. The old man seemed to be recovering from his rough handling and was able to bear his own weight by leaning unsteadily against a cupboard. Garrett still held his arm awhile lest he should tumble.

"This can't be your bed, Lachlan Mor. Surely, you don't sleep in this thing?"

The Ferryman's voice yet came thinly as he answered, "And why should I not. What better place to remind prideful man of his own mortality and the bridge yet to cross. It is cheering to be reminded each morning that I have been granted one more day, another chance to live a better life." He launched himself off from the cupboard. Garrett released his arm and the Ferryman stood swaying on his own feet. "There is always time for a new life, Garrett, a chance to begin again and make the best of what fate has decreed. The wheel turns, we have to go on whatever, even those in God's grace can't stem the stream for long. Now, let us celebrate. First we celebrate, then comes stillness."

"Celebrate?"

"Aye, for you were lost and now are found."

"What nonsense is this, old man. I have a ferry to catch. If you're well enough to celebrate you can damn well take me over to the mainland first."

"And can you walk up and down over the face of the earth forever? It is better to root yourself in one place than to wander about only to find that what you seek to avoid is already waiting for you at your destination. I'm not going to the mainland, you and I are going to celebrate this day of new beginnings." Lachlan opened the cupboard and removed an unopened bottle of malt. "I have not taken spirits for many a year, but today I make an exception." Garrett moved towards the door stopping to speak while his hand grasped the latch.

"Do you think I will share drink with you who said such vile things to me, even though they may be true? And do you imagine I have the stomach for celebrating?"

Lachlan put the bottle on the table, then came slowly to Garrett. He extended his huge arms and placed a hand on each of the young man's shoulders.

"They were not true, and you knew that. I just wanted to see what was in you. *Mairi boidheach*, she loved you well. It was the beginning and the end of everything for her."

"Oh God, God have mercy."

"Aye, on us all."

The two men sat down together and drank and talked of Mary. It was the first time since it happened, when he had been burned by red rage, that Garrett had spoken of Mary. As a soft dusk slowly removed the hills Lachlan found a leg of cured lamb and a knife in the cupboard so that they might eat.

Garrett woke with a heavy head the next morning. He had slept fitfully on a pile of woollen rugs. When he raised himself on his elbow the rising dust formed a shaft of sparkling light from the east window. Coughing in the musty air he made his way to the stream to splash his face in its icy water. He filled a large enamelled jug for Lachlan and returned to the house. He made the man a hot drink and took it to him. The Ferryman was still in bed. As Lachlan took the cup he winced in pain. "You were right about yon headache, even though it was no more than I deserved. I don't feel so well today, dizzy like, but the ferry must sail."

"If you are ill, it can't sail. I'll just have to put a notice on the jetty."

Garrett put his hand on the old man's head which was cool but when he reached for the pulse in his wrist his hand was thrown away.

"You will do no such thing, the boat must cross today, and stop pawing me with your mitts. Can't you see how sick I am?"

"Well, what do you suggest. Shall I fetch a doctor do you think."

"I don't need any doctor, I just need to rest and sleep. You will have to take the ferry today."

Garrett stood up so sharply he knocked the cup from Lachlan's hands. "Me, take the ferry? Let alone that it is probably illegal, what do I know of the boat or the current?"

"Now don't tell me you can't manage a motor boat, I know you can. And when did you ever lose sleep over the laws of the land? As for the current, at this season just take your bearing from Dun Beag on the far shore and that will take you to the harbour. Why it's just like a boy steering a pedal car, couldn't be simpler."

"No, really Lachlan …"

"In 38 years I have never missed a crossing to the mainland, are we to break that tradition now when there is a young fit lad standing here who can skim her across. There are important passengers waiting on the other side who must cross over today. You just make the one crossing, that's all I ask of you."

"Do I have a choice?"

The Ferryman laughed and groaned with pain. From a shelf by the bed he took something and threw it to Garrett. "These are the keys, begone now, standing here like *a' chailleach comhraideach* gossiping over her washing."

Garrett left him another drink and some bread and cheese and made his way to the shore, not without misgivings. Although late in the morning there was no one waiting to cross. Which was just as well, because Lachlan had given an over-optimistic impression of the docility of the current. A brisk wind was also blowing down the channel and Garrett found himself wrestling in the wheelhouse with the many course corrections he found he had to make. The heart of the antique diesel engine was strong, however, and he was able to reach the harbour, making only the smallest dent in the tender's prow as he moored her. He put his sailing board on the harbour wall and sat in the wheelhouse, glad of the respite. Two disappointed gulls landed on the deck, mistaking him for a fisherman. The harbour seemed far too big for the dying vestige of fishing vessels that still used it. Only two working boats and a handful of small sailing yachts were moored by the quayside. For the first time Garrett noticed the sheep dung on the deck of the ferry and prayed to all the saints that he would not have to take a flock of sheep over that day, he had visions of a woolly disaster. The quay and harbour wall ran long and narrow into the village, where a fuel store and some tin sheds separated the houses from the harbour. After about a quarter of an hour he noticed one lonely figure, struggling with a suitcase, walking out along the quay towards him. It didn't look like Lachlan would get rich today. It was a breathless and ruby-faced Susie Williams that took Garrett's hand as she clambered aboard.

"You're late," she said with an impish smile in her voice. The glossy, party animal had been left behind in Edinburgh's club land. This Susie wore baggy khaki fatigues, hiking boots and a blue, Aran sweater. Her frizzy blonde hair was tied back in a ponytail. Which, it must be said, suited her well enough. Leaning against the wheelhouse door she began to question Garrett. She was looking to pay her last respects to Mary Dalbeith and Ronan MacDonald and could he direct her to the kirkyard. After that, they talked.

When Garrett returned to the round cottage he would find no trace of Lachlan, nor his immediate belongings, including, thankfully, his morbid box bed. And although he searched for him on the island he never saw him nor spoke to him again. It was conjectured that a friend had taken him off the island in his fishing boat and that he'd gone to one of the outer isles, some even said to Iona.

But Garrett was not to know this yet, as he stood in the sunlight watching the sunshine playing around Susie's golden curls. It turned out that her suitcase was in fact a wicker carrying basket containing a small dog. "He's a Border Terrier. His name's Scamp and he's pleased to meet you. He likes sailors." She released him into the boat and the small animal immediately rushed to the foredeck where he stood, paws on the metal hull, nuzzling the wind, bravely barking at the waves. Susie laughed heartily to see Garrett's annoyance and with the warmth of her pink and white smile he also laughed. How could he laugh? To her delight, he let her take the wheel for a spell. The boat's engine set up a refrain in harmony with the sea and the wind. The steel prow cut through the waves as Garrett drove inexorably forward. It was all he could do, for good or evil. The Ferryman was heading for the shore.

No one knows how many turns of the wheel remain. In life there are no endings nor beginnings, just different states of being. There is no right or wrong only virtue or sin. There is no now, nor any moments in the past, just the temple of time and its relentless entropy. Happiness is the nearest the human condition comes to the absence of pain. Yet we can glimpse dreams and visions of the divine. That non-existential, spiritual experience which differentiates us from the beast. Gently, peacefully, listening in the silence for our own footfalls we take our first faltering steps. For a fleeting moment we see its rough masonry stretching out over the void, shrouded in mist. And then it is gone. *Drochaid*, the bridge between Heaven and Earth.

Scott McKenzie, born in Stirling and educated at the Royal High School, Edinburgh where his life-long love of literature was kindled, joined the school's Pipe Band and Literary Society. He acted in a dramatization of Huxley's *The Devils of Loudun* at the Edinburgh Fringe. A career in the Civil Service took him to London and Westminster where he drafted numerous Bills for ministers. In *Drochaid* there is much evidence of his Scottish roots and upbringing.